CONTAGION

INFINITY ENGINES BOOK VI

ANDREW HASTIE

To my K, A & E x

Other books in the Infinity Engines universe.

The Infinity Engines

1. Anachronist

2. Maelstrom

3. Eschaton

4. Aeons

5. Tesseract

6. Contagion

Infinity Engines Origins

Chimæra

Changeling

Infinity Engines Missions

1776

1888

1

ANTARCTICA

Halley VI research base, Antarctica. Present Day.

Doctor Melanie Braithwaite tutted and gently adjusted the focus on the eyepieces of her microscope, sharpening the image of the primordial single-cell organisms floating on the slide.

'Dave, how deep did you say these samples were taken?' she asked, not bothering to look up.

'Two and a half kilometres,' replied Dave Baskins, shifting his weight in the chair and pushing himself over to her desk. 'Think you've got something interesting?'

'Maybe.' She nodded to the microscope while moving away from her desk. 'Take a look.'

Dave was in his late forties and seriously overweight. As he studied the sample, she caught his musty scent. It wasn't too offensive; a not-so-subtle blend of body odour, tobacco and beer. He'd probably been wearing the same clothes for a month, which was normal for Antarctica.

The first thing Melanie noticed when she arrived at the base was how personal hygiene wasn't a top priority for the men, and some of the women were only marginally better.

Spending nine months cooped up in a glorified tin can with nothing but ice and snow for a view did things to people psychologically. Some withdrew, while others became more extrovert, the isolation magnifying their underlying idiosyncrasies. Melanie thought it would make a great study for a Mars mission.

She'd been analysing glacial cores as part of the British Antarctic Survey, one of a number of scientific research teams stationed on the vast subcontinent of the South Pole.

As a researcher, her role was to scrutinise the sedimentary layers buried deep in the ice for the last eight-hundred thousand years. It was a microbiologist's dream. Examining the ice cores was like looking back through the strata of millennia to some of the earliest forms of life on the planet. She was searching for rare species of single-celled bacteria and micro-algae in the hope of understanding what had triggered the explosion of life in the Cambrian period.

What made it even more attractive was the fact she was five thousand miles from London.

'Coccomyxa subellipsoidea,' Dave murmured, sitting back in his chair. 'Green algae.'

'Ten-million-year-old green algae,' she corrected him. 'And still capable of photosynthesis.'

'Resilient little buggers, I'll grant you that — but not going to win us any prizes back home. We need something juicy like an ancient strain of *Arthrobacter*. Chief McReedy says they're going to take one last shot at reaching Lake Vostok this week.' He pushed himself back to his desk.

Officially, Dave was the lead microbiologist on the project and her superior, but they both knew she outranked him in terms of experience and qualifications. Their project director, Professor Richardson, had made a point of questioning her about it during her interview for the posting. Melanie was clearly overqualified for the role, but her work at Imperial College and her medical training made her too useful to reject. The professor knew better than to ask what personal reasons could make her choose to spend the next nine months in one of the most inhospitable places on earth.

'We've got enough samples to keep us busy for the next ten years, why does the Chief think we need to go deeper?'

Dave shrugged, closing his laptop. 'Because he wants to go deeper? It's not every day you get to drill into a sub-glacial lake that's been sealed for at least thirty-million years.'

Melanie scoffed, tying her hair back in a pony tail and getting up from her desk. 'Sounds like a recipe for disaster. The last thing we need is to release some ancient super bug that's been safely locked away in the ice.'

'You've seen too many movies,' he said, checking his watch. 'On that note, it's definitely time for a drink.'

Opening the door to a large freezer unit, Melanie pulled out another slice of ice and dropped it into a Petri dish. 'You go ahead. I just want to check one more sample.'

Dave knew better than to argue, he always asked and she always made an excuse not to join them. It was five o'clock and nearing the end of the Antarctic summer. The Rec Room would be full of drilling crew and ops teams celebrating the end of their time on the base. In three days, they would have to start packing up their work and closing down the station for winter.

Unlike the others, Melanie wasn't looking forward to the flight back to civilisation.

After Dave left, she sat back down in her chair and rubbed her eyes.

Hard work and isolation were a perfect distraction from the shitstorm she'd left behind. There were too many unanswered emails in her mailbox, too many missed calls from her parents. She'd put her life on pause for the best part of a year, avoiding the subject of what drove her to this place or rather who — but soon she was going to have to go back and face him.

That wasn't today's problem — stay in the present, she reminded herself.

Standing up and stretching her arms over her head, Melanie felt the knots of tension releasing in her shoulders.

'One more and then we're done,' she muttered, dipping a pipette into the half-melted sample and dropping it onto a new slide.

Twenty minutes later, the unmistakable roar of snowmobiles broke her concentration.

It was too late to be one of their patrols. All of the guys would be in the bar. She wiped the condensation from the nearest port hole and peered out. Through the swirling eddies of snow, she could just make out the shape of three bikes heading towards the station.

As they drew closer, Melanie could see they weren't from BAS. These machines were too new and the Chief had sprayed all of their bikes red, white and blue after getting drunk at the party he'd organised for the Queen's birthday.

Which meant only one thing: one of their neighbouring research stations was in trouble. No one crossed the ice at this time of day — in less than an hour it would be minus forty degrees.

The base intercom crackled to life.

'Doctor Braithwaite to the sick bay,' Chief McReedy's voice echoed across the station.

She grabbed her jacket and made for the door.

2

OUTLIERS

Museum of Patents, South Kensington, London. 1858.

F red sighed deeply and read the letter again:

To: Frederick Ross Esq.
  Worshipful Company of Outliers,
  Patent Office Museum,
  London.
  1858-07-10-STD.

Dear Sir,
  Thank you for attending the recent physical evaluation. We are sorry to inform you that you have unfortunately failed to achieve the basic standard required for the position of Nautonnier in the Draconian Guild.
  Whilst we were impressed with your competency in all of the other fundamental prerequisites, your inability to achieve the minimum temporal

range required for the role excludes you from continuing with this application.

If you would consider re-applying for another position, we are currently recruiting for logistics officers at our forward base in 2019.

Thank you for considering the Draconian Guild.

Yours sincerely,

Master-Sergeant Finneas Frobisher,

Recruitment Division.

'Logistics,' Fred uttered the word like a curse, screwing up the note into a ball and throwing it at the wastebasket on the other side of his tiny office.

It missed, bouncing off the metal rim and joining a growing pile of rubbish beside the wire basket.

This was his third attempt at joining the Draconian Guild, and more specifically the Nautonniers; a specialist division responsible for exploring the darker periods of the deep past — parts of history that had fallen off the map.

Everyone expected Fred to join the Draconians. Generations of his father's family had served in the adventurer's guild, including his three older brothers, all of whom passed the induction on their first attempt without any issue.

'Sorry Dad,' he muttered, taking out his father's tachyon from his jacket pocket. It was all that was left of him now. The old chronometer bore the scars of its long years in service, the case worn and marked. Running his thumb over the fading metal insignia, Fred could feel the timelines rippling beneath the surface, but there was no use in trying to use it.

There was no limit on the number of times Fred could apply to the guild, but it was pointless unless he could master the time trial — it was a lost cause, what use was a temporal explorer who could only travel back a hundred years?

Every member of the Oblivion Order was born with the ability to move along the continuum at will; how far they could travel was commonly referred to as their *range*. It was a skill that could be enhanced with training and practice; using the right artefact, most could cross thousands if not hundreds of thousands of years in a blink of an eye.

And then there was the Paradox, Joshua Jones, whose range was rumoured to be infinite, vanquishing the Nihil by taking them back millions of years.

Fred's current record stood at one hundred and fifty-two.

Everything changed on his fourteenth birthday. Fred was the youngest of four sons, each of them raised listening to their father's adventures.

The man was a legend. One of the most famous Nautonniers in the history of the Draconian Guild, and they would sit around the dinner table, wide-eyed, hanging on to his every word as he told them of his latest mission.

Voyages into the unknown past were not for the faint-hearted, going beyond the edges of the map took courage and tenacity; widely accepted as one of the most dangerous jobs in the Order, it was one that would eventually kill him.

The news of his father's death was delivered by none other than the Grandmaster himself, Emilio Derado. Fred had run to the front door, assuming that his father had made a special effort to be home for his birthday. The stern face of Grandmaster Derado standing on the doorstep in the rain told him everything he needed to know.

Up until that day, everybody assumed Fred would follow in his family's footsteps. He was, after all, the son of the legendary Randolph Ross or *Wolfbeard* as he was affectionately called by his men.

They told his mother it would pass, that the issues with her youngest son's range were simply a form of post-traumatic shock; he was grieving, nothing more.

But months turned into years and he watched each of his siblings leave home, while his reduced range never improved.

When he turned eighteen, his brothers did their best to get him through the aptitude tests, but there were rules, and even with his legacy, nothing was going to alter the fact he could barely make it back to witness Captain James Cook land in Australia.

'Frederick?' came the reedy voice of Mr Woodcroft, Fred's boss, snapping him out of his reverie.

'Sir?' replied Fred, jumping awkwardly to his feet.

'Have you finished the report on the sea serpent?'

Clumsily fumbling around his desk, Fred knocked a tall pile of papers onto the floor with his elbow.

'Yes, it's here somewhere.'

Woodcroft tutted dismissively. Staring down at Fred over his spectacles, he had a certain way of standing that exuded impatience, and his formal black suit reminded Fred of an undertaker rather than the Head of the Outlier department.

'It was due yesterday.'

Fred's office was tiny, the lack of storage space meant his desk was a mess of disorganised notes, and no amount of shuffling seemed to help uncover the report he'd been working on for the last two weeks.

'I know it's here,' he explained, picking up a stack of documents and dumping them in a drawer.

'Never mind!' snapped Woodcroft. 'Bring it to my office by four o'clock.'

He turned and left, slamming the door behind him.

Fred collapsed into his chair and ran his hands through his ginger hair.

'Unbelievable,' he muttered under his breath. 'Three years and he still thinks I'm an idiot.'

His position at the Outlier Department was something of an accident. A friend of the family, knowing his issues with joining the Draconians, offered him the post after Fred completed his history degree at Cambridge.

At first, he was intrigued by the role. Outliers was a small research department of the Copernican Guild who investigated the more unlikely temporal scenarios: conspiracy theories, myths and legends that no right-minded actuary would ever entertain as a remote possibility.

Keen to study the more unusual beliefs of humanity, Fred threw himself into the job, but quickly discovered that the department attracted the more eccentric types, and was generally derided by the rest of the guild, and more importantly by his brothers, who began to call him 'Quirky.'

What began as a temporary job until he could join the Draconians had become a three-year stint in the filing division as a 'clipper'— someone whose main task it was to compile cuttings from the newspapers on subjects that may be of interest to the investigators.

In this case, it was a report on a 'Great Sea Serpent', which had allegedly been spotted by Captain McQuhae of *HMS Daedalus* and several of his officers and crew on their way to St Helena.

The articles recounted how the creature was sighted off the Cape of Good Hope in August, 1848. McQuhae declared the beast to be in excess of sixty feet long, with its head four feet out of the water as it passed their ship.

Fred knew that it was most likely a whale of some kind, but Woodcroft wanted everything on the subject of serpents and that meant digging through every publication for that year and the following five at least.

Most of his source material came from the newspaper archive of the British Library, somewhere he'd come to think of as his second office over the last few years, one that he preferred in many ways, not just because there was a rather pretty Scriptorian by the name of Katy

Preswick working behind the desk, but because he could while away a few hours without being under the constant scrutiny of Woodcroft and his cronies.

The clock struck the hour: thirteen bells. Time for lunch.

If he took his bicycle he could be at the library in ten minutes, and Katy would be eating her sandwiches in Bedford Square Garden.

3

CREWMAN

Melanie made it to the sick bay in under three minutes.

By the time she arrived, the Chief and two of his team had stripped the crewman of his expedition parka and dry suit.

Standing there in his long johns, the patient was an impressive specimen: over six feet tall with strawberry-blond hair and beard. By the look of him, Melanie guessed he was from the Swedish base at WASA, which was one of their nearest neighbours at over three hundred kilometres away.

He was ranting in a foreign language that sounded vaguely Nordic. His face was flushed, with wild, bloodshot eyes and spittle lacing his beard. There were two other men that she didn't recognise trying to calm him down, Melanie assumed they'd brought him in.

'What's happened?' she asked one of them, putting on a mask and a pair of latex gloves.

The man shrugged, as if he didn't understand the question.

'What's his name?'

'Johansson.'

The sick man roared at her when she attempted to take his pulse and had to be restrained.

'Get him on the bed,' she instructed the Chief and went over to unlock the medicine cabinet. 'I'll give him something to calm him down.'

Preparing the sedative meant estimating his weight. She knew McCreedy was the heavy side of ninety-five kilos from his last physical and she estimated that this patient was at least half as much again.

The medical bay came with a fully stocked drug cabinet, although the opioids were more strictly secured. As the only qualified doctor on the base she had free rein when it came to dispensing them, something that her predecessor had abused during the previous winter. Long, dark days and unfettered access to class A's was always a dangerous combination.

The man refused to lie down, and so they settled on him sitting on the bunk.

Walking over with the syringe, Melanie noticed a strange rash on his neck. 'What is this?' she asked, pointing at the unusual pattern.

Again the man's friend shrugged.

She was beginning to lose her patience. 'If you want my help, I need to know what I'm dealing with!'

Pulling up the man's sleeve to find a vein, she found the rash ran down over his forearms too. It was a complex, repetitive design that reminded her of a henna tattoo that she'd once got at Glastonbury Festival.

The man yanked his arm away, nearly knocking the syringe out of her hand.

'Hold him!' she ordered, stepping away until they had the patient under control.

His breathing was fast, his body rigid, knotted cords pulsed in his neck. While they struggled to hold him down, she placed two fingers against the beating artery in his neck and took his pulse.

Heart rate of one hundred and eighty, unusual rash, clear signs of confusion. Melanie's medical training calmly ticking off the patient's symptoms.

Infection, possibly meningitis or chemical poisoning?

She couldn't be sure until she could do more tests. The midazolam took a while to take effect, but she stayed with him until the man calmed and finally fell into a deep sleep.

'Thank you Chief,' she said, waving his crew out of the sick bay. 'I can handle it from here.'

The strangers refused to leave, which was when Melanie realised the insignias on their fleeces were not from the Swedish station.

'Where are you from?'

'The *Endurance*,' said the one who'd refused to speak before.

The name was vaguely familiar, but she couldn't put her finger on it.

'You're whalers?' she asked, knowing that the Weddell Sea to the North was notorious for illegal whaling.

He shook his head. 'Salvage.'

Melanie frowned. Antarctica was not somewhere most would come in search of shipwrecks.

'So what happened to your friend? They look like chemical burns?'

He shrugged once more. 'Soren came back to the ship, complaining of pain.' The man explained in broken English, pointing at his head. 'And hot?'

'Fever?' she said, taking out a digital thermometer and scanning the man's forehead, it was thirty-nine-point-seven centigrade.

'Fever, yes.'

Alarm bells were starting to go off in her head as she revised her initial diagnosis: *Fever, accelerated pulse, rash — Virus?*

'Okay, you need to stay here. I have to quarantine you until I know what he's got. It could be contagious.'

The men's eyes narrowed and they spoke to each other in a language that she couldn't understand.

'We go.'

'No,' she held up her hand. 'You stay here. You may be sick too!'

They walked past her as if she wasn't there.

She locked the door behind them, picked up the phone and dialled Professor Richardson's quarters.

'Professor, I need to speak to you urgently.'

While she was waiting for her boss, Melanie drew a blood sample from the sleeping man and set up monitors to check his vitals.

He was definitely fighting some kind of infection. She took the extra precautions that her years in virology labs had taught her. There was a hazmat suit in the locker, something that was only supposed to be used in an extreme biohazard situation, but she wasn't taking any chances.

Climbing inside the suit, she engaged the last of the seals as Professor Richardson knocked on the door.

'Sorry Professor, I can't let you in,' she shouted through the helmet into the intercom.

'What are you doing Doctor Braithwaite?' he asked, looking at her through the observation window as though she'd gone a little crazy.

'You need to quarantine those other men.'

'I can't, they've already left, along with most of the station. Apparently they've found the *Endurance*.'

'Their ship?'

He shook his head. 'From Shackleton's expedition. Was lost in 1915. It's quite something apparently. Completely frozen inside a glacier, less than thirty klicks from here.'

She tried not to scream.

'How many have gone?'

'Pretty much everyone in the Rec Room. Melanie, are you sure you're not overreacting?' he added calmly.

Am I? She thought, as the usual doubts came flooding in. *What proof did she have? What could she show him to substantiate her diagnosis? What if she was wrong?*

He smiled at her in that slightly condescending paternal way that her Research Director, Professor MacAllister, used to do before tearing her latest thesis apart.

'I'll run some tests,' she replied. 'Can you radio them? They need to come back.'

Richardson shrugged. 'I'm sure they'll be fine.'

4

KATY

Bedford Square Garden, London. 1858

K*aty Preswick's smile could light up the darkest room*, thought Fred, leaning his bicycle against the railings and spying her through the fence. She was sitting alone on a bench in the leafy gardens of Bedford Square throwing crusts to the pigeons that flocked on the grass around her.

'A little later than usual Frederick?' she said with a wink as he sat down beside her and unwrapped his own, rather flattened lunch.

'Unexpected visitation from Mr Woodcroft. He sends his regards.'

She laughed, it was a pure sound that made Fred's heart sing.

'You're a peculiar sort, and no mistaking.'

'He would tend to disagree,' he said, taking a bite of his cheese sandwich before sitting back on the bench and letting the sun warm his face.

Katy carefully folded up the brown paper and brushed the crumbs from her skirts. 'And how goes the search for the elusive Serpent?'

He sighed. 'That's something of a predicament. I have until four this afternoon to deliver my report on the sightings and I appear to have misplaced it.'

She smiled and produced a manila folder from her bag. 'Would it happen to be the one you left in my press archives yesterday?'

Fred dropped his sandwich and clapped his hands. He came very close to kissing her, but changed his mind at the last moment.

'Thank you!' he said, taking the document from her.

She blushed a little and turned her head away. 'You should take more care, Master Ross, if you're to make anything of yourself in this world. One needs to pay attention to the details.'

'I - I find the work a little mundane,' he stuttered, looking down at the half-eaten bread being devoured by the pigeons and wondering what Katy would think if he tried to recover it. 'My mind wanders.'

'Indeed it does. Sometimes, I wonder if you're so busy daydreaming about those explorers of yours that you forget to think about your own future.'

Fred knew he should tell Katy about his plans to join the Draconians, but somehow he could never seem to find the right moment. She was a member of the Scriptorian Guild, the keepers of books, and their worlds couldn't be more different. She enjoyed cataloguing dusty tomes while he wanted to wander the forgotten paths of history.

Somewhere a clock struck the half hour.

'Well, time does fly doesn't it?' she muttered, getting to her feet and smoothing down her skirts. 'Are you coming to the library?'

He nodded, tucking the folder under one arm and offering her the other, which she took with all the grace of a lady.

'What about your contraption?' she asked as they passed his bicycle.

'I'd rather walk,' he said with a smile.

The newly completed reading room of the British Museum was a circular building that took pride of place in the centre of the court-yard. It was a marvel of modern architecture, with a vast, domed ceiling whose architect was said to have been inspired by the Pantheon in Rome.

Inside the rotunda, towering stacks of cast iron shelves housed the collection which would one day become the British Library. It included the King's library of George III, the Magna Carta and note-books of Leonardo Da Vinci.

From the first moment he'd stepped inside, Fred had loved this space; a peaceful sanctuary away from the bustle and commotion of nineteenth century London. Officially, he was supposed to be researching the newspaper archives, but in reality he spent most of his time in the Exploration and Cartographic sections, poring over old charts and maps, hunting down first-hand accounts of adven-turers like Marco Polo.

Katy kissed him on the cheek and went back to her desk.

Hiding his blushes, Fred climbed the iron staircase to the mezza-nine and into 'Geographical History of Other Areas.'

It was a well-trodden path to the books relating to Antarctica, which in this time was still one of the last unexplored regions on the planet. In the last ten years, his namesake, James Clark Ross, had returned from discovering Mount Erebus, Mount Terror and Victoria Land, as well as claiming the Ross Ice Shelf and Sea in his name.

Fred knew what was to come of course; the so-called "heroic age" of exploration to the South Pole, led by the likes of Captain Robert Falcon Scott, Roald Amundsen and Sir Ernest Shackleton was less than fifty years away, but at this moment it was nothing more than an empty space on the map. 'Hic sunt dracones,' as the old cartogra-phers would say. 'Here be dragons.'

Whilst pondering over a map of Terra Australis in a first edition of *An Historical Collection of the Several Voyages and Discoveries in the South Pacific Ocean* by Alexander Dalrymple, a man suddenly appeared out of the bookcase — it was his friend, Montgomery Williams.

'Ross,' Montgomery greeted him with a cursory nod. 'Wondered if I'd find you here.'

He was a head taller than Fred, with a sharp nose and dark eyes, which always reminded him of a hawk. They'd met at Trinity College, Cambridge and found they had a mutual appreciation for adventure stories, especially those of Jules Verne and H.G. Wells — illegal contraband that Monty had smuggled back from the early twentieth century.

Monty's love of books had led naturally into a role in the Scriptorian Guild, where he now held a senior position in the twenty-first century, overseeing the collection of the Biblioteca Joanina, in Portugal, one of the only libraries that used bats to protect their manuscripts from insects.

He shared Fred's fascination for the golden age of exploration and made regular trips back to the nineteenth century for research purposes and to generally chat about the 'good old days'.

The twenty-first century was Fred's least favourite era. It was the nexus where the past met the future, and was commonly know as the 'Frontier' by members of the Order, while linears referred to it as the 'present'. He had visited it on several occasions, but had never felt compelled to stay. To Fred it was a terrible, soulless period, filled with an overabundance of technology, pollution and warfare.

More importantly, there was nothing left to explore, apart from the deep ocean and outer space, which Monty agreed was mostly empty except for the gas giants and barren, uninhabitable moons.

Fred preferred not to travel too far beyond the late nineteen hundreds, which for him was an amazing era filled with Victorian invention and exploration, celebrated in no small part by the Great Exhibition in London, 1851 and the Exposition Universelle in Paris, 1889.

He rented an attic apartment on Onslow Square, two doors down from Rear-Admiral Robert FitzRoy, who lived at number thirty eight. Fred had spent the last year trying to summon the courage to speak to the man who'd taken Darwin to the Galapagos on *HMS Beagle*, but failed miserably.

The garret was crammed with books and charts, leaving little space for a bed, wardrobe and a writing desk. It was not much, but it was his sanctuary.

Limited by his range, he'd come to appreciate the century in ways that most others did not, becoming something of a local expert.

It was also the period in which his mother lived.

As a linear, she had little choice, bound to the period by accident of birth. She married his father unaware of his ability to travel into the past, or that he would pass that ability to their sons.

She always likened it to marrying a sailor, who would be gone for months on end, never knowing if he would return from each voyage. In the case of a time traveller, months would indeed pass for his father yet he could still be sitting at the dining table every evening, usually with a new scar or a significantly longer beard.

It was unusual to marry outside of the Order, but not forbidden. To Fred the 1850s were home, and even though he hadn't seen her for a while, it was reassuring to know his mother was only a few years away.

'How goes the war?' Monty said, referring to Fred's battle to join the Draconians.

'Terribly. Third strike.'

Monty winced. 'How far did you manage this time?'

Fred sighed. 'A hundred and fifty. They had to come and get me. I couldn't make it back.'

His friend clapped him on the shoulder. 'Better than last time though! Anyway, I've something that might cheer you up — they've found the *Endurance*!'

'Shackleton's ship?' whispered Fred, looking around to see if anyone could overhear them.

Monty nodded, his dark eyes widening. 'Frozen inside a glacier.'

Although it was slightly strange to discuss the fate of an expedition that wouldn't set sail for another fifty years, the whereabouts of the missing *Endurance* had been an ongoing source of speculation for both of them.

'When?'

'Fifth of March, 2022.'

Fred folded his arms and frowned, narrowing his eyes in disbelief. 'Do you have the coordinates?'

'Of course,' Monty said, producing a slip of paper and handing it to him.

Fred unfolded the note and studied the temporal glyphs carefully. Navigating through time was not an easy task, most of their Order relied on the chronologies of artefacts to move along the continuum, but Draconians were different, and his father had taught him a long time ago how to travel 'without a compass' as he called it.

'Thank you,' he said, folding the note and shaking his friend's hand.

5

VIRUS

Halley VI research base, Antarctica, March 2022

Melanie put the crewman on a saline drip, secured him to the bunk and locked him in the sick bay. Making her way back to the science module, the station seemed unusually quiet, there was none of the usual background chatter from the Rec Room — no sounds of rowdy men getting drunk.

She carefully stepped out of the hazmat suit and stowed it into one of the sample freezers. The ultra-low temperature would kill off any active bacteria, if that's what it was. Viruses, however, were another matter, *those little buggers could survive anything*.

It would take at least an hour for the blood tests to process.

As a precaution she tested her own blood at the same time. It was standard procedure at the pathology lab at Imperial — *another habit acquired from MacAllister*.

While the antique haemo-analyser churned through its various tests, she made herself a green tea and pulled up the NIH medical database on her laptop.

Melanie knew there was little point in searching through the standard symptoms. The human immune system tended to react the same way in most cases, so she focused on the rash. Scrolling through the hundreds of photographs of petechial rashes, she looked for anything that matched the images she'd taken on her phone.

There was a strange fractal nature to the pattern, like a mandala, spreading over his chest, neck and arms. It wasn't like any physical symptom she'd ever seen, nor could she find anything close to it on the NIH database. Opening another browser tab, she used Google image search instead.

Discoid Lupus was the closest match. Raised red circles of thick, scaly lesions, that were symptomatic of the auto-immune disease, yet it was still nothing like the complex structures that the crewman was exhibiting.

A few minutes later, the analyser chimed and the first of the results appeared on the display.

His white cell count was incredibly high: twenty-two thousand per micro litre — more than double the normal range. Haemoglobin was low and so was his platelets count.

Everything is pointing towards a viral infection, but she would have to wait for the metabolic panel to know for sure.

The only way to confirm her suspicions was to test the samples using immunofluorescence. Melanie went over to the rack and booted up the nano imager. It hadn't been used since she'd persuaded Professor Richardson to have it flown down six months ago.

Her promise of being able to produce the best imaging of primordial organisms ever seen was a persuasive one; scientific journals like Nature and the Lancet were more likely to publish your paper if it was backed up by stunning micro photography.

Preparing the sample in paraformaldehyde took her back to her research days at Imperial College. The process was ingrained into her muscle memory after hours of repetitive work in the small cupboard of a lab she had been given by MacAllister.

Its size was irrelevant, those first two years were a joy. Like a child in a toy shop, she'd excelled at her work, and the results were astounding. As head of her department, Professor MacAllister, had taken her under his wing and together they made huge leaps in developing adenovirus viral vectors.

But in the final year, as the discussions began to turn to manufacturing patents and licensing, everything changed. Suddenly there were meetings that she wasn't invited to, with men in expensive suits from American pharmaceutical companies.

Then her security card stopped working and MacAllister stopped taking her calls.

After a week of waiting, trying not to think the worst, she received a cheque in the post and a letter from HR explaining how the departmental funding had been restructured and her position was now redundant.

Two months later MacAllister published the paper in Nature.

It earned him the Lasker Award and two hundred and fifty-thousand dollars in prize money. It was a well known fact that most laureates who win the Lasker go on to win the Nobel.

She read the article, twice, it was all her work.

The haemo-analyser pinged once more and her sample results flashed onto the screen: all her counts were normal.

6

WOODCROFT

British Library, London. 1858.

Leaving Monty reading a pamphlet on how the English explorer, John Hanning Speke, had discovered the source of the Nile, Fred reclaimed his bicycle and rode back to the office with the sea serpent report tucked safely under his arm.

He rode through Mayfair and down to the Wellington Arch, tipping a non-existent hat to the Duke's statue as he passed. The sky above it was a clear blue and a mild breeze stirred the trees. *Today was going to be a good day,* he thought, trying to contain the excitement stirring inside him.

The offices of the Outlier Department were housed in the Museum of Patents in South Kensington. A precursor to the Science Museum, the unassuming building was a storehouse for some of the most unique and obscure machines ever invented, including steam-powered carriages, various flying machines and a selection of mechanical hats.

Woodcroft's office was on the fifth floor, affording him a view across Kensington Gardens and Hyde Park.

The large grandfather clock in the hallway chimed four times as Fred knocked on the door, not waiting for a response before entering.

His boss was sitting behind a grand mahogany desk reading the latest edition of the *Inquirer*. He grimaced over the newspaper, reluctantly putting it down and taking the report.

Fred waited in silence as Woodcroft pored over his work.

'Natural phenomena,' he read aloud from Fred's conclusion a few minutes later. 'A cetacean, mostly likely of the *Balaenoptera borealis* species.'

Putting down the report, Woodcroft folded his arms over his chest. 'And what of the skeleton exhibited in New York in 1845?'

Fred smiled. 'Professor Wyman proved that the skull was mammalian and that the skeleton was comprised of bones from a number of different animals including an extinct species of whale.'

Woodcroft's expression softened, clearly impressed by the depth of Fred's research.

Fred wondered if this was the best time to mention the discovery of the *Endurance* and whether it would be worth investigating, even though getting there would be a challenge.

'Sir, I wondered if it would be possible to make a visit to the Frontier?'

'What an earth for?' Woodcroft asked, raising one eyebrow slightly.

'There's been a sighting of Shackleton's lost ship.'

'Has there indeed? I've seen no mention of it,' he said picking up the *Inquirer* once more and scanning the front page.

'I'd like to take a few days leave to confirm a theory.'

His face twisted into a sneer. 'Would you now? This would be the theory that Shackleton's crew were poisoned by lead in their tinned food?'

Fred nodded. 'I could take it as holiday, without pay?'

Woodcroft's face flushed as he got to his feet. 'This isn't the bloody Draconians, you can't just go gallivanting off whenever you feel the urge. No matter who your father was, there are rules, procedures that need to be followed.'

Fred tried to protest, but Woodcroft held up a hand. 'I've put up with your impertinence for the last three years. Don't think I don't know that you've been applying to join the Nautonniers! Half of the department are running a book on how far you'll get next time.'

The colour rose in Fred's cheeks as he tried to hold back the anger that was building inside him.

'With respect sir, let me prove I'm worthy of more than just clipping newspapers. If I fail on this mission, you will have my resignation.'

Woodcroft's expression softened, the idea obviously appealed to him. Sitting heavily down in his chair, he took a docket from one of his drawers and dipped a pen into his ink pot. 'This is highly irregular, but if it means an end to this obsession of yours I will make an exception.' He signed the travel document and handed it over. 'Don't forget to get your expenses chit from the treasury.'

Fred nodded and made for the door.

'And try to uphold the reputation of the department!'

Outliers were not allowed the freedom of roaming the time-lines, ever since Evander Pascal and the incident with Shakespeare their movements required the appropriate documentation.

The High Council imposed the limitation on travel after Pascal, one of the more radical members of the department, leaked future knowledge to the Bard. It was a form of punishment every Outlier was forced to bear, their movements tracked like school children asking for a hall pass.

Since then, none of the other guilds took them seriously. Hundreds of years later, their department was still the butt of most jokes, and excluded from events such as the Grand Temporal Ball. One of the many reasons why Fred was trying so desperately to get into the Draconians.

He knew Woodcroft expected him to fail, it was the only reason he would give him the travel permit.

Fred had forty-eight hours to prove him wrong.

7

LEVEL 4

Halley VI research base, Antarctica. Present day.

Melanie awoke with a start.

She'd been dreaming of falling through the ice and drowning in the cold, deep ocean below.

It was dark outside, which meant nothing in the Antarctic. The daylight would be gone altogether in a couple of months as winter closed in.

Rubbing the sleep out of her eyes, she opened her laptop, the time read 02:20.

'Shit.'

From the other side of the lab, the nano imager was blinking at her like a blue-eyed cyclops, making her wonder where Dave had got to. There was no way he would have let her sleep this long without wanting to know why she was using the single most expensive piece of equipment on the base.

Maybe he was too tired, she thought, trying not to let her mind wander into darker territories.

. . . .

Sipping cold tea to wash away the stale taste in her mouth, Melanie walked over to the imager and tapped on the screen.

Snapshots of the molecular structures of virus proteins appeared in gaudy purples and blues like deep-sea organisms floating in a sea of human cells.

Cursing, Melanie went back to her desk to find her glasses next to her keyboard, which had doubled as a pillow on more than one occasion.

Still half asleep, she squinted at the screen, tapping the display to zoom in on the strange, string-like shapes that hung there.

She printed the enlarged image and examined it under a lamp.

It was a virus, there was no doubt about it, just not one that she'd ever seen.

Ignoring the lateness of the hour, she picked up the phone and called Richardson's room, but there was no answer.

He would have to wait, for now she would need to check on her patient.

Walking through the station in a hazmat suit reminded Melanie of a space station from a seventies sci-fi movie. To conserve power, the motion sensors only lit the section she was moving through. The low-energy LEDs casting an eerie green glow over the metal bulkheads.

The Halley VI was built from separate compartments which were bolted together to create a long, cylindrical structure that stood on moveable legs.

The entire base had already been relocated twice during her tenancy, both times owing to shifts in the ice pack, which was unstable. Large crevasses could develop at any point and swallow them whole. When she first arrived, the thought of it would keep her awake at night, but slowly she got used to the grinding sounds of the shifting ice, until it became a kind of lullaby.

. . .

Pausing at the junction between the science pod and the main compartment, Melanie held her breath, straining to hear through her helmet, she listened for any sign of the crew.

But there was nothing beyond the hum of the environmental systems.

The base suddenly felt like a tomb.

Trying to ignore the icy knot that was forming in her stomach, she turned to the pressure hatch that led to the sick bay and pulled on the door release.

The man's screaming faintly echoed down the corridor, raising the hairs on the back of her neck.

It took everything she had to step over the threshold and into the pod.

Even at a distance she could see that the sick bay's observation window was smeared with blood. Taking a long, slow breath, she tried not to think about what was going on inside.

Melanie tested the handle and was relieved to find it was still locked.

Pushing the intercom next to the hatch she listened to the ranting inside.

A slow, methodical thudding was interspersed by outbursts in his native language.

'Hello? This is Doctor Braithwaite,' she said into the mic. 'Do you speak English?'

The gibbering stopped, and somehow the silence was worse. Melanie, her heart beating like a drum against her ribs, peered through the window.

'THEY'RE ALL DEAD! MY GOD IT'S COMING! DON'T LET IT TAKE MY EYES!'

There was a sickening thud as Johansson's head hit the glass, his face pressed against it.

Blood and spittle dripped from his mouth, his eyes were red with massively dilated pupils.

'DON'T LET IT OUT OF THE BOX!'

He was clearly delusional, the ravings of a deranged mind, but she knew better than to attempt to sedate him without backup.

Leaving the sick bay, Melanie tried to run down the corridor, but the suit was too cumbersome. Stumbling through the connecting door, she sealed it and made her way to the Rec Room.

It was empty, the tables still stacked with half-finished bottles of rum and whisky.

Melanie stopped and pulled off the hood of the suit so she could take a deep breath. Her heart was racing, and she felt nauseous. *This was no time for a panic attack*, she told herself, picking up one of the half-finished glasses, she knocked the rum back in one go.

'Guys!' she called out, straining her hearing for any response. Then, when there was no answer, she went over to the intercom and opened a base-wide channel.

'Professor Richardson, please respond.'

There was nothing but static when she released the button.

She tried again.

Walking to his quarters, she felt the effects of the alcohol kicking in. A warm glow relaxing the icy knot in her gut. Her breathing slowed and her mind cleared of the fear.

Where are they? She asked herself. The logical conclusion was that they hadn't returned to base. That they'd all bunked down at the salvage site, probably drunk. They hardly needed an excuse on a normal day, let alone the discovery of a ship that went missing over a hundred years ago.

Melanie could tell that something was wrong before she reached the door to his cabin. Objects from his room were strewn all over the corridor. Flipping the hood back over her head, she sealed herself back into the suit.

Richardson was lying on his bed, his head turned away from her, but the rash was there on his arms.

She quietly closed the door and locked it.

Her precautions may have saved her so far, but she couldn't say the same for the rest of the crew.

There will be protocols for this, she thought, trying desperately to remember what they were. The emergency procedures were kept in the command module, as was the VSAT and the HF radio, so she made her way there.

Removing the hood and taking off her gloves, she opened the thick blue arch folder labelled 'IN CASE OF EMERGENCY' underneath which the Chief had added a sticker of Homer Simpson asleep at the control desk of a nuclear power plant.

There were tabs for everything from fire, power outages, and oil spills to security threats and evacuation drills. There was nothing on quarantine for highly contagious hemorrhagic viruses, so she went with the next best thing...

In the case of a medical emergency:
1. Ensure that the patient is stable and there is no immediate danger to life
2. Contact Chief Medical Officer in Cambridge via VSAT on 2930
3. Check vessel itinerary and contact closest ship via GSMSS
4. Prepare the runway for airlift
5. Await further instructions

Sitting down at the radio, Melanie picked up the handset and changed the channel to twelve, the frequency reserved for field operatives. 'Chief McCreedy, this is Doctor Braithwaite, are you receiving me? Over.'

Releasing the call button, the speaker buzzed quietly with white noise.

She tried again.

'Chief? Do you read me? Over'

Nothing.

If there was one thing that she could rely on with the Chief is that he would never leave the station without his radio. He was a stickler for station procedure, getting lost on the ice was a serious possibility without GPS. The chances of survival outside of the climate-controlled base dropped to zero after thirty minutes, especially when the temperature fell to minus eighty degrees in the coldest months.

Melanie turned the dial through the other usual frequencies, getting nothing but more static. So she switched to the base-to-base channel and hailed the Swedish research facility at Princess Martha Coast.

'This is BAS Halley Six,' she began, trying to hide the fear in her voice. 'Are you receiving me? Over.'

In the long moment of silence, she closed her eyes and stilled her breathing.

'This is WASA, how can we help? Over,' came the unmistakeable warm tones of Igar Sorgenson, one of the more interesting characters on Antarctica.

'I'm just checking McCreedy isn't up there drinking your brännvin.'

'The Chief? Haven't seen him since Christmas. Tell him he still owes me a bottle of Absolut.'

'Roger that,' she said, trying to decide if she should mention the virus. 'Have you had any visitors lately?'

'No, why do you ask?'

'We had a salvage team turn up here yesterday, said they'd found the *Endurance*.'

'Really? Where?'

'Don't know, but wherever they went — the Chief has gone with them.'

The man laughed. 'He's a big boy, he knows how to look after himself.'

'Yeah, you're right, I'm sure he's fine,' she said, but something told her he wasn't.

The cold knot was reforming in her stomach as Melanie tried not to imagine what could have happened to the Chief and the rest of the team. Hypothermia was a terrible way to die, hallucinations were common and even paradoxical undressing; victims would be found naked in the snow, their clothes scattered over the ground where they lay.

Picking up the VSAT phone she dialled the number for the Chief Medical Officer.

The line clicked and chirped as the connection established.

'Hello, this is Doctor Malcolm Jenkins,' a voice responded in a calm, polite English accent. 'What is the nature of the medical emergency?'

Melanie forgot that Cambridge was eleven hours behind them, it was still afternoon in the UK.

It was so good to hear a friendly voice, her mind went blank. For a moment, she couldn't think of what to say.

'Hello?'

Focus.

'Er. Hi, I'm Doctor Melanie Braithwaite, stationed at Halley Six. There's been an outbreak of a hemorrhagic virus. I have two infected and many more missing, presumed to be also infected. I need help.' She wished she could have had made it sound more professional.

The line was silent for what seemed like minutes.

'Have you isolated the infected?'

'I don't know where they all are. There's a team off-base. They've been missing since yesterday. Patient zero is secure and Professor Richardson is catatonic.'

Again another ominous pause.

'Are you showing any signs of contagion yourself Doctor Braithwaite?'

The word was an odd one, it sounded like something from the days of the Black Death. She thought of those beak-like masks the plague doctors used to wear.

She pulled the suit cuffs up from her wrist, inspecting her forearms for any sign of patterning. 'No, I took hazmat precautions.'

'Good. Stay on the line. I need to talk to the Commissioner.'

The silence was deafening.

Melanie put the phone on speaker, and tried to distract herself by studying the print-out of the virus.

It was shaped like a snowflake, reminding her of an adenovirus, but it was wrong somehow. She couldn't explain what was bothering her, and she would need an electron microscope to be sure, which they didn't have. At least she could start an infectivity assay to try and identify the viral proteins.

MacAllister would know, she thought, if there was one thing the professor was good for it was identifying a virus, his encyclopaedic knowledge of deadly pathogens was what had attracted her to work for him in the first place.

'Doctor Braithwaite?' Jenkins's voice returned, snapping her out of her reverie. 'Are you still there?'

'Yes.'

'Look, we've got a slight issue. It's going to take thirty-six hours to get a team to you. Do you think you can hold on until we get there?'

'Sure,' she said, 'I'll run some tests in the mean time.'

'Look after yourself,' he added calmly. 'Try to establish a level four quarantine.'

8

ENDURANCE

Print Archive, British Library, London. 1858.

W hilst many members of the Order chose to use the time-lines of artefacts from museums, Fred preferred the feel of a book's time-line. There was something rather solid and reliable about a piece of well-bound print in his hand.

There were thousands of 'Vestige' books in the British Library, each one providing a route to a specific period in time. Linears typically referred to them as 'rare', but to members of the Order they were simply trail markers that could be followed.

Smiling coyly at Katy as he passed her desk, Fred wandered amongst the rare books until he found a first edition of Chaucer's Canterbury Tales.

Checking to ensure he was unobserved, he opened the glass case and ran his fingers over a page of Caxton's fourteenth century print, feeling the lines of temporal energy shifting beneath the surface as its chronology rose to his touch.

He could feel the age of the book come to life in his hand. Four hundred years of history unravelled like a web of fine silk, knotted with significant events along its thread. Fred could read the moments as they slipped through his fingers, and the longing to move back to the day it was printed was overwhelming, as was the disappointment in knowing that he couldn't.

Instead, he turned his attention to the short branch of time that spiralled away toward the Frontier. Closing his eyes, he took a deep breath and pushed himself towards the future.

He made it half way.

A hundred and sixty-four years was too great a leap in one go. It was late 1940 and Fred could hear the sound of air raid sirens. *The Blitz*, he thought, taking a deep breath and closing his eyes once more. The distant rumble of bombs was still ringing in his ears as he arrived at the Frontier.

The first time Fred visited the British Library in the present day, he'd been disappointed to find it was no longer part of the British Museum, but relocated to a rather unattractive new building near London's St Pancras Station.

It seemed that the storage of every book ever printed had become something of a problem for the linear librarians. They didn't have the advantage of the temporal architecture of the Scriptorian's Great Library, a collection that dwarfed theirs by some orders of magnitude.

Katy was very proud of her guild's work in the restoration of lost manuscripts. The Great Library held the entire collection of Alexandria, taken moments before the fire consumed it, the tablets of Uruk, lost for millennia and rescued from the floods that would have destroyed them, and the missing second book of *Poetics* by Aristotle.

At one point, after his first rejection from the Draconians, Fred had seriously considered joining the Retrievals Division of the Scriptorians, but Monty talked him out of it.

'Have you seen the state of them? Most have lost limbs, or have terrible burns that even Doctor Crooke can't heal properly.'

He was right, the retrievers risked everything to save the rare documents, taking them in the final moments before they were destroyed to ensure they weren't observed. This generally meant pulling them out of a fire, tsunami or volcanic eruption. 'Not for the faint-hearted,' was the motto above the entrance to their headquarters. Doctor Crooke's temporal healing had kept many from certain death.

The news archive was mostly online or stored on microfilm, which Fred saw as the lesser of two evils. Scrolling through reproductions of a 1917 edition of The Times, Fred found the last report. Wired from South Georgia, it described how the search was finally called off, an Argentinian vessel returning from the last known position empty-handed.

Shackleton and the crew of *Endurance* had disappeared without trace into the ice.

Reading the account, Fred's heart sank. Somehow he'd hoped that the outcome had changed, that perhaps some Draconian team, having heard the news of its discovery had used the ship to go back and correct the timeline, or at least allow them to be rescued.

Fred believed that, just like Franklin's ill-fated expedition to find the Northwest Passage in 1845, the *Endurance* had become trapped in the ice and the men poisoned by lead in the tinned food.

But without the ship, there was no way to prove his theory, and now his career depended on it.

The latest edition of The Times lay on the desk beside him, a much changed format than the broadsheet he was used to in 1858, but he was glad to feel the newsprint between his fingers.

The headlines spoke of war in Ukraine and escalating fuel prices, but buried on the fifth page was the report of the discovery. Trapped in the ice for over a hundred years, the American team that discovered *Endurance* had been funded by an anonymous organisation to the tune of ten million dollars.

Copying the coordinates of the wreck down into his almanac, Fred watched as they transformed into a beautiful map, adding to the other key locations of the voyage.

Shackleton's mission was an odd one, coming just five years after Roald Amundsen staked Norway's claim on the South Pole. He proposed to traverse the ice-bound continent, north to south. A trek of some eighteen-hundred miles over the most inhospitable terrain on the planet, to the Ross Sea on the southern side.

It was something that always bothered Fred. Overshadowed by the tragedy of the failed expedition, the original objective had seemed to be rather pointless.

Scratching his head, he flicked back through his notes.

The planning began in earnest on hearing the news of Captain Scott's failure to reach the pole in February 1913. By December, Ernest Shackleton had the financial backing he needed, including an unusual £10,000 grant from the British Government, but the question that was bothering Fred was *why*?

With tensions building in Europe, leading to the First World War, why would the Government invest such a large sum of money into a madcap adventure to the other side of the world?

After two hours of searching through the archives, Fred found the original accounts ledger for the mission in a sub-basement. Every library was overseen by the Scriptorian Guild, and one of the advantages of being a member of the Order was unrestricted access to the lower vaults.

Wearing thin cotton gloves, Fred handled the records with reverence, its marbled cover still carrying the beautifully scripted label, written in Shackleton's own hand.

Accounts of the Imperial Trans-Antarctic Expedition 1913.

Laying it carefully on the desk, he gently lifted the cover, wincing as the brittle bindings cracked, reminding him how long it had been since this book was last opened.

The pages of the ledger were filled with the details of every purchase and expense, each line written in fluid copperplate in fading black and red ink.

Reading through the provisions itinerary was intriguing. The meticulously recorded notes of each purchase making it seem more real somehow.

One thousand tins of meat, two hundred tins of beans, five tons of oats, fourteen sacks of dried fruit, sixteen sides of bacon, four barrels of cocoa powder.

Turning the pages, Fred scanned the columns of figures, looking for the income amongst the many lines of expenditure.

On the fifth page he found the sum of £10,000, and a line that simply read.

Dept. Psych. Res. For transport of cargo.

Copying the line into his almanac, he continued to search the ledger. There was no other mention of a Government grant, nor a sum equal to the ten thousand pounds – although there were considerable sums from wealthy donors like the playwright J.M. Barrie and Sir James Key Caird, the Scottish industrialist.

Sitting under the dim light of the single lamp, Fred chewed on the end of his pencil, wondering what cargo could be worth nearly as much as the ship itself.

And what was this mysterious Psych department?

There was only one way to know for sure.

Taking off one of his gloves, Fred traced his fingers over the entry, closing his eyes to feel for the time-line below the surface of the page.

Slowly, lines of temporal energy rose to meet his fingertips and he began to tease out the ledger's history.

It's just within my range, he thought, slowing his breathing as images of an office appeared in his mind. He caught the scent of leather and mahogany, heard the low, muffled sound of men talking in the next room, and focused on the moment.

As the vault around him dissolved away, replaced by the wood-panelled walls of the Royal Geographical Society, Fred took another deep breath, pushing against the fabric of time and felt it give way.

The room solidified as his presence in the timeline stabilised, the sense of dislocation passing almost instantaneously.

Treading lightly, he moved to the door.

He listened to their argument whilst trying hard not to make a sound, all the time knowing that one of his greatest heroes was standing on the other side.

'We need the money Ernest!' said a man in a broad Scottish accent.

'Not if it jeopardises the mission,' came the sharp reply.

'But it's ten thousand pounds man!'

'Who the hell are they anyway? I've never heard of the Department of Psychical Research?'

'Does it really matter? If the Government want to give us ten thousand pounds to ship something down there, who are we to argue? Could be the devil himself for all I care!'

Fred realised that the other man must be William Speirs Bruce, the leader of the Scottish National Antarctic Expedition, the one who'd given Shackleton the original idea for the crossing.

'I don't trust that Lieutenant Murray,' protested Shackleton. 'There's something shifty about his eyes.'

'You have little choice.'

There was a sound of movement, footsteps walking towards the door.

Fred hesitated for a second, caught with a sudden urge to stand his ground and meet the man in the flesh, but his presence in what was effectively a locked room would be too difficult to explain. So, closing his eyes, he let his mind draw his body back to the library.

. . .

After an hour of extensive searching, he could find no other reference to the Department of Psychical Research in the archives, which in itself was a little odd, since the Scriptorians prided themselves on their Government records.

Conscious that he'd already used too many hours of his allotted time, he made a note to follow it up.

He still had to get kitted out before he went down to see the ship.

9

ARRIVAL

Halley VI research base, Antarctica. Present day.

Melanie tried to keep herself busy, spending most of the day on her computer developing a mathematical infection model of the virus. She needed something to distract herself from the nagging dread that threatened to overwhelm her.

She was all alone.

Everyone else was dead.

By the time the sun rose, Johansson had succumbed to the virus.

Professor Richardson was close behind.

Melanie knew they would want her to start an autopsy, but couldn't face going in there. There were only two hazmat suits on the base and she'd already ruined one searching the station for any other survivors.

The sleeping quarters were all empty, as were the generator and plant modules.

She'd systematically locked each of the doors behind her as she went. Shutting down the heating, turning the entire station into a giant freezer. The temperature would quickly drop to minus forty degrees, reducing the chance of the virus replicating and creating a temporary morgue for the dead.

It's going to be a long day, she thought, pouring herself a thick, black coffee and taking a packet of biscuits from Dave's secret stash in his desk.

'On the upside,' Melanie said to herself. 'There had been some progress on the infectivity assay.'

Dunking the chocolate digestive into the steaming cup, she settled herself back into the chair and leaned into the microscope once more.

The virus had a double-stranded DNA, and from what she could deduce from her initial results the replication rate was incredible — it was doubling every two hours, far quicker than most single-stranded RNA.

This was like no other organism she'd ever seen.

Putting aside her feelings of impending doom, she did what any self-respecting virologist should do. Opening up an email, Melanie wrote a quick summary of her findings and attached the images from the fluoroscopy, then sent it to her old tutor at Imperial; copying in the BAS administrator and The World Health Organisation.

It was late and the sun was setting. Melanie's stomach reminded her that she needed to eat something. She'd survived on chocolate biscuits and coffee, but now she would need to venture out to the kitchen.

Putting on her Canada Goose parka, she left the warmth of the Science Module and stepped out into the corridor. Instantly, she could feel the heat draining from her cheeks. Frost coated the inside of the windows and her breath crystallised on the glass as she looked out over the glittering white landscape.

Wiping the fog away with a gloved hand, Melanie's eye caught something approaching the base. A black dot moving low over the horizon.

Her heart beat a little faster as she ran back to the lab to get her binoculars.

The aircraft approached like a bird of prey, swooping low, its dark wings stirring up white clouds of snow from the icy tundra. Melanie watched it from the observation deck on the roof of the Rec Room, the freezing air burning in her lungs.

They're too early. Her caffeine-overdosed brain tried to tell her, but she ignored it.

It didn't matter, the cavalry had arrived, she wasn't going to be alone any more.

As it flew closer she could see the plane was an Osprey with a tilt-rotor engine, not the usual type of aircraft that flew to Antarctica, most were C-17s or adapted Hercules LC-130s.

Rotating its turbines to make a vertical landing, the sound was deafening. Shielding her eyes from the swirl of biting ice that blossomed around it. Melanie caught sight of the insignia and her heart sank when she realised it wasn't the RAF, but bore the markings of the US military.

Climbing down from the platform, she made her way towards it.

As the rotor blades of the Osprey wound down, a door opened in the side of the fuselage and two armed men in bio-warfare suits jumped down.

One motioned to her to halt while the other aimed his weapon directly at her.

Shit. Melanie slumped to her knees and placed her hands behind her head.

'Where are the others?' asked the Colonel, looking through the window into the sick bay.

They had insisted on her wearing a bio-hazard suit with a two-way radio built into the helmet. It was more advanced than the standard BAS issue; these came with their own oxygen supply and climate control. Melanie felt like she could have walked on the moon.

According to the tag on the front of his uniform, the commander's name was Colonel Cooper. A stern looking man with a grey beard and a closely shaved head. His eyes were cold and emotionless, and there was a pallor to his skin that spoke of hard drinking and cigarettes. He carried himself like a man who could kill you with one hand.

He'd sent his men ahead to check there were no survivors on the base, even though she'd already told them there were none.

'They went with the other crew, back to the *Endurance*.'

He turned towards her, the lights in his helmet shining around his bald head like a halo. 'How long ago?'

The lack of sleep and stress was making it hard for Melanie to think clearly, the last twenty-four hours was something of a blur.

'Yesterday, they turned up with Johansson just after four pm'

'Sixteen hundred hours,' he noted. 'And the rest of your team went with them?'

'They seemed pretty excited.'

'I guess they would be. The ship's been missing for over a hundred years.'

She wanted to ask which base he'd come from. The Osprey had an operational range of a thousand miles at most. These were the kind of random facts that you learned when you spent too long in the company of the Chief and his engineers — it couldn't have made the flight from South Georgia.

Before she had the chance, the Colonel opened the sick bay door.

Johansson lay naked on the floor in a dark pool, a circle of runic symbols surrounding him, drawn in his own blood.

The fractal rash was fading, it was nothing more than a faint purple pattern stippling his back now.

Two soldiers walked in carrying a heavy-duty black bag and laid it next to his body. The bio-hazard symbols on the side were accompanied by a corporate logo, BioVage, the same US Pharmaceutical

Company that Professor McAllister was in discussions with when she got kicked out.

'Who told you to come?' asked Melanie. 'Did BAS contact you?'

The men lifted the body and placed it into the bag. The Colonel squatted down, examining the strange markings that Johansson had drawn on the floor.

'No, our orders came directly from the CDC.'

'And how did they know?' she asked, beginning to suspect that these guys weren't who they said they were.

Cooper got back to his feet with a grunt. 'Just be grateful we were in the vicinity. Chances are you'd be dead before your guys would've got here. Do you know what these mean?'

She glanced down at the floor.

'Looks like old Norse,' she said, having recently finished the last season of 'Vikings' on Prime, she recognised some of the symbols.

'Baskins, get in here and take some shots of this,' Cooper barked into his radio.

Walking back to the doorway, he examined the scratch marks on the back of the door. 'You locked him in here?'

'I didn't know what else to do.'

'Probably saved your life.'

10

QUIRKS

Bow Lane, London. Present Day.

Hidden away in the narrow alleys of Bow Lane; *Quirks & Co, Gentlemen's Outfitters*, could easily claim to be one of the oldest shops in London, even back in 1858.

The proprietor was an Antiquarian by the name of Jeremiah Quirk, and it was to him that any explorer worth their salt went to be fitted out for their adventures.

Standing in the pouring rain, Fred peered through the mullioned windows, marvelling at the leather flying coats and gabardine safari jackets. Having accompanied his father and brothers on numerous occasions, it had always been a dream to come here one day for his own fitting.

Quirk's tailored every Draconian uniform by hand, from materials that could withstand the rigours of long adventures into the past. Time had a strange way of failing modern materials. Polyesters and other man-made fibres wouldn't survive beyond the date they were invented.

. . .

To the unassuming passer-by, the establishment was nothing more than a bespoke tailor, overlooked and ignored by all but the most discerning of clientèle. Fred wasn't quite sure what kind of temporal shielding Quirk was using, but the shop was quite easy to miss if one wasn't looking for it — your gaze seemed to simply slip over it.

Taking a deep breath, he set his shoulders back, pushed open the door and walked inside.

A bell chimed as he stepped into the mahogany panelled boutique. The place smelled of old leather and sandalwood, like an old cricket bat, with the slightest hint of cologne.

'And how may I be of service?' intoned a smartly dressed man, appearing from behind a tall mirror.

Quirk wore a brown three-piece suit, and a dark blue shirt with a gold cravat tied around his neck. His hair was almost silver, as was his neatly trimmed goatee. He had a sharp nose on which he balanced a pair of half-moon glasses and olive skin drawn tightly over his cheekbones.

'I'm going to visit Antarctica,' said Fred, stumbling over his words. 'I need the appropriate kit.'

The tailor's eyes flashed and he seemed to glide towards Fred, a tape measure appearing in his hand out of thin air. 'And which century will sir be visiting?'

'Present day.'

'Ah the glorious Frontier,' said Quirk, running the tape across Fred's shoulders and down his arm. 'How I wish I had the time to pay it a visit.'

Fred thought it wise not to point out that they were actually in the present. The Antiquarian had lived so long he'd obviously lost track of what century he was in.

Standing still while the tailor continued with his measurements, Fred studied the racks of clothes in the cabinets.

They appeared to be changing as the tailor muttered to himself.

'Chest: forty-two. Shoulders: twenty-three. Back: thirty-six.'

A grey parka, its hood lined with white fur appeared next to a set of blue over-trousers and a set of thermal long johns. This was the benefit of temporal tailoring, Fred supposed, that clothes were being made to order somewhere in the past.

'And how many days will sir be staying at the South Pole?' Quirk said, kneeling down to measure his inside leg.

'Just the one,' Fred replied, wishing it could be more.

'Hmm, it's been a while since I've had the pleasure of dressing an *Outlier*,' he said, pronouncing the last word with a French accent. 'One hopes that there is nothing to concern us down there?'

'They've found the *Endurance*.'

Stepping back the tailor's eyes flashed once more as the tape measure disappeared. 'The *Endurance*? Yes, I had the pleasure of serving Sir Ernest and his officers. Fine fellow indeed, very resilient.'

Behind him, the rack of clothes was complete.

'Will you be needing the usual accessories?' Quirk asked as two assistants appeared and began to wrap the finished garments.

Fred had no idea what he meant, but nodded all the same.

Quirk pulled open a velvet lined drawer filled with an array of equipment: tortoise shell binoculars sat beside round-lensed, leather-bound sunglasses, pistols, ivory-handled knives and the most beautiful tachyon Fred had ever seen.

'The Mark Seven,' Quirk said, taking it delicately from the drawer. 'Possibly the most elegant chronometer ever made.'

Fred felt the weight of the tachyon in his hand, stroking its casement with his thumb, it truly was a masterpiece. The concentric dials whirred silently around the brass casing, each one marking the time in a different century. The buttons along its edge hardly protruded from the case, which itself had been inscribed with intricate chronographs.

He'd never owned his own timepiece, and had no intention of starting now.

'No, thank you,' Fred said, handing it back. 'I have my own.'

Fred pulled his tachyon from his waistcoat and held it up.

Balancing a pair of pince-nez glasses in front of his spectacles, Quirk studied the watch.

'A Mark Three Timemaster, well I never! I haven't seen one of those in a long while, and in such good condition. I have to admit I'm something of a collector, do you know they only made a hundred of these?'

'It was my father's,' Fred explained, not particularly comfortable with the way the man was admiring it.

Quirk licked his lips. 'I don't suppose you would be interested in selling it? Or maybe a trade?'

Fred shook his head. 'No. Sorry.'

A flicker of disappointment crossed the tailor's face. 'Well, never mind. Here are your packages — how would you like to pay?'

There was an awkward moment while Fred searched his pockets for the chit from the Outlier treasurer. He unfolded the promissory note and handed it to Quirk. 'The department is paying.'

'Of course they are.' Quirk sneered, holding the note between two fingers like a soiled nappy.

11

PRISONER

Halley VI research base, Antarctica, March 2022

Melanie was too angry to cry.

This was the second time in her career she'd been sidelined just as she was about to make a major discovery.

For her own safety, Colonel Cooper instructed his men to keep her under quarantine on the Osprey. She tried to argue with him as they marched her out of the station towards the plane, but he just ignored her.

They confiscated all of her work, making some excuse about it being 'an issue of national security,' which was bullshit as far as she was concerned. Antarctica was governed by a treaty signed in 1959, designating it as a continent devoted to peace and science. Halley VI was effectively on British soil, it had sovereignty, just like an embassy in a foreign country.

They had no right to do this, she thought, *treating me like a prisoner*. But it was hard to argue when you were staring at the business end of an M60.

. . .

The inside of the Osprey was just like any other transport plane; webbing hung down from the walls and cold metal jump seats lined each side of the fuselage. *This wasn't designed for long-haul flights*, she thought, *so where's the ship?*

It was well known that the US Navy made regular tours below the sixtieth parallel, supposedly in the name of supply and survey, but Chief McCreedy had his own theories on what they were really doing — especially when he was drunk.

'Submarine base,' he would whisper conspiratorially as if the Rec Room was bugged. 'Right beneath us.' Then he'd stomp on the floor with his boot. 'Los Angeles class - 688i's, designed for under-ice operations.'

In Melanie's opinion, it was highly unlikely there was a secret base beneath the ice, the treaty banned any military activity in Antarctica, but McCreedy was right about one thing: there was a near-permanent US Navy presence in the Southern Ocean beyond McMurdo Sound.

After an hour, she heard men talking outside. They were moving closer to the bulkhead that separated the passenger compartment from the cargo section, she recognised Colonel Cooper's unmistakable Southern drawl as he barked orders.

The whirr of hydraulics from the tailgate lowering was followed by the unmistakable revving of snowmobile engines. Melanie smelled the gasoline fumes as they drove them out of the back of the aircraft.

If they were planning to head over to the *Endurance*; she could only imagine what they were going to find when they got there.

What was the ship carrying that could have caused this? She wondered, watching through an icy window as the men rode off into the distance. An abandoned exploration ship didn't really fit the profile for a previously unknown virus source. It was unlikely to have evolved from some old tins of food that had been in a natural freezer for over a hundred years.

12

THE SHIP

Endurance, **Weddell Sea, Antarctica. Present Day.**

Surveying the endless white plain around him, Fred wondered where everybody was.

Quirk's goggles were fitted with special lensing glass, allowing him to view the time-lines of those who had passed by in the last few hours.

But the temporal landscape was just as devoid of life as the physical one.

Rising up before him, suspended inside a glacial rift, the *Endurance* sat like an insect trapped in amber, its masts and rigging still intact as if frozen in time — which it quite literally was.

It was truly a majestic sight. The three-masted barquentine was one hundred and forty-four feet long and had a gross tonnage measuring over three hundred and fifty. Her bow was still intact. Lifted high out of the sea, it was made to meet the ice head on, each timber being fashioned from a separate oak tree and at least fifty inches thick.

The masts had faired less well, Fred could see that only the fore-mast was still rigged for sail; he assumed that the others had been cut down and used for shelter. She was fitted with a coal-fired steam engine that was capable of speeds up to ten knots, so a lack of sail wasn't necessarily a recipe for disaster.

He shivered at the thought of being trapped here. Even with his goose-down expedition parka and double-worsted long johns, his body was still acclimatising to the sudden drop in temperature. Less than ten minutes ago, he'd been standing in a nice warm hotel room in St Pancras station wondering whether he needed to take the ridiculous hat that Quirk had insisted on giving him as a gift — now he was glad of it.

A huddle of tents and rigid huts had been assembled to the right of the ship. His lenses told him they too were empty, but he still avoided the basecamp and followed the safety line to the access tunnel bored into the side of the glacier.

Inside the entrance, the walls were smooth like glass, melted with some kind of thermal lance, and the floor rose by degrees so that within a few minutes he was standing on the deck of the ship.

Still no one appeared to challenge him.

Helpfully, the salvage team had hollowed out most of the upper deck, like a bubble inside a snow globe, Fred looked out at the distorted view of the world beyond.

The air was warm inside, and the deck awash with meltwater. Taking off his hat and goggles, it was hard to believe he was standing on the Weather Deck of the fabled *Endurance* after so long.

Fred considered taking off one of his gloves to touch something and revisit a moment from before the mission went awry — partly to find out what had happened, but also to experience the thrill of being among the crew.

The threat of frostbite changed his mind.

Something was wrong, his instincts told him. *This was too easy.*

He couldn't ignore the fact that a find like this should have men guarding the entrance, let alone working around the base.

The distant sound of engines brought him back to reality.

Through the magnified prism of the glacial walls he caught the flicker of movement. A group of men were moving fast across the ice, riding strange motorised sleds and carrying weapons.

Soldiers? He thought, his heart beginning to beat a little faster, *there weren't supposed to be military on Antarctica.* It was a place for peaceful, scientific research.

Pulling off one of his gloves with his teeth, he reached inside his parka, and took out his father's tachyon.

It felt cool to the touch, as it always did. Flicking open the outer casing, he stroked his thumb across the concentric dials, lingering on the three temporal markers. Set just as they had been when his father last used it. Fred couldn't bring himself to change them and had no intention of revisiting them either.

The stomp of heavy boots coming up the tunnel snapped him out of his reverie and he hastily put it into an outer pocket of his coat.

Men with guns barked orders to each other as they moved swiftly towards the deck.

Frantically, Fred looked around for somewhere to hide. The doors to the cabins were all sealed, still covered in a layer of ice.

Moving quickly towards the open hatch on the deck, he looked down into the hold.

As his eyes acclimatised to the darkness, he saw the bodies, lots of them, and they were not all from Shackleton's crew.

'Stand still!' came a command from behind him. 'Put your hands where I can see them!'

13

OSPREY

Osprey, Halley VI Station, Antarctica, March 2022

The hatch in the fuselage cracked opened and a blinding white light poured into the compartment.

Melanie blinked, shading her eyes as two guards manhandled someone through the door and threw them into a seat on the opposite side from her.

'Stay there!' one of the men barked, 'Any more trouble from you and I'll cuff you to the wall.'

Their prisoner was already sporting a cut lip and a bruise below his left eye. He said something to the men which she didn't catch and one raised the butt of his rifle.

'Enough!' said the other soldier, grabbing his arm. 'The Colonel wants to question him later.'

The bigger man grunted and left without a word. His colleague followed, slamming the hatch closed behind him.

The red-headed man shrugged and gave her a twisted smile.

'Are you okay?' she said, getting up from her seat. 'I'm a doctor.'

'I think so,' he replied, probing his cheek with his tongue.

'Although I think they may have loosened one or two of my teeth. Rather uncouth chaps, don't you think?'

Melanie laughed inadvertently, his accent was like something from a Charles Dickens novel. 'Where are you from?' she asked, checking his pupils, trying to ignore the fact that his eyes were a deep shade of brown.

The man looked a little confused. 'Great Britain?'

Suspecting concussion, Melanie kept him talking. 'Can you follow my finger?'

His pupils tracked her movements perfectly.

'I meant which base are you from?'

'Ah, I see. Yes. That's a little tricky. I'm not actually supposed to be here you see. It's all a bit hush-hush.'

She stepped back, looking him up and down. 'You're a spy?'

The man's cheeks coloured a little. 'Not exactly, no. My name's Frederick, Frederick Ross. Although most call me Fred.' Raising one eyebrow, he held out his hand. 'Pleased to meet you.'

'Melanie Braithwaite,' she responded, taking his hand and shaking it. 'Are you from MI6?'

He shook his head. 'Goodness no. I'm researching the *Endurance*. That's where they captured me.'

Her eyes widened. 'You saw it?'

Fred sighed. 'Yes, and it wasn't a pretty sight.'

'My team went over there two days ago. None of them returned.'

His gaze dropped to the floor. 'And I'm afraid they never will.'

She settled back in her chair, an awkward silence growing between them as they contemplated the dead.

'It's a virus,' she said quietly after a few minutes.

'A what?' he replied, his voice echoing down the body of the plane.

Melanie tried a different tack. 'An infectious disease that can be passed by contact?'

'Ah, a contagion — like the plague?'

'Yes, I suppose so,' she replied, a little confused by his odd terminology.

Frowning, Fred began searching through the inner pockets of his parka. 'There were no reports of any infection in the Captain's last report. Perhaps it was something that occurred after the crew left the boat.'

'You've read the reports?'

He took out a leather-bound notebook and flicked through the pages. Each was covered in tiny handwriting and strange diagrams that, for a second, looked as if they were moving.

'No, definitely no report of sickness, other than the usual frostbite and scurvy of course,' he said, holding up one particular section and tapping it with his finger.

Squinting, she tried to read the tiny notes.

'Captain Worsley kept exceedingly good records all the way down to South Georgia.'

Melanie scanned the text, diary entries from the voyage were copied down in a beautiful copperplate script. Fred ran his finger along the edge of the page and the contents scrolled as if it were in a browser window.

'What kind of device is this?' she asked, taking the book from him.

'Probably shouldn't have shown you that. May I have it back please?'

She flicked through the rest of the book, stopping every so often to study the animating diagrams and maps that formed across the surface of the page.

'It's incredible,' she whispered. 'Is this new? It feels like paper.'

He leaned forward and took it from her, putting it back inside his coat. 'No, actually it's very old.'

Melanie's eyes narrowed, her expression hardening. 'Who are you exactly — where are you from?'

Fred sighed and ran a hand through his red hair. 'I'm from 1858. I guess you would call me something of a time traveller.'

She laughed. 'And I'm the Queen of Sheba.'

His tone became serious. 'Listen. I was sent here to investigate the ship. I didn't know about this plague thingy, but from the look of our current situation I don't think we should linger here. Since I've already broken one of our most fundamental laws in showing you the almanac, I believe the best course of action is for us to leave.'

She scoffed. 'And where do you suggest we go? It's minus forty outside and the nearest base is over two hundred miles away. Not to mention there's a storm coming in.' She pointed to the flakes of snow smashing into the window.

'Back to 1858,' he said, taking out an antique pocket watch and holding it up.

The face was a series of concentric dials, all turning at different speeds.

'And what is that? Your time machine?'

Fred grimaced at the thought of using it. 'It's called a tachyon. It was my father's. It records where I've been, the paths I've taken.'

'Like a Sat Nav?'

He stared at her blankly. 'What is a Sat Nav?'

She rolled her eyes. 'Satellite Navigation. It's a type of interactive map. Like the ones in your journal.'

Fred rubbed his head as if the concept was making it hurt. 'No, not like that. It's different. More like a phonograph.'

There were noises outside.

'Well, whatever it is, you'd better do something quickly. They're coming back.'

Fred closed his eyes and let the timelines unwind from the tachyon. His short routes were clear to see, a fine web of journeys back and forth from 1858, but behind them, fading into the background were his father's last jumps. Long, sprawling paths reaching far back into the past.

This was no time for sentimentality, he told himself gritting his teeth and reaching for the closest point, he took Melanie by the hand.

14

THE ROADS LESS TRAVELLED

The Shadow Realm.

L yra studied the map for a moment, then made a note against a small illustration of a tower.

Not Rivendell. She wrote carefully in a child-like hand, drawing a line to attach the text to the tower where it fluttered like a kite in the wind.

Looking up from her journal, her eyes scanned the bleak landscape beyond the crooked pile of stones that she imagined was once a mighty fortress.

Overhead, the sky was dark and filled with boiling storm clouds, always threatening to rain, but never quite delivering. Since the first time she'd visited, the realm had seemed permanently trapped in a state of dusk, leeching the colour out of the world and painting the landscape in shades of grey and brown.

A dusty path stretched out through the coarse moorland towards the East, and another went North.

To Mordor? Lyra pondered, knowing that the Northern route almost always ended at a high mountain range — one she'd never been able to find a way through.

Not today.

Putting her journal away, Lyra pulled her coat tightly around her and turned towards the East, setting off in the direction of Gondor.

It was one of the thirteen kingdoms she'd already discovered — or at least where it should have been the last time she came this way.

That was one of the major issues with mapping the Shadow Realm. As her predecessor E.M. Williams noted in her book: 'The Wanderer', the paths were not fixed. They changed at random, her maps were covered with notes and amendments.

Eventually, Williams came to the conclusion that approaching the same junction from a different direction seemed to lead to a new set of trails — the journey becoming as important as the destination.

Lyra spent almost a year trying to understand them, making her own charts and updating the ones that Williams had created.

To make it more memorable, Lyra decided to use locations from Tolkien's *Lord of the Rings*. Inventing names for places like Rivendell, Mordor and Gondor, gave the realm a familiarity, made it more interesting than it probably was.

But the more she discovered, the more relevant Tolkien's naming seemed to be, and she was beginning to wonder whether the author might have visited the realm himself.

This was a shadow dimension; a parallel world made up of redundant branches of time, forgotten corners left to crumble and fade. Ruined epochs whose paths Lyra had wandered since she was a child. For a seer of her abilities, exploring the empty streets behind the mirrors was more interesting than the harsh reality of the continuum — and quieter too.

According to the foreword in her book, E.M. Williams spent over a century in this world, searching for the elusive god-like figure known as 'The Wanderer', although he had many other names, mostly

Nordic: Odin, the Allfather, Shepherd of Shadows. Every culture had a version of the elusive god.

Lyra believed she'd met him once. On that occasion, he called himself Abandon. The ancient spirit gave her a gift, a key, that changed her life, enhancing her abilities to 'See'.

Now it was more of a curse than a gift. The constant chatter of other people's fates distracted her to the point of madness in the real world. She no longer needed physical contact with others to experience their destiny, making it impossible to stay in anyone's company for too long, even Benoir's.

And it was driving a wedge between them.

When they'd first met, Lyra had promised him that she would never look into his future, but it was becoming impossible. His fate unfolded around him like a shroud and no amount of training with the Grand Seer was helping her to control it.

The Shadow Realm had become a sanctuary.

But in all her time of searching, she'd yet to find Abandon again. Lyra hoped he would have answers, and that perhaps he could take back the gift he'd given her, make her normal, whatever that was.

Because Lyra knew what would happen if she didn't, Bedlam was full of Seers that couldn't control their abilities, driven mad by the relentless visions of the future.

The road to Gondor was a desolate one, littered with dead things; the skeletons of tiny creatures lay half covered in lichen and moss, like a pet cemetery that had been ransacked by wolves. Lyra picked her way amongst them, trying to avoid the sickening crunch of bone under her boots.

Reaching one of the stone bridges, she took out her water bottle and rested against the wall. The bridge spanned a giant chasm of darkness, whose sheer granite walls disappeared into the void like a crack in the very fabric of reality.

'Abandon,' she shouted into the chasm. 'Where are you?'

There was no echo, and no response, just as there hadn't been whenever she'd called out his name.

Sighing, Lyra put the water bottle back in her pack and hunched it onto her shoulders.

Looking across to the other side of the bridge she could make out the tall towers of the gates that led into Gondor. It was a welcome sight, but she knew it was still another hour's walk and her feet were aching.

'Perhaps we should go home,' she said to no one in particular. 'He'll be wondering where I am.'

She took out her notebook and marked a spot on her map, then took out a small mirror and placed it on the stone floor.

A circle of daylight shone out of the glass, lighting her face, and she felt the warmth returning to her cheeks. Taking a deep breath, she relished the familiar smell of home.

Slowly the light expanded and Lyra stepped into the wide cone of colour and sound, allowing it to encompass her.

'Benoir,' she whispered and disappeared.

15

THE JOURNAL

Endurance, **Antarctica, Present Day**

Colonel Cooper stepped down from his snowmobile and pulled off his goggles. The snow storm had reduced visibility to less than thirty yards. If it hadn't been for GPS tracking they would never have found the ship.

One of his officers, Lieutenant Miller, walked towards him as quickly as the driving snow would allow.

'Where are we at?' Cooper shouted over the howling wind, squinting up at the ruined ship trapped in the ice.

'The hazmat team is in there now. Looks like the doc was right, they found her team plus most of the salvage crew in the hold.' Miller pointed to the small shanty town of temporary shacks. 'Two of them are still in their bunks.'

Cooper grimaced. 'Any survivors?'

Miller shook his head. 'Apart from the limey, negative sir.'

The colonel sucked in a lungful of cold air and blew it out in a stream of vapour which froze instantly on his thick grey beard. 'I want the whole area locked down. Bring in the Osprey and get the bodies sealed and ready for shipping.'

Miller looked up into the storm. 'Not sure she'll be able to fly in these conditions.'

'Just do it.'

The lieutenant stepped away and took out his radio.

Cooper pulled a cigar out of his jacket pocket and clamped his teeth around it. His physician had warned him that smoking could make things worse, but he didn't say he couldn't chew on it.

Miller returned a minute later.

'Sir, we've just got word that the prisoners have escaped. Do you want me to organise a search party?'

The colonel grunted. 'In this?' He waved at the whirling vortex of snow around them. 'Where are they gonna go? It's minus forty and they're two hundred miles from the nearest base. Far as I'm concerned the less witnesses the better.'

His men were lining the body bags beside the rope that led to the *Endurance,* the incongruous black shapes standing out starkly in the white landscape. Cooper counted twenty-five bodies, that would account for the salvage team he'd sent to find the ship and at least seven from the Halley VI.

Chewing on the end of the cigar, he savoured the taste of the tobacco rolling around in his mouth, it helped him to ignore the nagging ache at the back of his skull.

The entrance to the glacier was hidden behind a series of domed tents linked together to make a quarantine zone, a kind of medical airlock.

The white canvas shook in the wind as he stepped inside.

Cooper found the advanced team being hosed down with steam, their hazmat suits glistening with ice crystals.

One of the men pulled off his hood, saluting as he walked towards him.

It was Science Officer Garcia.

'I've instigated a class four containment around the ship, sir.' He held up a titanium biohazard container. 'And taken samples. Should have a better idea of what caused it in a few hours.'

'Are all the bodies out?'

Garcia shook his head. 'We've cleared the recent victims, but Shackleton's crew are frozen to the hull, we're trying to separate them without damaging the tissue.'

Cooper nodded and continued into the next compartment.

Positive Pressure Suits were specifically designed for bio-containment. With their own air supply, it felt more like a spacesuit as Cooper climbed inside it.

There was a time when he considered joining NASA — when they still had the support of the Senate, before they lost Columbia and their funding. No one was going to back a project that ended the lives of seven American heroes quite so publicly.

Instead, he became the Director of the Medical Research and Development Division at Fort Detrick, a secure military facility for the storage and study of every deadly pathogen known to mankind.

Walking slowly up the ice tunnel, the colonel noted the marks of the thermal lances where the salvage team had carved through the glacier. It would have taken a squad of four less than a day to cut through the fifty feet of ice to reach the ship.

Officially, they were a private salvage contractor, hired by a holding company. Unofficially, they were an elite unit of specialists hand-picked by Cooper to extract documents from the ship before the rest of the world had a chance to get anywhere near it.

The Captain's Log.

But they'd failed.

Something had gone wrong.

He'd prayed that it was still there.

. . .

The cargo hatch lay to one side, leaving a gaping dark hole into the hold. Garcia's team had rigged a winch over it to haul out the dead.

Like a crime scene, the closer he got, the more signs of conflict he noticed: deep scratches gouged into the wooden planks, broken rigging and bullet holes. *Something terrible happened here*, he thought, staring down into the dark space below the deck.

Bodies lay broken and blackened against the hull, desiccated by the cold like mummified remains. It was some, but not all of Shackleton's crew, which gave him a small spark of hope.

Garcia's extraction team returned with heat guns and more body bags.

The colonel headed for the captain's cabin.

Manoeuvring through the small hatchway was difficult in the bulky suit. Although it was supposed to be tough enough to deal with any tears or punctures, Cooper wasn't taking any chances, and he took his time navigating through the passageway to the stern.

The beams of the cabin were still hung with equipment: binoculars, hats and belts, as if Shackleton or Worsley had stepped out a moment before.

A chart table was covered in nautical maps held down by a solid pair of compasses, sextant and a small journal with the initials F.W. embossed into its cover.

The log book. Cooper smiled, picking it up with his over-sized gloves and dropping it into one of the pockets on the front of his suit.

Primary mission objective accomplished.

16

BENOIR

Paris, 1889

L yra stepped out of the long mirror and into the study.

The room was empty, except for the ghosts.

Grandma Cousineau sat in the corner, rocking back and forth in her usual chair, whispering prayers to the holy mother as she knitted socks.

Bertie the crippled boy limped through the wall and paused to adjust his leg brace, before passing into another room.

The twins took turns at toasting slices of bread in front of the dying embers of the fire, which crackled in the grate.

There were more of course, past and future occupants of the house that Benoir had inherited from his grandparents. Lyra tried to think of them as extended family, but sometimes they felt more like part of the furniture. On a good day she could shut them out for a few hours, but this was not a good day, she was tired and they were noisy.

The study was just how she left it hours before — time passed differently in the shadow world.

She listened for any sign of movement in the house.

Benoir was not home yet.

Putting her journal beside the others on the shelf, Lyra hung up her backpack and made her way upstairs to the bathroom.

Bathing had become something of a ritual whenever she returned from her wandering. 'Washing off the dust of neglect', she explained to Benoir. Her skin always felt unclean when she came back to the real world, as though she'd walked through a waterfall of ash.

Immersing herself in the steaming waters of the bath, Lyra relished the warmth on her skin. It helped soothe her mind. She took a long, slow breath and slipped further down into the tub, letting the water cover her face.

It was over a year since they returned from the world of the Anunnaki. Unlike the others, who seemed to remember nothing of their exploits, Lyra's memories remained intact.

She had no idea why, perhaps it was part of her enhanced abilities, but it made it impossible to return to any kind of normal.

Abandon had changed her, and not for the better.

Her consciousness could leave her body at will now, the linears called it 'astral projection'.

Lyra closed her eyes and felt the incredible lightness as she separated from her physical self and floated up towards the ceiling until she found herself looking down at a pale figure floating in the petal strewn waters.

The astral plane was filled with the glowing auras of the living. It was very different from the way she usually experienced the destinies of strangers. The first time she'd encountered it, she'd thought it must be heaven.

Spectral beings glowed like candles around her, it was only later that she realised these were the time-lines of living people, woven around them like beautiful cocoons.

Rising out through the roof, she ascended into the sky above Paris. It was a clear, cloudless sky filled with stars. The moon was almost full and painted the streets in a silver light. Lyra slowed her ascent to take in the view of the city at night. It was the late nineteenth century, a beautifully decadent time, filled with artists, philosophers and inventors. The Exposition Universelle was drawing the great and the good from all corners of the globe.

Somewhere over towards the Champs de Mars, beyond the newly built Eiffel Tower, Benoir would be tending to his sabre-tooths, bedding them down for the night. Lyra considered visiting him, she loved to watch him working with his animals. He would be so absorbed with his beasts that she was sure he wouldn't notice her ghostly presence.

Perhaps later, she told herself.

Turning east, she started in the direction of London.

Flying low over the countryside towards the Channel, Lyra sought out the familiar auras of her friends, following their lights like beacons shining out amongst a cloud of glowing souls.

Caitlin's pattern was one of the easiest to identify. It was so strong and vital. She was in the Chapter House, playing with her son in his bedroom. Josh was downstairs in the kitchen with Rufius, his aura was like a small star compared to the candle-like flickering of the old watchman.

As Lyra suspected, their home had relocated since she'd last visited. A staging post, hostel and general sanctuary for weary time travellers, the Chapter House had a tendency to change address often, mostly for secrecy.

When Lyra was a child, she was convinced that the building had a short attention span and liked a change of scenery every now and then.

It was now residing in a small terrace in Notting Hill.

Which was somewhere it would always go when her parents left for their summer expedition.

. . .

Watching Caitlin playing with Zack through the fourth storey window, Lyra smiled at the memory of what he might become, the sacrifice he made to save them from Tiamat. His abilities as a Seer had been greater than anyone she'd ever met, even Kelly; he would be the next Grand Seer at least, if not more.

Caitlin was a caring, loving mother and Lyra could see there were more children to come — something that she herself would never have, a fact that she kept hidden from Benoir because she knew it would break his heart — if she ever finally summoned the courage to tell him.

Not yet, she thought, *let me have him for a little while longer.*

She drifted down through two floors, finding Sim, her brother, who was busy working in his study, covering a large blackboard with equations and algebra. He would become a Copernican Grandmaster one day, and a very good one, but there would be tragedy too.

Knowing was the terrible burden of every Seer, to see the fates of others, especially loved ones, was what eventually drove most of them to madness.

Before she could ponder on it, something pulled her back to her physical body, like a line snapping tightly on a fishing rod.

Benoir's hand slipped into the water and behind her head, lifting her gently out of the water. She gasped for breath as he bent down to kiss her.

'Too long,' he whispered. 'Ma chérie, you forget that you are not a fish?'

Lyra giggled. 'I like the way you save me,' she said, before kissing him back.

He began to strip off his clothes, peeling off the braces and unbuttoning his shirt. 'Another trip into the shadows?'

'I found a new route into Gondor,' she replied, sitting up to make room as he stepped into the water.

There were new scratches on his chest, three red welts where something had slashed at him. She took a cloth and gently dabbed at the wounds. 'Another day playing with the sabre-tooths?'

He winced. 'No, it was a Panthera atrox, a cave lion. Caught me off guard when I was feeding the bears.'

Lyra traced her fingers over his muscled chest, white scars ran across his skin like a map.

'So many,' she said, kissing some of the older ones.

He wrapped his arms around her and pulled her close to him. 'All the more for you to heal.'

They kissed deeply, she closed her eyes and tried to focus on the way his body felt against hers, but it was no use, his timeline unravelled around them like fire.

Instantly she pulled away.

'Merde!' he cursed, 'What's the matter with you?'

Lyra tried not to cry. Her eyes welling with hot tears. 'I'm sorry. I can't.'

She got out of the bath and wrapped a towel around herself.

'Lyra!' he called after her as she went to leave.

'You wouldn't understand even if I told you!' she said, her hand on the door handle. 'I'm sorry.'

And with that she left.

17

HOLIDAY

Draconian Stores. Present Day.

Rufius strode ahead of the others picking various pieces of equipment from the well-stocked shelves and muttering about the quality, before throwing it into his shopping trolley.

Josh had never visited the Draconian stores. It appeared to be a vast warehouse packed with the most unusual things, like an enormous camping store with everything from firelighters to Challenger II battle tanks.

'We're going to need weapons,' Caitlin reminded Rufius, pushing her cart past the old watchman.

Zack sat on her back in a papoose, his eyes shining with joy at catching sight of his father.

Josh pulled a face and his son cackled.

'Where's the list?' asked Caitlin, turning back to Josh, seemingly unimpressed by his goofing around.

'Er, I think I left it on the table.'

Her eyes rolled. 'Great,' she said, 'sometimes I wonder whether it would be easier doing this on my own.'

'I can remember most of it,' said Rufius, coming to Josh's aid. 'And Alixia's team will have their own supplies.'

Caitlin's scowl only seemed to deepen. 'Have you been to the Cretaceous lately? The flies are the size of rats, and the rats could take on a tiger. Don't get me started on how big the mosquitoes can be.'

'Then why exactly are we going?' This was not the first time Josh had asked the question.

She sighed. 'Because I thought it would be good to do something together, as a family? It's what we used to do when I was a kid. I want Zack to have a similar experience.'

Josh wanted to point out that their baby would be too young to remember this, but bit his tongue. He knew Cat too well to provoke her when she was in this kind of mood.

'It's only for a few days, lad,' said Rufius, clapping him on the shoulder. 'It'll be good for you to get away from work and spend some quality time with the little one.'

He was right, of course, ever since the baby was born, there had been one crisis after another. As watchmen, Josh and Rufius had spent most of the last three months on missions.

'Does it have to be the Cretaceous? Surely we could start with something a little more civilised? At least somewhere with flushing toilets.'

Zack made a strange gurgling noise and the smell wafted slowly through the group. Rufius made a hasty retreat into the weapons section.

'I thought you'd like a bit of an adventure,' Caitlin said, calmly unbuckling the baby carrier.

Josh lifted his son out of his papoose and sniffed his backside.

The smell made his eyes water.

'I would if it was just us, but Zack's another matter,' he said, taking a fresh nappy from the changing bag.

She smiled and stroked the side of his face, running her fingers through his beard. 'He's stronger than you think, and the sooner we test his range the more chance he has of becoming a millennial.'

· · ·

Soon after Zack was born, Caitlin explained to Josh about the abilities of babies of the Order and how they needed to be carefully nurtured. That the sooner they were taken into the past, the higher the likelihood of them being able to travel further and deeper.

This would be his maiden voyage, and it was to be a long one, back into the Cretaceous, sixty-six million years ago — to the extinction event that ended the epoch of the dinosaur.

'Anyway, Alixia is expecting us and so are Lyra and Benoir,' she added, handing him a pot of Doctor Crooke's nappy rash cream.

Josh thought the lotion smelled worse than the soiled nappy, but the other parents swore Crooke's lotions were the best — somehow the doctor's potions could accelerate time at cellular level.

Rufius returned soon after the change was complete. For a man who had no qualms with fighting the nightmarish demons of the Maelstrom — he seemed to have a strong aversion to soiled nappies.

His shopping trolley was overflowing with leather sacks, spears and a pair of lethal looking crossbows.

'They've got a superior penetrating power to the bow,' he explained, pulling one out proudly and levelling it at Josh. 'Could take down a rhino at full pelt, so should be pretty handy against a T-Rex.'

'Which are extinct by the Cretaceous,' corrected Caitlin, putting Zack into a sling across her chest. 'But a Mastodon would do as much damage if it charged.'

Rufius picked up a bolt and held it between his teeth while he cranked back the bowstring.

Handing the primed crossbow to Josh, he showed him how to brace it into his shoulder. It felt heavy, but then it was made from materials that would be present back in the Cretaceous.

Placing the bolt into the notch on the top of the stock, Rufius pointed at a stack of animal skins on the far side of the warehouse. 'Give it a go.'

Josh took careful aim at a large dark spot on one of the skins and gently squeezed the trigger until he loosed the bolt.

It buried itself deep into the stack with a satisfying thud.

'Great! So as long as you take it down with the first shot we'll be fine,' Caitlin snapped, pushing the trolley away from them. 'Because you won't have time for a second.'

Rufius and Josh shrugged at each other and followed her along the aisle towards the largest wigwam Josh had ever seen.

18

PROSTITUTE, MAID OR NUN?

Patent Office Museum, South Kensington, London. 1858.

Fred landed badly, lost his balance and tried to steady himself using the edge of his desk, but missed and fell backwards into a stack of old newspapers.

Getting quickly to his feet, he dusted himself off and peeked through the blinds hoping that no one had noticed. Luckily, the rest of the department were still at lunch, all except for Roberts and Pascoe who liked to play temporal chess.

He opened his tachyon and checked the date. He'd made it back to exactly the right moment, a quarter to two, a comfortable two hours and fifteen minutes before his travel pass expired — which was something of a minor triumph, considering he was carrying a passenger.

Except Melanie was nowhere to be seen.

There were very few in the Order that could chaperone; the ability to carry others with you into the past was incredibly rare. Most who could were conscripted into the Protectorate to transport prisoners, which was why his family had kept it a secret for most of his life.

For years, Fred thought it might explain why his range was so limited — but recently he'd read an article in the *Outlier Inquirer* about an incident in 1965 when a young Draconian transported an entire school bus of students into the Pliocene as part of a college fraternity prank.

Closing the tachyon, Fred rubbed the casing affectionately with his thumb. His father would have been proud to know that he'd finally used it, and for a good cause — rescuing a damsel in distress.

At least that was what he'd hoped had happened.

Suddenly, there was a noise from outside and Fred opened his office door to find Melanie naked, trying her best to hide her modesty as the two chess masters looked on in amazement.

Grabbing his overcoat from the coat stand, he wrapped her in it as she leapt into his office.

'What the hell just happened? Where are my clothes?' she asked as Fred closed the door and locked it. Woodcroft wasn't going to be happy about a linear in the office, especially a woman.

If his job was under threat before, this would pretty much seal his fate.

Blushing, Fred looked away while she put on the coat. 'My apologies. I should have mentioned that modern materials tend to disappear when travelling past the point they were invented. Which unfortunately seems to include all of the fibres in your clothes.'

It was then that he saw the realisation dawn in her face. Her eyes widening as she took in her surroundings.

'You're seriously telling me that we're actually in 1858?'

Picking up The Times from his desk, Fred held it up and tapped on the date with his finger. 'We are indeed.'

Spotting the colour draining from her face, Fred guided her into a chair and went to find the bottle of brandy he kept for special occasions.

. . .

'I don't understand. How?' she muttered, taking large sips from the glass.

Fred poured himself a generous measure and joined her, after all he'd had quite a momentous day too.

He grimaced. 'Well, firstly I should remind you that I wasn't supposed to reveal our existence, let alone bring you back to my office. To be honest, I'm surprised the Protectorate haven't shown up already.'

He got up and went to look through the blinds on his office window. Pascoe and Roberts had returned to their game and the others were slowly returning to their desks. Woodcroft was nowhere to be seen, *perhaps he's still at lunch*, Fred hoped.

'The Protectorate?' Melanie repeated, finishing her drink in one long gulp.

Fred stepped back from the window. 'Temporal Police. Very sneaky.'

'Time Police, of course.' She shrugged as if it were the most normal of explanations. 'Guess someone needs to keep order. Can I have some more of that brandy please?'

Fred poured her another large glass. 'It's a Cognac actually, a Gautier 1762. Farley in accounts gets them shipped up — they're really only twenty years old.'

'So,' she continued, ignoring him. 'You really can travel through time?'

'We can.'

'And there are more of you?'

He paused for a moment, considering how much to reveal, then decided if the Protectorate were going to come they would have done so by now.

'Several thousand to be somewhat imprecise.'

Melanie drained the second measure in one go.

Fred followed suit, the heat on the back of his throat making him cough.

She put down her glass and stared at him, her eyes widening with a fierce determination. 'I want to see.'

Fred shook his head. 'I think the less you know the better.'

Melanie stood up unsteadily and pulled the coat tightly around her. 'No, I want to go outside.' Then staring at what she was wearing added: 'Do you have any other clothes?'

Somewhat relieved, Fred went over to a cupboard and twisted the key first one way and then the other. Opening the door, Melanie realised it wasn't a cupboard at all, but seemed to lead into a very large walk-in wardrobe.

'We keep a small collection of period garments here for emergencies,' he explained, walking into the room. Rails of period costumes from the fifteen hundreds hung on both sides on what appeared to be a series of rotating racks. Each section carried a brass plaque with a date embossed into it. Fred went over to a mechanical control unit and moved a few of the dials. The racks rotated slowly, replacing the medieval garments with dresses from the nineteenth century.

Melanie chose the most practical outfit she could find, although even a simple dress still seemed to require a petticoat, corset and numerous layers of lace.

When she was finished, she could hardly breathe, her breasts felt like they were going to pop out of her corset and her ribs ached.

Fred was waiting patiently in his office.

'Well I never!' he exclaimed, looking her up and down.

She couldn't help but smile, there was something quaintly cute about Fred's turn of phrase. 'That reminds me. Aren't people going to notice the way I speak.'

He laughed and waved it away. 'No, I'll just say you're visiting from the Americas. They all speak strangely.'

'Are there any female doctors in this period?'

He thought for a moment. 'No, I think Elizabeth Garrett doesn't start practising until 1865.'

'You've taken me back to the dark ages,' she joked.

Fred scoffed. 'Hardly, in those times your choices would have been dramatically reduced, you would either be a prostitute, a maid or a nun.'

19

MOUNTAINS OF MADNESS

Vinson Massif, Antarctica. Present Day.

Sitting in the relative warmth of the snow-cat, Colonel Cooper watched the GPS coordinates closely as they travelled across the ice field. The captain's journal documented the exact latitude and longitude of the cave's location, just as he'd been told, but as the mountain range loomed up towards them, he began to wonder if they should have brought climbing gear.

Opening up the logbook, his numb fingers flicked through the pages of handwritten notes until he found the relevant entry.

Day 317, June 20ᵗʰ 1915.

The men are anxious to be rid of this foul cargo.

We anchored in the bay yesterday as the weather closed in. A terrible storm from the South forced us to remain on the ship. It was as though even this godforsaken place was trying to tell us it didn't want it.

Shackleton has hardly left his cabin since we left South Georgia, he complains of terrible nightmares and the doctor has prescribed laudanum to calm him.

I leave him to oversee the base-camp while we make for the cave.
I can only pray that this will be the end of the whole terrible affair.
Captain Frank Worsley.

The cargo, Cooper repeated to himself, *a rather abstract term*. There was no mention in the expedition accounts of what exactly the *Endurance* had carried for the Department of Psychical Research, it had been a closely guarded secret.

But he knew, and it had the power to save him.

His doctor hadn't pulled any punches when he gave him the prognosis eighteen months ago.

'It's an aggressive tumour. You've got six months, maybe a year at most.'

He'd been suffering from chronic migraines for months before they found the tumour sitting in the cerebellum. Which also explained the involuntary spasms he was getting in his arms, and the tremor in his hands.

They started him on chemo, he didn't want to, but the doctor persuaded him. His hair fell out and he was as sick as a dog. After five treatments he stopped going, but the hair didn't grow back, the tumour however continued unabated.

When he told his wife, she cried, which was the first real emotion he'd seen her express in years. Cooper left the house and never went back.

He wasn't about to waste the little time he had left with a woman who was just waiting to cash in the life insurance.

He took a leave of absence from the Army and went travelling. There were things he wanted to do, places he wanted to see, before he died.

What he discovered gave him a glimmer of hope, one that Western medicine could never have offered.

. . .

The snow-cat shuddered to a dead stop at the base of the Vinson Massif. Clouds clung to the craggy peaks of the mountain which towered over them at nearly five thousand metres. Putting on his gloves, Cooper stepped out of the vehicle and took out his binoculars.

Scanning the slopes for any signs of an entrance, it took a few minutes before he found the depression in the otherwise blank canvas of ice and snow.

It wasn't too far up the slope, he couldn't imagine Worsley's crew would have been able to drag the crate very far in these conditions.

'Up there,' he said to First Officer Ramirez, who was attaching crampons to his boots.

Thirty minutes later, explosives blew a beautiful white plume of snow a hundred feet into the blue sky.

It took them two hours to clear away the rubble from the entrance, and another before the team were appropriately suited-up to go in.

The cave had obviously been collapsed on purpose. A few yards inside, they found the first of the bodies. The man's hand was still frozen around the detonator that brought down the roof. Extreme cold had preserved his corpse, and although his skin was blackened and his features distorted, he was still easily recognisable as one of *Endurance's* crew.

Cooper sent a team ahead, watching the beams of their torches lighting up the walls as they moved further inside.

As the ice turned to rock, the Colonel noticed markings carved into the stone. Thin lines scored into the granite, mapping out constellations like a star chart.

Shining his torch along the walls, he picked out the Plough, Cassiopeia and Orion's Belt. It was like some ancient observatory from a time before the ice had formed, when men could have survived down here without Goretex, electrically heated gloves and layers of thermal padding.

Which he guessed must have been one hell of a long time ago.

The radio clicked and Ramirez's voice came through his helmet comms.

'All clear sir, but you're never going to believe this.'

20

MUSEUM

British Museum of Natural History, London. 1889.

Josh and Caitlin were late.

They followed a squat little curator as he led them through the labyrinthine vaults beneath the museum. It was slow going, not helped by the fact that Josh kept being distracted by the bodies of strange creatures preserved in the glass display cases on either side — much to Caitlin's annoyance.

'The Xeno department has requisitioned the entire vault,' explained the man, tapping on the glass with his cane as he passed. 'Not your usual exhibits.'

Most of the exhibits resembled something from a horrific biological experiment: tentacles with eyes, limbs encrusted in shell, and bodies with translucent skin exposing all of their internal organs. These were holotypes, specimens captured from the chaotic realm for further study. Josh shivered at the thought of going back into the Maelstrom; it made venturing back into the final epoch of the dinosaurs look like a summer vacation.

Somewhere he had no intention of ever returning.

. . .

Finally, they came to an empty chamber with a large circular disc inlaid into the floor. It was made from a series of brass concentric rings, each one inscribed with temporal markings.

'Portal Forty-Four,' the curator said, taking an ornate key from his jacket and placing it in the lock at its centre. 'Cretaceous wasn't it?'

Caitlin nodded. 'Base fifteen.'

There was a deep, resounding grinding of gears as the rings began to rotate and then slowly pivoted out of the floor to form an astrolabe.

The curator waved them inside.

'The rest of your party have already gone through, they're waiting on the other side with your luggage.'

The noise woke Zack, who moaned at the disruption and Caitlin took him from Josh, calming him down before stepping inside the sphere of slowly rotating rings.

Josh joined them, feeling the hairs rising on the back of his neck as the rotation of the rings accelerated and the temporal fields established themselves.

When she was planning the trip, Caitlin was adamant they should use a safety portal.

During the early days of her research, Alixia had insisted the Draconian engineers construct a series of quantum corridors to connect the deep outposts to the nineteenth century. It was a form of temporal breach, developed from studying the attacks on the chronosphere by monads, temporal vampires that evolved in the chaos of the Maelstrom.

Used mostly for defence, breaching gates would seal a rupture in the temporal field, but they could also be paired to create portals between two points in time. It was a safety measure to ensure the research teams could make the sixty-six million year jump without ending up inside a volcano.

Josh wasn't convinced they needed it, he'd travelled back further than anyone else in the Order, except perhaps the founder. Caitlin reminded him that their first trip was an accident that left them stranded in the Mesolithic, and the second time he'd just absorbed the power of an Infinity Engine.

It would have been easier to use Caitlin's parents' ship, the *Nautilus II*, but her engines were still untested for long trips and Zack's grandparents were unwilling to risk it.

In the centre of the astrolabe rose a thin metal pedestal with a single artefact sitting on a small square plate. The carved object was a tiny figurine, no more than six inches tall, carved from the tusk of a mammoth.

Holding Zack close to her, Caitlin took Josh's hand and they touched the surface of the ivory. It was cold and the time-line was nothing more than a vague whisper beneath the aged white bone.

Slowly, he coaxed the time-line out of its distant history, letting the lines of energy weave around his fingers. Caitlin was doing the same, the fractal pattern rolling over her forearms as she searched for the origin point.

She was right, it felt like a long time since Josh had travelled back so far. He'd forgotten how difficult it was to do it intentionally. He smiled, remembering the first time he'd dragged Caitlin back to that prehistoric cave, trying to avoid Dalton and his stupid Monad.

As the quantum field of the gate established itself, he felt the millennia stretching away before him. Millions of years twisting like fine gossamer threads caught in the wind. Spreading out along its length were the usual markers left by previous Nautonniers, those brave pioneers that blazed a trail into the dark, unmapped parts of history.

'Ready?' asked Caitlin, turning towards him.

He could tell from her expression that she'd already located the terminus. She was always so much quicker than him at this, but then she'd grown up with it.

'Go for it,' he said, wishing just once that he could have got there first.

21

THE SCIENCE OF SMALL THINGS

South Kensington, London. 1858.

'Please try not to point,' Fred whispered to Melanie, grabbing her hand as they walked along the pavement towards Belgravia.

Her expression reminded him of a child in a toy shop: eyes wide and mouth open, pointing at the most mundane of things as if they were made of gold.

It was getting so bad, that he wondered whether he shouldn't hail a hansom cab. At least that way she could gawp at the passers-by without drawing so much attention to herself. He took out the coins from his trouser pocket, three shillings and sixpence, that would probably be enough for a trip to the museum.

Outliers were not the most well paid members of the Order. Not that money was ever really an issue, but one was supposed to subsist on the earnings of the period. His lodgings were by far his largest expense. He could have lived in a cheaper area or an earlier period, and commuted, but he liked to play the part of a linear and live in the time that he worked.

. . .

'But it's so different,' she said, raising a finger of her other hand towards a horse-drawn tram. 'Aren't they supposed to be electric?'

'Not until 1901,' said Fred, gently pushing her hand down.

'And there are so many horses,' she added, watching the constant stream of carriages.

Fred waved down a cab as it turned out of Queen's Gate.

'Twenty-five thousand at last count.'

Melanie gasped. 'Christ! How much manure does that produce?'

The cab stopped beside them, Fred opened the door for her and offered her his hand.

She scowled at it. 'You don't have to do that. I'm perfectly capable.'

He sighed. 'Sorry, but these are different times, it is expected, not to do it would look entirely out of place.'

She shrugged and then fell over her skirts as she tried to step inside.

'How does anyone do anything in these dresses?' Melanie complained, as he helped her into a sitting position.

'With practice.'

While she adjusted her skirts, trying to find a way to sit comfortably, Fred instructed the driver to make for the British Museum.

'So, how long were you stationed in Antarctica?' he asked as the carriage set off at a trot.

'Nearly nine months,' she replied, already distracted by the streets of Piccadilly rolling past the window. 'I was studying ice cores for primordial organisms. I'm a microbiologist.'

Fred folded his arms and leaned back into the leather seat. 'The science of small things.'

Melanie suddenly turned away from the window, her eyes filled with awe and excitement. 'What year did you say this was?'

'1858.'

Fred could see the wheels turning in her mind. He'd already noticed that she played with her fingers as though counting when she was thinking deeply about something.

'Eighteen fifty-eight. Louis Pasteur will be working on Germ Theory in Paris. Joseph Lister won't read his papers for another seven years. My God, these are the men that changed the world.'

'Before you ask, the answer is no.'

She scowled. 'But, these men are legends. Can't I at least shake their hands?'

Fred knew this question would come, or at least one like it. It was the first thing any normal person would ask once they realised time travel was actually possible — besides killing Hitler's parents, most linears wanted to meet one of their heroes.

'There are rules about interacting with the past. We try to do as little as possible, especially since the Shakespeare incident.'

'Shakespeare?'

He winced. 'Probably shouldn't have mentioned that.'

Melanie wasn't about to be dissuaded. 'These men changed our understanding of bacteria, infection and disease. They have literally saved millions of lives over the last hundred and fifty years. They stood up to the established doctrines on miasma and other equally ridiculous theories. They revolutionised public health!'

'It only takes one wrong word, one slip of the tongue. The advancement of knowledge can have an exponential impact on the future. The Copernicans would have the Protectorate down on us like a ton of bricks.'

She pouted, sitting back and crossing her arms over her chest. 'And who the hell are the Copernicans?'

'Actually, if there is a threat of plague, the Copernican Guild may be exactly who we need to help us. They specialise in statistical modelling, determining course corrections to keep the continuum on the right track.'

Melanie leaned forward. 'Course corrections?'

Fred bit his lip. 'Pretend I never said that.'

But she'd already made the leap. 'You change the past?'

Fred stared out of the window, his cheeks flushing red. He wasn't used to talking to linears, and there was something about this woman that made it difficult to hold his tongue.

Her eyes were ablaze, the world outside the cab window forgotten. 'You're telling me these Copernicans calculate changes to the past? What kind of computers do they have that could do that? The factorials for the model would be astronomical.'

He gritted his teeth, grinding his jaw and then sighed. 'It's hard to explain. It'll be easier if I just show you. They're probably going to redact your memory anyway.'

She scoffed. 'They can wipe my mind? Next you'll be telling me that they can predict the future.'

He raised one eyebrow and smiled. 'Never underestimate the power of the Infinity Engine.'

Tapping on the roof of the cab, he gave the driver a new destination.

22

SAMPLES

Cave, Antarctica. Present Day

Cooper found it hard to distinguish the human remains from the jumble of bones that lay scattered around the damaged crate. The cavern was like a crime scene, frozen in place for over a century.

The container was over twelve feet tall, built from sturdy looking oak beams with iron bands bolted around it at three sections. The creature they'd kept inside had broken through one wall, the wood splintered outwards as though a cannon shot had blasted through it.

His keen eyes spotted the signs of fire, scorch marks seared the wood, as if there had been a last ditch effort to destroy whatever was inside the crate.

Walking further into the cave, Cooper found the skeleton of the beast. A long sinuous body, like the skeleton of a giant snake, lay coiled at the bottom of the slope, its skull resting on one side.

He whispered a silent prayer for the men who sacrificed themselves to keep it from escaping.

The shape of the creature's head reminded him of a dragon, which was obviously impossible, this was just some throwback to the dinosaur, he told himself, but if the old man's story was authentic, this creature held the cure he needed.

'Take samples of everything,' he barked into the radio. 'Then vaporise the whole thing.'

Walking out of quarantine and into the snow, Cooper took a few deep breaths, letting his heart rate settle back to somewhere close to normal. Part of him had never believed it would be there, that the story was too crazy to be true. The curse at least seemed to be genuine; everyone who'd come into contact with the creature had died.

Checking he was alone, he took out his phone and called Fort Detrick.

There was a delay while it switched to an encrypted line and the voice at the other end said:

'Sir.'

'Salvage crew dead. BAS team also compromised. Bringing samples back for analysis.'

'Understood.'

'Prepare for a biohazard seven protocol.'

'Seven?'

'Roger that.'

23

PREMONITION

Northern China, Cretaceous.

The air in the jungle was humid and heavy.

Josh adjusted the heavy pack on his back, feeling the sweat trickle down between his shoulder blades as they trekked in single file beneath a canopy of gigantic conifers.

Above their heads, unseen creatures screeched, shaking the branches in anger, sending coconut-sized fruits crashing to the ground. Clouds of large flying insects buzzed around them, their bodies as thick as Josh's finger, only being held at bay by one of Doctor Crooke's fouling smelling lotions.

The path from the arrival point to Alixia's encampment was hard to follow, and if it hadn't been for Benoir carving his way through the bush with a machete, Josh was sure they would have got lost.

Lyra's husband was waiting for them when they appeared at the landing site; a clearing surrounded by monolithic stones like a primeval Stonehenge. Standing in its centre was a much larger version of the figurine they'd used in the museum, carved from the same enormous tusk, the material obviously had a sympathetic relationship connecting them over millennia.

Lyra was there too, looking paler than ever. She hugged them both and took Zack while Josh and Caitlin helped Rufius with the bags.

The base camp was in the bottom of a deep basin, the high sides creating a natural protection from most of the larger predators. They descended using a series of switchback paths hewn out of the rock by Draconian engineers. When they came to a break in the foliage Josh caught sight of the whole valley, it looked as though some ancient god had scooped out an enormous handful of earth.

'Meteorite strike,' explained Benoir, coming back to admire the view. 'Couple of million years ago,' he added nonchalantly as if it was yesterday.

Josh took off the rag that he'd been using as a makeshift bandana and soaked it in water. Squeezing it on the back of his neck, he shivered as the cold sensation rolled down his spine. By the position of the sun it was nearly midday and he guessed that the temperature was close to forty degrees.

Caitlin stopped beside him. 'You okay?' she asked, taking his hand.

He wiped the cloth over his forehead. 'I'm boiling in this.' He tugged at the heavy cotton shirt, which was drenched with sweat.

She nodded, tugging at her own shirt, which was equally damp. 'No such thing as wicking back in these times. Just think of it like you're wearing a mosquito net.'

Josh laughed. 'Have you seen the size of them? You need a baseball bat not a net.' He swatted at an imaginary bug.

'It'll be easier when we get to the camp.'

'What about Zack?'

Caitlin looked ahead to Lyra who seemed completely unaffected by the heat or the insects.

'He's fine. I think she's using her abilities to keep the bugs away.'

Josh reopened his flask and drank thirstily.

'Take it easy on the water, it's got to last another couple of hours.'

He scoffed, pouring some more onto his rag and wrapping it around his head. 'There's a whole river of it down there.'

She winced. 'Full of bacteria that your body has never encountered. Just assume everything here is trying to kill you and you won't go far wrong.'

'Remind me why the landing point isn't nearer the camp?'

Caitlin sighed. 'Because Alixia prefers to work outside of any latent temporal fields. It's standard safety procedure when working in a hostile environment. You wouldn't want a real T-Rex turning up at the Museum.'

'Hostile?' Josh repeated.

She kissed him. 'What's happened to you? Ever since Zack was born you've become a complete wuss.'

Josh couldn't put a finger on what it was exactly. There was something lingering in the back of his mind about losing his son. A premonition of sorts, but he couldn't bring himself to tell Caitlin, nor anyone else for that matter. He'd played with the idea of going to see the Grand Seer about it, and then remembered how unhelpful that would probably be.

'I just want to keep him safe is all,' he replied, 'that's my job right?'

Her eyes glinted with the hint of tears. 'It is, but don't wrap him up in cotton wool either. I want our son to grow up to be strong and independent.'

Putting away the water bottle, Josh started back along the trail. 'Just like his mother.'

24

COPERNICANS

Hall of Copernicus. 1580

It took Fred three jumps to reach the sixteenth century. Melanie recovered from each one more quickly than the last, unaware of the embarrassment he was feeling at not being able to make the journey in one.

Which was immediately forgotten the moment they stepped into the Great Hall of Copernicus. It was a breathtaking sight, the walls of the vast clockwork-cathedral reaching up to the stained-glass ceiling, with beams of coloured light glinting off the slowly turning gears of the massive mechanism.

This was the headquarters of the Copernican Guild, somewhere that Fred had only visited once before with his father when he was ten. They had been invited to the investiture of the new Grandmaster. It was a fancy affair, one that required formal robes and haircuts, but all Fred could remember was the gigantic celestial clock that hung at one end of the hall. It marked time in a hundred different centuries.

Above them, hundreds of engineers worked on the metal gantries, making adjustments to the gearing or oiling its many parts. Actuaries and statisticians cluttered the concourse, striding purposely about their business carrying stacks of punched cards, abacuses and slide rules. Each was dressed in robes of varying shades of blue.

'It's a difference engine?' asked Melanie, craning her head towards the upper floors.

'An analytical engine,' came a voice from behind them. 'Capable of two-thousand petaflops a minute.'

'Simeon!' exclaimed Fred, turning towards the man. 'How the devil are you?'

Melanie turned too.

Simeon was a tall, blonde-haired young man with pale skin. His eyes were bright but ringed by dark shadows that spoke of too many long nights.

Fred shook the man's hand enthusiastically. 'Bloody good to see you, old chap.'

His friend looked rather uncomfortable at the display of affection. 'You too,' he stammered. 'It's been a while. How's the Draconian application going?'

'Not so well,' replied Fred, his enthusiasm waning. 'But where are my manners? May I introduce, Doctor Melanie Braithwaite.' Taking a step back, Fred nodded to Melanie.

Simeon smiled nervously and held out a hand. 'Pleased to meet you Doctor Braithwaite.'

She shook it, his hand was soft and his grip gentle.

'And you,' she replied.

'Are you related to Gilligan Braithwaite? The xenobiologyst?'

Melanie shook her head.

Simeon's eyes narrowed and he snatched back his hand as if he'd been burned.

'You're a linear!'

Turning to Fred, his voice dropped to a low whisper. 'You know how much trouble you could get me into, bringing a linear into the guild?'

Fred puffed out his chest and folded his arms. 'I think you need to hear what she has to say. It's important.'

Simeon paused for a moment, his gaze flicking across the hall as a group of steely-eyed soldiers dressed in black armour made their way through the crowds.

Melanie realised that no one was looking at them directly, everyone was avoiding their gaze.

'Protectorate,' he hissed. 'Come with me.'

They followed the young Copernican away from the officers and towards an ornate set of elevators.

'Why is he so annoyed?' whispered Melanie.

'You're not supposed to be here. Linears aren't supposed to know we exist. It ruins their calculations.'

'Putting it mildly,' murmured Simeon over his shoulder.

'Linears?'

'Those who travel through time at one-second per second, with the general flow of the continuum,' Fred explained.

'You mean the ones that follow the general laws of physics?'

He nodded.

'And knowing that you exist would change your manipulation of the timeline. Like adding an observer effect to a quantum wave function.'

Simeon look impressed. 'Why exactly are you hanging around with this Outlier?'

Melanie stopped, her cheeks colouring. 'And what's so wrong with that?'

'Long story,' replied Fred, calmly taking her arm. 'We're not well respected amongst the Copernicans. Ever since the episode with Shakespeare they've been petitioning to have us disbanded.'

'What exactly did happen with Shakespeare?' she asked a little too loudly as they reached the lift.

Simeon scoffed, pulling open the safety grille. 'Do you want to tell her or shall I?'

'One of my former colleagues decided to impart certain future knowledge to the Bard, hoping the playwright would immortalise it, and in doing so, influence the outcome of an event that was to occur two hundred years later.'

'Suitably vague,' Simeon agreed, closing the doors and pressing one of the brass buttons on a panel of hundreds.

Fred continued. 'The subsequent three plays that were penned on the subject were intentionally 'lost', but not before enough of the public had watched them. It caused a great deal of work for the Copernicans to undo the consequences.

'To be exact, four hundred actuaries took thirty years — twelve thousand years of effort.'

Fred looked down at his feet. 'We've been excommunicated.'

'You've had your wings clipped, ' corrected Simeon. 'And rightly so.'

A bell pinged, signalling that they had reached their floor.

Simeon took them along a corridor of clattering gears and into a small chamber with a large brass sphere sat in the middle of the floor. Its surface was covered in lenses like a projector from a planetarium. On one side, a panel hung open, exposing its inner workings.

The walls were lined with shelving filled with the broken parts of other complex clockwork machines. It reminded Melanie of the workshop of a watchmaker.

'This is repair and maintenance, no one will bother us in here,' he said, folding his arms over his chest. 'So what is so important that you had to break the prime directive?'

Fred began to explain about how he discovered Melanie being held prisoner in the Antarctic, and the bodies he'd seen in the hold of the *Endurance*.

Simeon's eyes widened as he processed the information. 'A plague?'

Melanie felt the need to take over. 'A virus to be exact. One that the planet hasn't encountered in millions of years. I've no idea how it got onto the *Endurance*, but it's incredibly contagious and deadly within twenty-four hours.'

'And you know this how?'

'Because I have a doctorate in microbiology.'

Again Simeon looked impressed. 'And this was in 1915?' he asked, taking out his journal.

'The Frontier,' replied Fred. 'Has anything shown up on your latest horizon scans?'

The Copernican leafed through the animating pages of his book, and shook his head. 'I will need to do some checking. Environmental factors like pandemics are a very difficult thing to model, they tend to be excluded from our standard calculus.'

'Which is why you need the Outlier department.'

Simeon ignored the comment. 'I'll schedule some time on the engine, but Professor Eddington has prioritised the realignment of the Michelson interferometer, so processing time is limited at the moment.'

'This has the potential to be the next Black Death!' snapped Melanie. 'Millions could die.'

Simeon's expression hardened. 'Believe me, we've dealt with far worse.'

Melanie glanced at Fred, who simply shrugged.

'Ross, you'll need to get her back to her own time before the Protectorate catch on to you.'

Fred nodded. 'Would you mind not mentioning our visit to the Professor?'

'I don't think he'd believe me even if I told him.'

25

RETIREMENT

Base Camp 15, Northern China. Cretaceous.

The sky was darkening by the time they reached Alixia's camp. Stars glimmered in the deepening blue, their positions in the heavens unchanged from the present, making Josh feel suddenly very insignificant.

The base reminded him of a frontier fortress more than a research station; a tented encampment surrounded by high wooden palisades cut from the surrounding forest. A column of smoke curled up above the walls, bringing with it the welcome smell of cooking meat.

Alixia was standing at the open gate to welcome the weary travellers with her usual amount of motherly fussing, hugging each one of them in turn and commenting on how tired they looked.

While she clucked and cooed over Zack and Caitlin, Josh and Rufius were gratefully enlisted by her husband, Methuselah, to discuss the supplies they'd brought with them.

· · ·

'How's the water purification?' asked Rufius, opening one of the hessian sacks and fishing out a clay amphora of wine.

'We've got the carbon filtration up and running.' Methuselah's eyes widened. 'How in the name of Chronos did you manage that?'

'Ah, well that would be telling.' Rufius winked, then pulled the cork out with his teeth. 'What do you do for glasses around here?'

Alixia's husband went into one of the tents and returned a few moments later with cups made out of horn.

'Rhino?' Rufius asked, examining the patina.

'Triceratops,' replied Methuselah, 'we found a graveyard not far from here. Looks like an entire herd walked off the edge of a cliff.'

Rufius grimaced, pouring the wine. 'Not a great way to go.'

'Not for me,' said Josh, sniffing his shirt. 'Do you have anything like a shower? I could really do with a cold one?'

Methuselah nodded proudly towards a series of canvas stalls at the end of a row of tents. 'There is indeed! With both hot and cold running water.'

Josh thanked him and made his way towards the showers, shedding his shirt as he went.

'How's the new father?' Methuselah asked, watching him go.

'Tired, nervous, over-cautious, but otherwise well enough, although I've a notion that Caitlin is doing most of the work.'

'First year's the worst.' Methuselah raised his horn. 'Here's to never changing another nappy!'

Rufius chuckled. 'I'll drink to that.'

'I hear he's decided to join the watch?'

'Indeed he has. Although he's still got a few rough edges that need smoothing off, coming so late to the Order as he did. It's been a traumatic couple of years. A veritable trial by fire.'

His friend laughed and patted him hard on the back. 'Sounds like someone else I know.'

Rufius grunted and took a swig of wine, rolling it around in his mouth before swallowing. 'Vintages of this age never travel as well as you think.' He picked up the amphora and poured them both another cup. 'Beginning to know how it feels.'

'So what are your plans old man?' said Methuselah, sitting down on a rock next to the Repenomamus giganticus that was being slowly roasted on a spit. 'Will you be staying long?'

Rufius sat down on the opposite side of the fire and scratched his beard. 'Well, you know I'm starting to wonder about that. These days I wake up and parts of me feel a little worn.'

Methuselah laughed and rubbed his hand into the small of his back. 'Don't we all my friend, but I'm not surprised, you've certainly pushed yourself to the limits.'

'I'm not talking about the aches and pains — that's just part of the job.' He took another long sip of the wine. 'It's more subtle than that. I've run out of challenges. There's nothing I haven't seen. I've travelled up and down the time-lines for so long.'

'You need a wife!' Methuselah said, slapping his friend on the knee. 'No such thing as a boring life when you're married.'

Rufius shook his head. 'Tried that once. I doubt there are many women who'd put up with me, except maybe yours, and she's already taken. No, I think I need to find something else, something that satisfies my soul.'

His friend's eyebrows arched. 'You're not thinking of retiring?'

'It's crossed my mind lately.'

'Where would you go?'

The old watchman looked up into the night sky, watching the embers circling up into the darkness. 'I always wanted to visit the gold rush of mid-nineteenth century America. Then perhaps onto twelfth-century Japan, to spend some time with the Samurai of the Kamakura shogunate.' He rubbed his shoulder, 'I have some unfinished business with Yoritomo.'

Methuselah nodded solemnly. 'So not so much settling down, as settling old scores?'

Rufius grinned. 'Need to get my accounts in order.'

. . .

Later, the others joined them around the campfire.

'Welcome to our family and friends,' toasted Alixia, getting to her feet and raising a small, carved horn of wine towards Josh, Caitlin and Zack. 'And especially to their beautiful boy.' Her eyes glittered in the firelight as she stared at the baby.

Everyone raised their cups.

Methuselah carved the roasted mammal with an obsidian blade while Alixia handed out wooden bowls to the camp.

Lyra stood up and walked away into the dark with Benoir following close behind.

'What's the matter with you?' he asked when he finally caught up to her.

'Do you ever think about our future?' she said wistfully, staring up into the night sky. 'What fate has in store for us?'

She could feel his confusion without needing to look at him.

'Not really.'

Lyra turned towards him. 'You've not thought about us starting a family? Of having children?'

He shrugged. 'Maybe, but not for a while yet.'

She could feel the heat rising in her cheeks and the sting of tears. She took a deep breath to hold them back. 'What if I told you that I've seen what we become? That I know that we shouldn't try to have kids?'

'You promised me you wouldn't — ' he began, but she cut him off.

'I know! But it's different now. I can see without even trying, without touching you. My powers are getting stronger every day.'

Now the tears came, and she let them. 'You deserve a better wife.'

He tried to take her hand. 'Don't say that!'

'No! Don't touch me. It makes it so much worse! It's driving me crazy. All I want to do is curl up in your arms, but then the visions come, and they're terrible Benoir. So many dark futures writhing around you like black snakes. I can't stand it.'

Sobbing, she ran off towards the tents.

26

ENDURANCE

Patent Office Museum, South Kensington, London. 1858.

After a small detour to observe the Black Death in the rookeries of London, 1665, which Melanie insisted was not caused by bad air, Fred was relieved to return to the relative safety of his office.

'So, what exactly do you do here?' she asked, opening one of the dossiers on his desk. It was filled with newspaper clippings from reports about the giant sea serpent.

'We investigate the unusual,' he recited with pride. 'While the Copernicans concentrate on events that are statistically likely, we look beyond the algorithm and into the events that defy explanation. We work at the edge of the possible.'

Melanie seemed impressed, just as Fred had been when he first heard it during his induction. The Head of the Outlier Department, Tellamar Vornick, was something of a poet, albeit a mad one, but she did make a good speech.

'Sounds a bit like the X-Files,' Melanie said, holding up a woodcut illustration of the serpent attacking a ship.

Fred blinked, staring at her blankly. 'What's the X-Files?'

'It was one of my favourite shows. They used to investigate weird events and aliens.'

'At the theatre?'

She laughed. 'No on TV. It was a cult show on BBC2 in the nineties.'

'The nineteen nineties?' he said, mentally trying to calculate her age.

Melanie nodded. 'My dad taped them all. I grew up watching them on VHS.'

He waved his hands and pulled out a pad from his desk drawer. 'Wait, that's too many acronyms. What is the BBC2?'

'Don't you spend any time in the twentieth century?'

Fred shook his head. 'As little as possible, it's too close to the Frontier. Far too dangerous.'

She perched against the edge of his desk and explained about the X-Files, television, and the British Broadcasting Corporation, while he jotted down copious notes, his eyes filling with wonder.

'And VHS was a way of recording sound and image on magnetic tape?' he asked when she'd finished.

'Yes, I can't remember what it stands for, but we had all eleven series. I've watched the whole thing at least three times.'

She smiled at the memory of those moments with her father, sitting on the old leather sofa in his study discussing the doomsday storylines of the alien invasion. He was already something of a conspiracy theorist before it came out, and she loved the way he deconstructed the plots of each episode.

'Now don't tell me,' Fred said, raising his finger. 'A series is a collection of shows?'

'They made a couple of movies too, but we don't talk about them.'

'Movies?'

Melanie was beginning to lose the will to live. 'Moving images, on film.'

'And the aliens were from outer space?'

'That was the general premise, there were some other wacky

storylines, but the main one was about alien colonisation — there are quite a few Americans who believe they've been abducted by extraterrestrials.'

Fred put the end of his pencil in his mouth. 'Interesting. I wonder if it was a by-product of the space race. My friend Monty told me about the twentieth century's obsession with reaching the moon.'

'Well, they found a spaceship hidden under the ice in Antarctica.'

He looked shocked. 'They did?'

'In the movie.'

'Ah, I was going to say. I'm sure we would have heard about that.'

She continued. 'And they believed the aliens were using a virus, called "Black Oil", to infiltrate the human race.'

'Well, that would make a stuffed bird laugh! Who thinks of these stories? It's worthy of H.G. Wells!'

'It is, at least I thought so until the *Endurance*, suddenly I think it's more science fact than science fiction.'

Fred took out another dossier and opened it. 'I've been studying the Imperial Trans-Antarctic Expedition for some time now. There's more than one oddity concerning their mission.'

Melanie walked around to the other side of the desk and peered over his shoulder.

'Since the loss of Captain Scott, and with Amundsen reaching the South Pole first, the expedition had been struggling to raise funding.'

Fred handed her a copy of the expenses.

'See here,' he pointed at a line of beautiful copperplate script. 'There's a rather generous donation from a government department listed as "Psychical Research", for the transport of cargo. I tried to learn more about them, but there's little record of their existence.'

'Ten thousand pounds? How much would that be in my time?'

Fred took out an antiquated calculating machine and began to punch in numbers and adjust gear wheels. Melanie wondered how the human race managed to make it out of the nineteenth century in one piece, there would be more computing power in her phone than on the entire planet at that moment.

'Approximately, one million two hundred and twenty-nine

pounds,' he said, pointing at the enamelled digits along the brass casing.

'For transporting cargo?' she exclaimed. 'What was it, radioactive waste?'

Fred shrugged. 'Whatever it was, Shackleton wasn't happy about taking it, but he needed the money.'

Melanie folded her arms over her chest. 'Well, whatever they were doing. They found something that wiped out my entire team in less than twenty-four hours. And now some crazy American Major has got his hands on it and my research.'

'Colonel,' Fred corrected.

'I don't care what his rank is. I want to find out what the hell is going on and hopefully stop it from spreading across the globe!'

'The Copernicans will ensure that it is dealt with.'

'And how long will that take? Your friend didn't seem that convinced.'

'I'll admit they're notoriously slow, but they do have the benefit of time. It's a hard concept to appreciate for a linear, but the Copernicans could spend the next hundred years working on a solution, and then apply it in a matter of moments.' Fred snapped his fingers to emphasise the point.

Melanie frowned. 'I don't have that luxury. I need to do something now!'

Fred's eyes lit up. 'I have an idea,' he began, closing the dossier. 'Although it might be a little bit tricky getting you there.'

'Where?'

'A whaling station on South Georgia, circa 1914.'

27

BAD DREAM

Base Camp 15, Northern China. Cretaceous.

L yra slept fitfully that night. Her dreams were troubled by terrible visions: entire cities laid waste by a terrible plague; the bodies of millions of people lying dead in the streets covered in clouds of flies, their skin covered in strange fractal patterns.

She walked among them like a ghost, trying not to breathe the fetid air. A miasma of death floated over everything, the taste of it burning her throat, making her want to gag.

With every step, she appeared to move between countries: Paris, London, Mumbai, New York and Rome — nothing had survived, not even the birds. The world was as silent as the grave, it was as though it had become the Shadow Realm.

Waking with a start, Lyra realised she was no longer inside the tent.

It was dark and there was a man standing over her, or at least the shape of one. His head was covered with a cowl, out of which a pair of shining eyes glowed like fiery coals.

'Abandon?' she gasped.

His face was obscured by shadow, making it impossible to be sure, but there was something about his aura that seemed familiar.

'What are you?' he hissed, his hand reaching out towards her.

She dug her heels into the earth, scrabbling to get away from him.

'Stay back,' she screamed, but he lurched forward.

Somehow Lyra got to her feet and turned to run, but his hand closed around her wrist. 'You have seen the future,' he continued. 'I am waiting there.'

Spinning on her heel, she grasped at his hood and pulled it back.

The man's head was bald, and silvered in the moonlight, on its crown was tattooed a star, which glowed with the same effervescence as his eyes.

'Who are you?' she asked, trying to free her hand, digging her nails into his skin.

The man released her and pulled the cowl back over his head. 'I am eternal.'

He bowed and vanished into thin air.

Lyra woke up.

A dream within a dream. She realised, staring up at the canvas roof of their tent.

Benoir stirred in the bed next to her and turned over.

Closing her eyes, she breathed in the warm morning air, waiting for her heartbeat to settle back into a normal rhythm. As with every vision she'd ever had, Lyra felt totally disconnected from the real world. She focused on the sounds of the camp waking and the clatter of pans as the fires were being lit for breakfast.

Slowly, she felt her spirit settle back inside the shell of her body.

Sunlight played over the tent, a soft breeze rustling the canvas, and on it came the musky scent of Benoir, distracting her from the lingering post-dream despondency. She savoured the moment, remembering the first time she'd met him. A tall, strong, man who was busy feeding sabre-tooth cats. He'd been so darkly handsome, and she knew without needing to rely on her abilities that he was part of her destiny.

She fought back the urge to wrap her arms around him, knowing that it would only end in disappointment.

Lyra rose slowly from her cot and put on a thin cotton dress. Benoir had set out fresh fruit on the small dining table and she picked up a peach. Biting into the flesh, it tasted sweet and the juice ran down her chin, making her laugh.

Benoir woke with a snort and sat up.

'Hey,' he said, rubbing the sleep from his eyes. 'It's early. Are you okay?'

'Bad dream.'

'Vision?'

She tried to smile, to make out it was okay, but her dark, haunted eyes told a different story.

He sighed stoically. 'You need to go.'

She nodded. 'I need to tell the Grand Seer. It's my duty.'

'I know.'

She came back to the bed, took his face in her hands and kissed him. 'I will find a way to fix this, I promise.'

28

FORT DETRICK

U.S. Army Medical Research and Development Command, Fort Detrick, Maryland. Present Day.

C ooper gripped his grandfather's medal in the palm of his hand, watching the Hercules C-130 transport on its final approach to the airstrip. The feel of the cool metal between his fingers had always calmed him, ever since he'd been a cadet at West Point. Lately, it had become useful for something else: testing the sensation in his fingertips on the points of its star — there was no feeling in three of them now.

Time was running out.

The day his grandfather gave it to him was one of his strongest memories. The man was a war hero, he'd been awarded the Silver Star for saving his commanding officer during a raid on Hill 1062 in the Korean War in 1951.

Four generations of Coopers had served their country, and all had gone to the Military Academy at West Point, every one had seen conflict. 'We were born to be soldiers.' his father used to proudly remind him and his brothers.

. . .

Cooper served his time in Iraq with the 2nd Battalion, 23rd Marines, losing one of the fingers on his left hand in the process. It was a small price to pay, many of his comrades lost a lot more to IEDs.

Now he was attached to the bio-defence research agency of the U.S. Army, at the Medical Research Institute of Infectious Diseases (USAMRIID). In reality it was a biological weapons facility, but the Senate funding committee preferred to think they were saving the world from the next pandemic, rather than averting bio-terrorism.

The Hercules came in fast and landed hard, slamming on the brakes as the heavy plane struggled to stop before the end of the airfield.

'Alpha Charlie Zulu, make your way to hangar five,' instructed the air traffic controller standing beside him.

'Hanger seven,' corrected Cooper. 'I want them in lockdown.'

The controller turned towards him, an unspoken question fading from his eyes. 'Seven, yes sir!'

Hangar seven was a specialised decontamination facility, designed for high level toxic materials. Cooper had taken care to keep the cargo a secret on its journey back from Antarctica, strictly a need-to-know basis, but questions would be asked when his CO discovered that he'd put it into quarantine.

Procedures would need to be followed.

Fort Detrick went by another name: "Fort Doom" which it earned producing Anthrax bombs during WWII. Cooper thought it was still fitting, considering the number of lethal pathogens that were sitting in cold storage in the vaults below his feet.

Leaving the control tower, he marched over to hangar seven. Spotting Lieutenant Miller ahead, he increased his pace to catch him up.

'You've put them in seven?' the man said, keeping his tone neutral so as not to question his authority. They had worked together for ten years and he was one of the few men Cooper knew he could trust.

'You have a better idea lieutenant?'

'No sir, but the flight crew.'

'Will spend the next ten days in quarantine, until we can be sure that they've not been infected.'

Guards were posted at the doors to the hangar. They snapped to attention and saluted as Cooper approached.

'As you were,' he said, placing his hand on the security console and pressing his eye to the scanner. It took a few seconds for the system to recognise him and unlock the door.

Moving through a series of airlocks, they pulled on the pressure suits and walked into the building.

The suit's heads-up display told Cooper the temperature inside the hangar was constant at sixty-four degrees Fahrenheit, far warmer than the chilly thirty degrees outside. The specialised sealed environment filtered and circulated the air — nothing got in or out of the facility that was bigger than point-two-five of a micron.

A team were already busy unloading body bags from the back of the Hercules while the flight crew were being led away to a decontamination unit at the far end of the hangar.

'I want preliminary autopsy reports on them by seventeen hundred hours,' Cooper said to Miller over the radio. 'And get the samples from the creature to the path lab ASAP.'

Without waiting for a response he walked into the back of the plane and towards the large sealed biohazard container that was strapped securely to the fuselage.

The lock accepted his security card and he lifted the lid, letting the freezing gas dissipate before looking down into the icy interior.

The head of the creature stared back at him with hollow, unblinking eye sockets.

29

KELLY

House of the Grand Seer, Mortlake. 1595.

The Grand Seer raised his eyes from the page as Lyra stepped out of the mirror at the end of his study.

'My little bird,' he said, putting down his quill and blotting the entry in his journal. 'I have been expecting you.'

She feigned a smile, but he could tell from the look in her haunted eyes that things were not well.

'I have seen something,' she said, sitting down in one of the leather chairs beside the fire.

Kelly went to his extensive collection of scrying orbs and picked out a small purple one. Then he opened a drawer in his apothecary's cabinet and removed a flask of dark liquid and a raven's feather.

Shaking the bottle until it cleared, he sat opposite her and placed the items on the table.

'Well now,' he said calmly, judging by her expression that the vision must have been quite terrible. 'Drink a measure of this and then we can begin.'

She took the pipette from the top of the flask and let three drops fall onto her tongue. Kelly held up the glass sphere to his eye and stared into it, tilting his head at different angles as if trying to see around something.

He had known Lyra since the day she was born. Her talents were some of the most powerful in the seers guild, but they came at a price, as the pale scars on her arms testified.

'You've been walking in the Shadow Realm again?'

She nodded, pouting like a scolded child. 'It's the only place I can find peace.'

Sucking air through his teeth, Kelly put down the sphere and rolled up his sleeve. 'You're still wrapped in the skeins of forgotten lives. I cannot see clearly.'

Picking up the raven's feather, he sliced the end off the quill with a knife and drew it down his forearm. A dark line appeared with finer ones branching off like veins over his skin.

Staring into the fire, Lyra's lip trembled. 'I saw the end. A world filled with dead.'

The Grand Seer sighed, drawing runes into the growing lattice of lines on his forearm. 'As have I, many times, it is our burden to carry.'

'No,' she raised her voice. 'This was different! I wasn't alone.'

Kelly's hand paused and he looked up, his dark eyes narrowing. 'Tell me what you saw.'

She described the devastation, the cities laid to waste and the bodies left to rot on the streets. Unlike dreams which faded quickly once the dreamer awoke, visions retained their clarity and Lyra could remember every detail. It pained her to repeat the things that she'd seen, but Kelly insisted on knowing everything, the most trivial thing could be the most important.

'No crows?' he interrupted. 'An unusual sign.'

'No life at all.'

Lyra took a deep breath and continued, explaining how she woke from the first vision to find herself in another, with a man standing over her.

'Then it was his dream you walked in,' Kelly noted and held out his rune-covered hand. 'I must see.'

She nodded and took hold of it.

The Grand Seer's eyes rolled back into his head and his lips whispered silent incantations as he entered her mind.

Lyra felt the warm, feather-like touch of his consciousness on her own. It was something she'd become familiar with since she was a teenager when Kelly had helped her learn to control her darker emotions, showing her how to reroute the negative pathways, stopping her from wanting to end it all.

Since then, they had shared so many visions, her mental defences were used to the intervention; he could delve into her most private thoughts, not that he did, but she wondered if he could see the effect that Abandon's gift had wrought on her abilities.

When he was finished, Kelly slumped back in his chair. He looked drained and his hooded eyes were glazed with a distant, vacant stare.

'Master?' Lyra whispered. 'What did you see?'

Her voice brought him out of his reverie, but his hand shook as he stroked his beard.

'I believe the figure was a manifestation, an avatar, of someone who clearly wishes to cause a great deal of harm.'

Reaching over to a side table, he poured himself a large brandy and another for Lyra. 'I've not heard of any other seers reporting such premonitions, which is usually the case when something so catastrophic is imminent. Nevertheless it is clearly a portent of a possible calamity.'

Taking a long sip of his drink, Kelly sank lower into the chair.

'I should probably inform the Copernicans, although Eddington will be wanting specifics.'

'It felt close, less than a year,' Lyra said, taking her glass and tasting the liquor. Enjoying the feeling as the warmth of the alcohol slowly spread down her neck and into her chest.

'The star on his head was familiar. Have you seen it before?'

Lyra shook her head.

Putting down the glass, the Grand Seer rolled down his sleeve and got up from the chair.

'I have,' he said, walking over to one of his bookcases.

He ran his long fingers along the rows of the leather bound spines, reading their contents by touch like a blind man used braille. Finally, he came to one particular tome and levered it out.

'Have you heard of the Argenteum Astrum?'

Lyra shook her head.

'It was a society created by the occult magician Aleister Crowley.'

Her eyes widened. 'The exile?'

Kelly's expression hardened. 'My finest pupil and my greatest failure.'

Lyra had heard the story of Crowley's fall from grace, it was used as a solemn warning for them all. He'd been a talented seer who abused his powers to gain favour amongst the linears of the nineteenth century.

That was until the day he lost his talents, and became trapped in the late Victorian age.

'*Argenteum Astrum* is Latin for silver star — it is also the name of an organisation devoted to the practice of "scientific illuminism".'

The Grand Seer opened the book and handed it to her.

'Crowley convinced his followers that he was in contact with spiritual beings whom he called the "Secret Chiefs". They were supposed to have dictated two Books of Law, the first of which you hold in your hand. It seems to have struck a chord with the Victorians as he acquired many initiates and inspired other societies such as the Order of the Golden Dawn and Rosy Cross.'

'How did he lose his talents?' she asked, leafing through the pages which were filled with esoteric texts and cabalistic diagrams.

'No one knows. The man has delved into the darkest reaches of the continuum, studied the mysticisms of the universe and supposedly consorted with elder gods.' Kelly made a swift movement with his right hand as if casting a protection spell.

'Creatures of the Maelstrom?'

He shrugged. 'Perhaps, or even from your shadow world,' he said, nodding towards the mirror. 'There are more things in heaven and earth, Horatio, than are dreamt of in your philosophy.'

Lyra put down the book and walked over to the mirror. She stroked the glass with her finger, feeling the pull of the realm beneath its surface.

'Do you think he's met Abandon?'

'That is a question only he can answer.'

The grandfather clock stuck the hour and the Grand Seer lifted his feather cloak from the coat stand. 'I'm afraid I must leave you now. I have an appointment with the Founder. I will discuss your vision with him. Since I know you will ignore any warning I give you not to follow this, I won't bother.'

She bowed her head. 'I have no choice.'

He patted her on the shoulder and smiled benevolently. 'I know child.'

30

GREAT LIBRARY

The Great Library. 1858.

Their journey began in the restricted section of the British Library, which Melanie was surprised to find was still in the rotunda of the British Museum.

Fred led her through the stacks until he came to a metal security grille, with a sign clearly stating that this area was off limits to the general public. The lock was a series of dials with strange symbols on each ring. Fred twisted the brass circles until they aligned with a click and the door slid open.

Beyond the grille was a dark maze of bookcases. It had the musty smell of mouldering paper and old leather, 'the scent of history', her father would call it, sniffing an old book he'd found in some second-hand bookshop. He collected old legal documents, spending most weekends rifling through antique rooms and rare book stores.

Once inside, Fred took out his 'pocket watch' and tapped one of the buttons, and the face of the tachyon glowed with a blue-white incandescence creating a sphere of light around them.

'Should be just down here,' he said, pointing the torch towards a particularly dark corner of shelves.

Melanie wasn't quite sure what was down there. Wondering how exactly he was going to get them to South Georgia without an aeroplane, she followed him all the same.

Finally, they reached a tall bookcase of ancient manuscripts, each one attached to the shelf by a fine metal chain. Fred produced a brass key and slid it in between two leather spines.

Melanie heard the grinding of gears and watched as the entire bookcase seemed to recede in on itself, creating an archway into a corridor that shouldn't exist.

'The Great Library,' he said, waving her through. 'Tradesmen's entrance.'

Confused, she stepped over the threshold and into the largest library she had ever seen.

Towers of books stretched hundreds of feet upwards towards a distant ceiling. Linked by wrought iron walkways they formed a giant maze that went on for miles in all directions.

'How?'

'Temporal architects,' Fred explained, closing the portal behind her. 'It's actually fourteen different libraries stitched together. Although some of them may have been used more than once, at different times of course.'

'Of course,' she repeated, craning her neck towards the roof.

Fred went on to explain that it contained every lost book and misplaced manuscript from history. A vast repository of all human knowledge, curated by the guild of Scriptorians.

Melanie trailed behind him, watching the small figures moving between the stacks like acrobats on metal wires.

'They're indexing,' Fred explained, 'it's a thankless task.'

She squinted, pointing at one particular pair. 'They look more like they're fighting.'

He followed the line of her finger. 'Yes, that happens too. There are a lot of differing opinions about the right system of classification — men have died over it.'

. . .

After an hour and what felt like three miles of walking in very uncomfortable boots, they finally reached the cartography section. Fred explained that it held every chart and map that had ever been drawn, and many that had been forgotten.

The wall of the circular room was lined with mahogany plan chests and lacquered old globes. Above their heads hung a large sphere on which a world map had been drawn in incredible detail. When Melanie looked closer, she could see illustrated warships moving across the oceans and the tiny figures of armies marching across Russia.

'It's the Napoleonic war of 1812, the cartography curator is something of a military buff,' said Fred, hardly paying it any attention. 'Come on, the chart we need is this way.'

He went to one of the taller plan chests, its long thin wooden drawers set with beautiful copper plaques inscribed with the names of each mapmaker.

'These are the first maps ever made of the island.' He opened a drawer marked *Captain James Cook*. 'Captain Cook took possession of South Georgia in the name of His Majesty King George III in 1775.'

The map was a simple black and white drawing, bordered with the chequered markings of latitude and longitude. A dotted path had been plotted around the island with soundings and dates, weaving between place names such as: Pickergills, Possession Bay, Cape Disappointment and Clerkes Rocks.

Closing his eyes, Fred ran his fingers over the soft vellum.

'What are you doing?'

'We call it weaving,' he said in a quiet voice. 'I'm opening the threads of its timeline, reading the chronology.'

'And you can all do this?'

'Some better than others,' he replied, hoping he wouldn't have to explain about his limited range.

'I thought we were supposed to be going to 1914?'

His eyes snapped open. 'We are, but it's not every day you get to witness Captain Cook at work.'

She folded her arms. 'How is this helping us get there?'

He smiled. 'Maps are mostly copies of earlier versions. Charts handed down through generations of navigators. Good ones especially so, and Cook was one of the best. I can see where this was used and by whom, including a Norwegian sea captain by the name of Carl Larsen who founded a Whaling Station in Grytviken in 1904.'

'Still ten years out.'

Fred shrugged. 'It's close enough.'

'Why don't you just use something from Shackleton's expedition? Didn't you say you had some of his books?'

'All of the useful documents are still on the *Endurance*.'

Melanie scoffed. 'Which you were trying to steal when you got caught by Cooper.'

Fred tried not to be offended. 'I was trying to retrieve them for posterity.'

'This is pointless,' she snapped. 'I want to go back to my time. I need to warn the authorities about what's going to happen.'

'Without any proof? How do you think they'll take that?'

He had a point. Thanks to Professor MacAllister, Melanie was already discredited academically, turning up without any evidence was only going to make her look more of a laughing stock.

She grunted. 'What about other ships? Surely there would have been a regular fleet of whaling vessels using the station?'

Fred's eyes lit up and he placed his hand once more on the map. 'Indeed there were.'

31

CROWLEY

Boleskine House, Loch Ness, Scotland. 1914

L yra stepped out of the mirror and onto a wide mantelpiece above the fireplace. Climbing lightly down onto the thick Persian rug, she found herself in what appeared to be the study of a magician. The room was filled with esoteric objects, including a painted wooden Egyptian coffin and a glass case with a mummified hand, and books, lots of books.

Hundreds lined the walls. There were mystical treatises from many different religions and doctrines, each well-thumbed, their spines worn and cracked by use. She ran her finger over them, letting them tell their stories. Many were collected from Crowley's travels through Mexico, India, Egypt and Nepal.

That was not all he acquired on his tour. Her nose caught the subtle scents of hashish, opium and other exotic substances. A copper crucible sat on a low, round table in the centre of the room, the ashes of something recently burned still warm inside it.

Taking a deep breath, Lyra calmed her mind, opening herself to the timelines of those who had recently been in the room.

As if summoning ghosts, she felt the lives of Crowley's guests, their pasts and futures unfurling around her like a cloak.

Crowley and his acolytes had been preparing for a ritual invocation over the last six months. One that would apparently bring forth his guardian angel. Other members of his Order were helping in the process, bringing him gifts from all over the world.

Ethereal images danced around her: there was George Cecil Jones, a chemist and co-founder of the Argenteum Astrum; Gerald Kelly, a painter and his sister Rose, who married Crowley the year before in Paris.

She could see all of them except the man himself. His was like a missing jigsaw piece in the complex network of patterns swirling around her; somehow Crowley's timeline was an unreadable blur.

'And who in the name of the twelve dukes of hell are you?' a deep voice said from behind her.

Lyra turned, finding a paunchy, bald man in a long white robe standing in the doorway. She knew immediately that it was Aleister Crowley, but he was not the man from her dream.

'Anna,' she said with a small curtsey. 'Anna Blavatsky.'

Crowley's eyes were lined with black kohl liner like a pharaoh and his cheeks daubed with white powder. Lyra tried not to laugh at the ridiculous sight.

He stared at her, as if unsure whether she had been conjured up by one of his rituals.

'Daughter of Helena?' His eyes narrowed as he asked in a dramatic baritone that reminded Lyra of a Shakespearean actor.

She'd done her homework, Crowley had never met the co-founder of the American Theosophical Society. Helena Blavatsky was a spiritualist who claimed to have contacted 'Masters of Ancient Wisdom,' and Crowley would have read her work. The sudden appearance of her daughter at his house would be too interesting for him to turn her away.

She nodded, stepping towards him and holding out her hand. 'My mother spoke of you often,' she said in a smooth American accent.

He took it, bowing his head to kiss it. 'Madame Blavatsky was a visionary, it is an honour to meet her daughter.'

Instinctively, Lyra felt for his timeline. It had a strange structure, like that of a broken tree.

As if sensing her prying, Crowley released her hand and stepped back. 'And what pray brings you to my humble sanctuary?'

Lyra took a moment to compose herself. There was a glimmer of suspicion in his eyes. 'I seek enlightenment.'

Taking hold of her hand once more, he turned and led her out of the room. 'Come, we have much to discuss.'

32

GRYTVIKEN

Grytviken, South Georgia. December 4, 1914

The carcass of a huge whale lay on the slipway as oil-skinned fishermen worked with long-handled flensing knives to cut away the blubber in long strips. The sight of its ruined body and the smell of fat rendering in the large copper kettles alongside it made Melanie feel physically sick.

The whaling station was a cold, stark place. Its wooden buildings sat hunched against the shoreline like old men in a gale, their weathered boards stained with salt and patched with driftwood. Broken-toothed mountains towered over the bay, sheltering the harbour from the worst of the weather.

Even though it was supposed to be the warmer season, she still shivered.

Before they left the library, Fred insisted on dressing her in fur-lined oilskins, ramming a hat down over her head to hide most of her features. There were very few women in Grytviken, he explained, and certainly no single ones.

There were hardly any other options in the tiny clothes closet of the cartography department. When Fred dialled in the year and location, it offered three different types of oilskin or an Inuit style fur coat.

He chose something similar for himself. His red hair fitted in well amongst the other whalers, who she guessed were all Nordic or Scandinavian. However, his lack of beard made him look much younger.

Melanie looked back to the ship that they'd arrived on, glad to be standing on solid ground. *The Petrel* was the best link Fred could find to the date they needed to reach. A whaler from Norway, the boat was still at sea when they appeared, stowing away for hours in a hold full of dead sperm whales until it docked was not her idea of fun.

Fred stared out into the bay, admiring the *Endurance* which sat low in the grey waters of King Edward Cove. Melanie was still struggling to understand how anyone would take such a small boat on such a long journey.

'How are we going to get on board?' she asked, coming to stand beside him.

'The Captain will take on final supplies before he leaves. We can slip on board with them.'

Melanie looked out to the ship anchored beyond the smaller whaling vessels. 'How long will it take for them to reach the Weddell Sea?'

Fred took a deep breath and let it out slowly. 'Two months, maybe more, it depends on the pack ice.'

She thought about her own journey to Antarctica, the flight from Punta Arenas in Chile had taken just two hours, although it took over a day to get there. That had been a nightmare journey, twenty-four hours of trying to forget the past three years, it had felt as though she were on the run.

'We're not going to be able to stow away on there for two months?'

He smiled. 'No, we're going to skip the boring parts and jump forward to the end.'

'Sounds like most books I've been reading lately,' she joked.

A group of men were loading a barge with barrels of whale oil on the quay. Two crewmen from the *Endurance* were going over the manifest with one of the longshoremen. Fred picked up a sack of grain and heaved it onto his shoulder, Melanie did the same, keeping her head down as they passed them.

Stepping onto the boat, Fred found a space between two large crates and sat down.

'That was Shackleton,' he whispered, 'and Thomas Orde-Lees, the quartermaster.'

Melanie squeezed in beside him and pulled a crate across to block their entrance.

'They're coming on board,' he said at the sound of heavy boots on the deck.

The journey to the *Endurance* was a slow one. The barge was being towed by a fishing boat with an old steam engine that chugged out putrid black smoke that smelled of rancid fish.

'Must be burning whale oil,' Fred said, sticking his head out to check on their progress.'

'It's disgusting,' sneered Melanie.

'Not a lot in the way of wood and coal down here,' he said, sitting back down.

The wind rose as they left the shelter of the bay, and the chill bit at her fingers. Tucking her hands under her arms, she shifted closer to Fred to keep warm.

'Did you always want to be an Outlier?' she asked, distracting herself from the heavy waves that had begun to buffet the barge.

Fred chuckled. 'No, I've spent the last three years trying to leave.'

'Why?'

He took a deep breath. 'Because my family has been Draconian for generations. My father was something of a legend.' He tapped on his coat pocket, where he kept the old man's watch. 'Saved a lot of his comrades, was awarded the Order of the Dragon for gallantry.'

'Draconian?'

'They're the adventurers guild. The explorers who go into the darker, unmapped areas of the past and defend us from the creatures of the Maelstrom.'

'What kind of creatures?' Melanie asked, trying to convince herself that this was a normal conversation.

'Things that live outside of the temporal continuum. I've only seen a monad, it's a nightmarish ghoul that preys on your memories, but apparently there are thousands of others. The *Outlier Inquirer* did a piece on them only recently.'

She held up her hand. 'Just so we're clear, you're telling me that there are monsters waiting outside of time to devour my mind?'

'Yes, the article wrote about a Draconian department dedicated to studying them, they're called xenobiologysts. Apparently they've discovered all manner of hideous things. The Maelstrom is a terrible place by all accounts.'

Melanie blinked. 'And you want to join them?'

Fred seemed to shrink inside his sou'wester. 'It's all I've ever wanted to do, but I can't pass the basic requirements. My range is too limited.'

She stared at him blankly.

The barge bucked and cold, grey water sloshed over the gunwale and into the boat.

He shifted position to stop the water running underneath him. 'Everyone in the Order has an ability to travel through time, some can go further back than others. You need to be able to travel at least a thousand years in one leap to be eligible for Draconian basic training. Something my brothers have taken great pleasure in reminding me.'

There was a tinge of sadness in his voice and Melanie tried to change the subject.

'My sister's in a band. They're quite famous. She's got her own plane.'

It was Fred's turn to look confused. 'She's a musician or a pilot?'

'Both actually, it's very annoying. I get a PhD from Imperial and can't afford to pay the rent. Ruth gets a GCSE in Music Production, hooks up with a DJ in Ibiza and writes a bestselling album.'

'At least you weren't named after a Pope.'

'What?'

'All of my brothers were named after kings: William, Edward, Henry.' He counted them off on his fingers and then pointed at himself. 'Pope Frederick II.'

She winced. 'You could always use your middle name.'

He sighed. 'Rudolf.'

Melanie tried hard not to laugh, but his face was a picture of misery.

33

THREAT MODEL

U.S. Army Medical Research and Development Command, Fort Detrick, Maryland. Present Day.

The grainy images of the last moments at the Antarctic base-camp played across the wall of screens in the command centre. Cooper watched the faces of the Joint Chiefs, all hardened military men with years of experience in the field, and saw the horror in their eyes at what was playing out before them.

The footage, taken from one of the team's bodycams, showed the insanity of the salvage crew as they attacked the members of the British Antarctic Survey the moment they arrived to help them.

'The pathogen was initially believed to be airborne,' he said, walking in front of the screens. 'We estimate that the first symptoms took between eight and twelve hours to appear. But when the virus is introduced directly into the bloodstream, via a bite, it seems to take hold more rapidly, literally within a few minutes.'

They were like rabid dogs, tearing at each others' flesh, dragging their victims into the hold of the ship.

Cooper signalled to Miller, who stopped the film and the screen went black.

General Armitage turned towards him, the veins in his neck pulsing against his stiff collar. 'And you've brought this back?'

Cooper nodded. 'It's in containment.'

'Do we have any idea where it came from?' asked Admiral Casey.

The colonel shook his head, unwilling to tell them about the cave or the creature they found inside it. 'Either it was something on-board the *Endurance*, or the salvage crew found it when they got down there. My lab is still working on the profile of the virus, we should have an initial assay in the next twenty-four hours.'

Armitage nodded, the answer seeming to reassure him.

Admiral Casey was not so easily satisfied. 'Have you modelled the potential threat to the wider population?'

Cooper tapped a button on his tablet and a three-dimensional model of the globe appeared on the screens. Small red dots began to appear around New York and spread out over most of North America as a clock counted hours in seconds.

'This is a worst case scenario based on patient zero entering a heavily populated area. It's using an R estimate of two point two.'

The dots spread rapidly, within a week, half of the Midwest was red, but by the end of the second week the infection covered half the map.

'A month?' said Admiral Casey. 'You're saying it would overwhelm the USA in less than a month?'

Cooper tapped on the screen and the globe began to rotate, showing that most of the planet was now covered in red. 'No sir, I'm saying that it could annihilate the human race in under a month.'

They looked at him as if he were mad, unable to comprehend the threat that stood before them.

'Who else knows about this?'

'Other than the men in this room. No one.'

'What about the BAS? Aren't they going to wonder where their team has got to?'

Cooper smiled. 'There was an unfortunate accident, a fissure opened up right beneath Halley VI, it swallowed the base whole.'

The admiral nodded. 'Seems like you have everything under control. How long before we have a viral profile?'

'Ten days. Maybe fourteen at the max.'

34

UNUSUAL DEATHS

Northern China. Cretaceous.

Alixia stood amongst the bodies of the dead creatures. Her fists balled on her hips and her lips clamped together in a tight white line as she studied the carnage. The rest of the group stood back a little, mostly because of the smell, but also because they knew when to leave her alone.

One of her rangers had returned to the camp the night before and reported unusual activity amongst the herd he'd been observing. They were *Chenanisaurus*, one of the last of the T-Rex family, a predator that could reach eight metres in length. These were not full grown, Alixia guessed that they were less than two years old, immature adults at best.

The herd lay in strange formation, their bodies creating a circle around a mound of even younger siblings. *As if trying to protect them?* Alixia thought, trying to imagine what could have happened during the night.

Nothing about the scene made any sense. These were alpha predators, the only threat to them was an older, dominant male from another herd. She paced around the perimeter looking at the tracks embedded in the soft mud and trampled grasses.

There was nothing but their own footprints.

Yet the damage inflicted on them was clearly from a larger beast.

She looked skyward, *unless it had wings.*

Benoir approached her, his face set like stone.

'They came from the south,' he said, raising his hand in the general direction. 'Looks like a stampede, as if they were running from something.'

Alixia nodded, she trusted the Frenchman's tracking skills as much as her own. 'Winged predator,' she said, kneeling down and measuring one of the wounds on the nearest body. 'I would estimate the claw was at least two feet in length.'

'Pterosaur?' Benoir wondered.

'I'm not sure. I've never seen anything attack like this before. This is killing for killing's sake, not for food.'

She stood up and brushed the dirt from her skirt.

'Take blood and tissue samples and then burn the bodies.'

He nodded and went off to organise the team.

Caitlin and Zack were sitting playing in the flower meadow outside of camp when they spotted the party returning.

Caitlin could tell from the expression on Alixia's face that something wasn't right, she was not one for hiding her displeasure.

'What's wrong?' she asked, picking up Zack.

'We may have a rogue predator,' Alixia responded in a tone that she usually reserved for chastising her husband. 'Probably a Pterosaur.'

Caitlin fell in step next to Alixia as she continued back towards the gate. 'For now it's probably wise not to travel too far from the camp.'

'What is it? Should we go home?'

'I'm not sure. I need to speak with Rufius.'

With that she strode on, leaving Caitlin behind.

Josh appeared from a stand of trees carrying a small bundle of fur. As he came closer Caitlin could see it was a mammal of some kind, a cross between a bush baby and a monkey.

Zack's eyes lit up at the sight of the furry creature and small fingers reached out towards it.

'He likes him,' said Josh, holding a small piece of fruit in front of the creature. 'I was thinking of calling him Bert.'

Caitlin frowned and stepped back. 'He's probably covered in parasites!'

'He's cute,' Josh insisted as Bert took the fruit and stuffed the entire thing into his mouth, making his cheeks bulge like a hamster.

'Put it down!' she snapped.

Josh did as he was told and Bert scurried back into the under-growth with a grateful chirrup.

'What's the matter with Mummy?' he asked, tickling Zack under the chin.

Caitlin nodded towards the retreating figure of Alixia who was nearly at camp. 'Alixia says there's a rogue pterosaur hunting nearby. I've never seen her look so worried.'

'Pterosaur?'

'Flying dinosaurs,' she explained, looking up at the sky.

Josh scratched his head, pulling out a bug and squashing it between his fingernails. 'I thought they were supposed to be extinct by now.'

'The asteroid collision changed the climate. It took hundreds of thousands of years for them to die out. If anything those that survived are going to be more resilient, more adaptive.'

'So we should probably get out of here then?'

Caitlin nodded. 'I think so, Alixia's gone to talk to Rufius. I'm guessing to work out how to get back to the linking stones without being attacked.'

She could see Josh holding back the "I told you so".

'I know, I know. You were right we shouldn't have come,' she said.

His expression changed. 'Let's get back to the camp and find out what's happened.'

35

BASECAMP

Endurance, Weddell Sea, Antarctica. 1915.

T he *Endurance* was surrounded by ice in all directions. The sound of the floes grinding against the hull reminded Fred of a dying whale.

The deck was tilting to one side, forced over by the pressure of the encroaching ice. The crew had already abandoned ship and he could see a small camp made from lifeboats, sails and cargo out in the distance.

'Where are they?' asked Melanie, stepping out of the forward cabin.

Fred pointed towards the shanty town. 'We've overshot. They've already abandoned the ship.'

Trying to hide her disappointment, she went over to the gunwale and looked down at the rope ladder. 'I thought we were supposed to see what happened.'

'Time travel is harder than it looks, it's not an exact science.'

Turning back towards him, her eyes narrowed. 'When exactly were you going to tell me that?'

Fred pulled up the collar of his coat and stepped over the rail onto the ladder. 'It's going to get cold, we'll freeze if we don't get inside and near a fire. I suggest we continue this discussion somewhere warmer.'

Melanie grunted and followed him.

The crunch of the ice beneath her feet reminded her that it was probably less than twenty-four hours since she'd left Antarctica. Instinctively, she went to check her watch, only to realise that it was gone, lost in the first jump back to 1858, along with her clothes.

It was hard to keep track of time when you were moving around in history, but her body clock was telling her it was definitely time to rest, to sleep.

Trekking across the white field towards the ramshackle encampment, Melanie was more excited about the idea of a hot meal and a warm bed than meeting the famous Shackleton and his intrepid crew.

The first hut was empty, as was the next tent and the one after that.

Everyone was gone.

They went back to the hut and found some wood and coal. It took twenty minutes of hard work and grunting before Fred managed to get the stove working.

'Where's the crew?' Melanie said, warming her hands.

Fred had taken off his fur-lined coat and was sitting on one of the bunks, eating beans out of a tin with a bent spoon.

'My guess is they've gone inland. The dogs and sleds are missing, as well as some of the supplies. They're continuing with their mission.'

She unbuckled her coat and sat on an empty cot opposite him.

He leaned over and picked up another tin from the wooden crate. 'So, we've beans, or rice pudding.'

Melanie opted for the pudding. She needed something sweet, her blood sugar was low and she could feel a headache brewing.

The shack warmed quickly and after they'd eaten, both of them fell asleep in a matter of minutes.

. . .

It was dark when Melanie awoke and for a second she forgot where she was. The smell of the wooden hut and the smoke from the fire reminding her of a camping trip from when she was eleven.

Her parents were never the most adventurous holiday planners, for most of her childhood they would go to the same location, a cabin by Thirlmere in the Lake District.

Spending two weeks drying out your socks and shoes on a wood burner was character building, according to her father, as was yomping up the Cumbrian hillside in the sleeting rain.

But right now, she would have done anything to have been back there.

The weak glow of the stove gave the cabin a strange otherworldly hue. There were spare coats and hats hanging on pegs, cups and plates stacked neatly on the table as if the men had stepped out of the room for a moment. She listened to the wind whistling through the cracks in the window panes, hoping to hear the sound of dogs, but there was nothing but the grinding of the ice against the ship.

Fred was snoring and muttering in his sleep.

She rose quietly and added some more coal to the stove. Then lit one of the oil lamps and went over to a small writing desk that sat in one corner.

Charts of the area were laid out across the desktop. Annotations in a shaky hand had been added to the vast areas of white space, plotting a route from their boat to a site near the mountains of Vinson Massif.

Melanie followed the dotted line with a pair of compasses, measuring the distance. It was over twenty miles to their destination, a journey that would take less than an hour on a skidoo, but with heavily-laden sleds it could take as long as four days, without allowing for the crossing of crevasses.

Shackleton's goal was marked with an 'x' alongside the latitude and longitude.

'What time is it?' asked a bleary-eyed Fred, rising from his cot with a yawn and scratching the two-day old stubble on his chin.

'Nineteen fifteen,' she replied sarcastically.

He laughed. 'Never gets old that one.'

She held up the map. 'I've found where they were heading.'

Fred opened the stove and stoked the fire, adding a few more coals to it until it was burning brightly once more.

'Good! Now let's see if they have any decent coffee.'

After a breakfast of powdered eggs and beans, Fred picked up the chart.

His fingers touched the paper as if it were made of tissue, gently caressing the lines and words that were inscribed upon it.

'Can you take us there?' Melanie asked, hoping that they wouldn't have to make the journey on foot.

He closed his eyes and drew in a deep breath.

Fred felt the room changing around him as he followed the chart's chronology back to the moment the men left. As if at the end of a tunnel, he heard their voices, caught glimpses of them walking past him like ghosts. This was the *prelude*, the moment before he shifted entirely into the timeline, allowing him to observe, but not interact.

As the vision stabilised he caught snippets of conversation.

'Just throw it into the sea,' one man said.

'Who would know?' agreed another.

Faces came in and out of focus around him. Shackleton, Worsley and Wild, each now sporting a beard and looking exhausted.

'We have a job to do,' insisted Shackleton. 'Let's be rid of it, and then we shall make for the *Aurora*.'

. . .

Taking his hand away from the map, the cabin regained its solidity.

'What did you see?' Melanie asked, handing him a hot cup of black coffee.

'They took the cargo about ten days ago.' He got up and went to the small window. 'They should've been back by now.'

'Did you see what it was?'

Fred shook his head. 'No, but the crew were scared of it. They couldn't wait to be rid of it.'

Melanie sat down at the desk and took down one of the journals from the small shelf above it.

'What are you looking for?' asked Fred.

'They were either infected by something they found here or brought it with them. Since they weren't sick on the voyage — I'm assuming the former. Whatever it was, it led to their deaths, and potentially a global pandemic in the future. We need to find a way to stop them.'

Fred looked shocked. 'We can't just jump back and change history.'

She turned towards him, a fire burning in her eyes. 'Why not? I thought that's what you guys do.'

'Because there are procedures to follow, to ensure we don't create a catastrophe. It's why we need the Copernicans.'

Melanie scoffed. 'I've already modelled the outbreak. You don't need them to tell you this is going to end badly if we don't do something about it.'

36

YAOGUAI

Boleskine House, Loch Ness, Scotland. 1914

Lyra followed Crowley through the dark-panelled corridors of the manor house, marvelling at the strange and unusual creatures that sat stuffed in glass display cases in the alcoves along the route. There were mermaid-like children, skulls with unicorn horns and deformed arachnids with over-sized heads and mandibles. All were obviously fake, meant to impress his guests, but they were very convincing.

Lyra shivered at the thought of meeting such a spider in real life.

'I have been collecting specimens from all over the globe,' he began with a flourish of his hand, Lyra noticed his nails were painted black. 'Some have incredibly interesting magical properties. There is one in particular that I wish to show you.'

They passed a room decorated in the style of an Egyptian temple. Two women sat on the floor, naked except for the hieroglyphs painted over their skin. Censers burned above their heads filling the air with the heady aromas of jasmine and sandalwood.

. . .

At the rear of the house was a large conservatory. Its iron and glass construction was similar to Alixia's roof garden, a replica of the Palm House at Kew.

In the centre of the palm-fronded space was a sculpture of a Chinese dragon, and water ran out of its mouth and along its long winding tail.

'The Yaoguai,' Crowley announced bowing reverentially towards it. 'One of my most prized possessions. The Taoist Alchemists of the Qin Dynasty believed they had the power to assume human form and that their blood could preserve life. I have several of their early scrolls, supposedly written by Lao Tzu himself, if you would like to see them. Perhaps over a cup of tea?' He pointed towards a small table laid out with a Chinese tea set.

Lyra sat in the seat nearest to the fountain while Crowley went to find the scrolls. She ran her fingers over the marble statue, letting the cool water run through her hands.

Its time-line was over a thousand years old.

She caught glimpses of a beautiful walled palace, with pagodas and dragon pennants flying over golden roofed palaces.

The Forbidden City, a voice whispered to her and she turned to see if there was someone else in the room.

Studying the dragon closely, she realised it was more of a serpent with wings, the sculptor taking great pains to carve every scale along its body in incredible detail. A tiny symbol had been etched into every one of the diamond-shaped patterns.

She contemplated following the time-line.

Kelly had been wrong, Crowley wasn't the man in her vision, but he had lost his abilities and Lyra wanted to know how.

Crowley returned a few minutes later. He'd washed off the clownish make-up and was now wearing a three-piece suit, looking every part the Scottish country squire.

Several bamboo scrolls were tucked under one arm, whilst he carried a decorated china pot in the other hand.

'I've always wondered about your mother's time in Tibet. She claimed to have been taught an ancient, unknown language by the Masters of Mahatmas,' he said, placing the pot and the scrolls on the table and sitting heavily into the cane chair opposite.

Lyra nodded. 'Senzar, a tongue absent from the nomenclature of languages and dialects with which philology is acquainted,' she quoted from Blavatsky's *Secret Doctrine*.

She could tell by his reaction that this was some kind of test.

'And the Book of Dyzan?' he continued.

Another test, Lyra thought. 'The book composed in Atlantis? That I never saw. Nor did she pass on the knowledge of how to read it.'

He shrugged and picked up the teapot. 'I myself have had similar experiences with Aiwass,' he said, pouring the hot water onto the leaves while stirring it gently with a bamboo whisk.

Lyra accepted the tea bowl gracefully, raising it in respect to her host before rotating it to sip from the other side.

'It's very good,' she said, before taking another sip.

Crowley nodded deferentially and took up his own bowl. 'It's from Wuyishan, picked from the nearly extinct mother-trees of their ancient forests.'

She savoured the flavour, knowing better than to try and enter its timeline. Natural objects had a tendency to leave you stranded in the most unlikely corners of the deep past.

'You wanted to show me something?' Lyra said, nodding towards the scrolls.

'Ah yes! Indeed I did.'

He unrolled the first of them and laid it out across the table.

'These are some of the Qin Alchemists' earliest manuscripts. I have been working on the translation, but it's proving a little tricky. I wondered if you might cast your eyes over it?'

Lyra picked up the first of the scrolls and studied it. The symbols looked a little like Kanji, but seemed to make no sense. In the margins the alchemists had drawn beautiful rich illustrations of dragon serpents, their eyes burning with a golden fire.

She glanced up at Crowley who was observing her closely.

'It is not a language I recognise,' she said, putting down the document. 'Sorry.'

'But what about its timeline?' he asked, leaning forward and pushing the scroll back towards her. 'You're a seer, are you not? One of the Order? Tell me what you *see* girl.'

There was an underlying menace to his voice now. Lyra felt the threat, taken aback by the fact he'd seen through her pretence.

'I'm not sure what you mean,' she replied coyly, hoping that it was just another one of his tests.

Crowley laughed, it was a cruel, hard sound that made her shrink away from him.

'You cannot fool me. I may have lost my abilities, but I can still sense yours.' He sniffed the air. 'You positively reek of time. Who sent you? The Grand Seer?'

She nodded, unable to think of another lie, her head was beginning to feel woozy, and she found it difficult to think clearly. *He's drugged me.*

Crowley's lips twisted into a wicked grin. 'Then I must be close.' He gathered up the scrolls and grabbed her by the wrist. 'I've been waiting a long time for him to send someone.'

37

CAVE

Vinson Massif. Antarctica. 1915

The distant sound of men's voices echoed along the cave walls. Fred held his hand up, signalling to Melanie to stop.

Pressing herself against the cave wall, she realised it was no longer formed of ice, but smooth rock, worn down by thousands of years of water erosion. Taking off one of her gloves, she ran her hand over its granite contours, her fingers finding markings scratched into its surface. Holding up the lamp, she could make out crude pictograms of men and beasts carved by stone tools.

The presence of a prehistoric civilisation on Antarctica was something that Dave and the Chief argued over many times, mostly late at night in the Rec Room when they were drunk. The idea that the ice-bound continent could once have been a fertile land with a climate that supported life was a regular bone of contention between them.

A few years ago, a German science team found evidence of an ancient forest beneath the sea floor near the Pine Island glacier. They dated it to the Cretaceous, around ninety-million years ago, which would have been far too early even for humanity's earliest ancestor,

Australopithecus Afarensis, let alone a tool-using hominid like *Homo Habilis*.

Yet someone had made these marks. A sentient being that was clearly aware of its environment and the desire to memorialise their story in stone.

The Chief's usual argument was based on a theory about a sixteenth-century chart that showed the original coastline of Antarctica. Named after the Portuguese Admiral who discovered it, the "Piri Reis" map was supposed to have plotted the northern edge of Antarctica in detail that would only be visible if it were free of ice. Dave protested that the map was an obvious fake, but the Chief insisted that the coastline was confirmed by a Canadian mapping team using ground radar.

She missed their bickering, which would last for hours; it was one of the only reasons to go to the bar, that and movie night.

Fred tapped her on the shoulder and motioned for her to follow him, setting off quietly into the dark.

The cave was over twenty feet in diameter by this point, with a smooth floor scored only by the marks of the sledge the crew were using to haul the cargo.

Ahead she could see the dim glow of lamps, illuminating the edges of a wider, cavernous space.

Reaching the end of the tunnel, they crouched in the shadows.

Rows of stalactites hung menacingly from the ceiling like the teeth of an ancient shark, their calcified points threatening to crush anyone who walked beneath them.

The cavern floor sloped away from the crew of the *Endurance*, who were struggling to manoeuvre an iron-bound wooden crate, which was over ten feet tall, using chains encircling it on both axes.

A star symbol had been burned into one of the sides.

'Stay here,' whispered Fred, moving out of cover and down into the cavern.

Melanie went to stop him, everything about this situation was ringing alarm bells, but he was gone before she had a chance.

Watching him weave carefully between the stalagmites, she wondered what on earth he was planning to do.

Some of the crew were removing the ropes that bound the crate to the sledge, others stood guard with rifles, aimed directly at the wooden box.

'Leave the sledge,' said one man. 'And let's get out of this godforsaken place.'

'We can't spare it,' replied another, who Fred recognised from his accent as Captain Worsley. 'Use the poles and we'll have it off in no time.'

Four men took long poles and used them as levers to hoist the back edge of the crate away from the sled, but the cargo was too heavy. Worsley ordered the guards to put down their rifles and assist before the box began to move.

Disturbed by the movement, something roared from inside, a chilling cry that froze the marrow in Fred's bones. He looked back nervously at Melanie, considering whether it wouldn't have been wiser to leave her back at the ship.

The crew grunted and heaved until the sledge suddenly tipped forward, causing the crate to slip off its base and tumble down the rocky slope. The sharp crack of splintering wood echoed through the chamber as the ropes slipped through the crew's hands, losing control of its descent.

It rolled end over end towards the cavern floor, fifty yards below.

Fred shifted position, watching the thick planks of the crate buckle and split with every turn until it came to rest amongst the stalagmites.

For a brief moment the crew stood agape, expressions of disbelief and shock on their faces.

Fred motioned to Melanie to go back, but she shook her head.

Suddenly, the silence was punctuated by the sounds of something clawing its way out of the wreckage, snapping the crew out of their reverie. Leaving the sledge behind, they ran. Tripping over the uneven floor, the men scrambled back towards the cave, but the beast was upon them in a heartbeat.

Tentacles and teeth tore into their bodies, tossing them aside like rag dolls.

Fred couldn't move. His brain unable to process the carnage unfolding before him. The creature was a whirlwind of teeth, scales and claws. The men flailed around trying to fend it off with their poles, but it swept them aside like matchwood.

The guards shot indiscriminately, firing wide and high as their hands shook with fear.

In less than a minute the creature had slain half of the company, the other half having made it to the relative safety of the cave.

'Set the charges,' barked Worsley, throwing a large rucksack towards some of his men. 'Bring it down. We'll buy you some time.'

Melanie shrank back into a dark crevice as the crew rushed passed her, clenching her jaw tightly to stifle the scream. Once they were out of sight, she peered around the edge to find Fred crouching behind a large stalagmite no more than ten yards from her.

His eyes were closed and he appeared to be talking to himself. Holding the tachyon clutched to his chest, she could see he was too afraid to move.

Lamps lay scattered over the floor, their oil burning in pools of orange light.

In the flickering shadows she caught the silhouette of the creature, moving slowly towards the remaining men.

'Hold the line,' barked Worsley, reloading his rifle and taking aim.

At the sound of his shot the creature was upon them, its long, barbed tail brushing three men aside and into the walls. Melanie heard their bones breaking on impact.

She had little time to think. Worsley was planning to collapse the tunnel, and the beast was closing in on Fred and the last of the crew.

The Captain stood his ground as the creature swayed from side to side. In the fading light she could just make out a long, serpentine body covered in scales, its dragon-like head bearded with tentacles.

Its eyes changed for a second and for a moment Melanie thought she saw a flicker of intelligence, then they darkened once more as it charged.

The flames from the lamp oil were dying out, soon it would be too dark to see. Melanie looked around her for anything to use as a diversion.

Her hand found the butt of a rifle and she slowly pulled it towards her. Feeling along the stock until she found the magazine, she broke open the remaining three cartridges and poured the gunpowder into one of her gloves, then added flint shards from the cave floor. Closing the opening with a leather thong, she threw it into the last of the burning puddles.

Counting to five, Melanie pushed herself out of the cave and slid down shale towards Fred.

The creature's head snapped towards the noise of the loose stones, but before it could move, the glove exploded sending hot splinters of flint in all directions.

It screamed as the knife-like edges seared into its flesh and fell back down the slope towards the wreckage.

Melanie reached Fred a second later and took his hand.

'Fred, you've got to get us out of here!' she screamed at him, shaking his shoulder.

His eyes opened, blinking in the semi-darkness. 'I can't,' he groaned.

'You have to try!' she pleaded, 'they're going to seal the cave. We'll be trapped in here with it!'

Melanie could see blood seeping through his shirt.

'What happened? Did it cut you?'

He nodded. 'It hit me with its tail. Hurt's like the devil.'

Melanie opened his coat to examine the wound, trying to hide the look of concern at the amount of blood pouring out of it.

'Am I going to die?' he asked meekly.

She took off her scarf and rolled it up before pressing it against the wound.

'Not if we can stop the bleeding. Keep pressure on it,' she said, putting his hand back on the wound.

Noises from below told her the creature was recovering from the shock of the blast. Melanie helped Fred to his feet and put one arm around his waist as they made their way towards the exit.

The sound of its claws on the cavern floor made her quicken the pace, but Fred dragged his feet.

'Come on Fred, don't give up yet!'

There was a series of deafening booms further up the tunnel and she pushed him against the wall as the percussion wave hit them.

Her ears were ringing and she could taste dust in her mouth when she came around.

Fred was lying beneath her, his eyes glazed, staring over her shoulder. She could feel the hot breath of the creature on the back of her neck. Fred opened his hand, the watch case was dented where something had scratched it.

'It's okay,' he whispered in her ear, 'I know what to do now.'

38

CRYPTIDS

Boleskine House, Loch Ness, Scotland. 1914

Crowley dragged Lyra down a flight of stone stairs and into a large vaulted basement. She struggled weakly against him. His grip was like iron and the soporific effects of the drugs he laced in her tea made it hard for her to fight back.

The basement had been converted into a laboratory, its walls lined with tall glass tubes containing pallid creatures preserved in a luminous green liquid. They were all hideously deformed, tissue falling off their bones like mouldering paper.

'Doctor Lind!' Crowley called out. 'Where are you man?'

A small, weasel-faced man appeared from behind one of the largest glass chambers, he was wearing a white coat stained with drops of blood, and holding a vicious-looking saw in one hand.

'Master.' He had a scar through his upper lip, which affected his speech, giving him a lisp that elongated the 's'.

The man leered at Lyra through the thick lenses of his spectacles. 'Is this the one you foretold?'

'Indeed it is.' He pushed Lyra forward. 'This is Miss Blavatsky, although I doubt that is your real name.'

He stared at her, as if waiting for her to answer.

She tried to resist, but the drugs softened her resolve.

'Lyra.'

Crowley smiled. 'Lyra, this is Doctor Lind. He's a cryptozoologist, best in his field.'

Waving his hand at the morbid exhibits, he continued. 'He specialises in cryptids — creatures that science has chosen to ignore. Ones that evolution has discarded. Come, doctor let us show her your masterpiece.'

They followed Lind through a series of vaults, each one a storehouse of more unusual specimens. It reminded Lyra of Doctor Shika's specimens at the Xenobiology lab, except hers were generally in better condition and most were still alive.

Finally, they arrived at what Lyra mistook for an operating theatre. On the table, surrounded by numerous mechanical devices were the bones of a massive snake-like creature, the body was over twenty feet long and its skull was propped up on an articulated arm, as if posed for a museum display.

'My acolytes discovered the remains on the island of Penglai, in China. The local legends had talked of a dragon that had lived in the mountains. Lind believes the fossil to be truly ancient.' His eyes glinted as he stared at the skeleton.

Doctor Lind was busying himself in another part of the laboratory.

'What are you trying to do?' Lyra asked, looking back at the rotting corpses floating in the tanks.

Crowley smiled. 'Trying? No, my dear, we've gone far beyond trying! Behold what we have achieved!'

The doctor cranked an iron handle connected to a mechanical winch, raising a series of metal screens along one wall and revealing a long window onto what Lyra assumed was the bottom of the loch.

Squinting into the murky green water she caught the subtlest of movement, a dark shape slipping between the waving weeds, a long sleek body weaving towards them.

Lyra gasped as it glided past. The creature was enormous, its head shaped like a dragon's, with tentacle-like feelers trailing from its jaws. The scales of its body glistened in the dappled light, silver and gold.

'What is it?'

'My yaoguai.'

'How?'

It wasn't the first aquatic dinosaur Lyra had ever seen, her mother had raised many extinct species in the flooded caves beneath the Chapter House, but this one was different, like something from Chinese mythology.

'There was a legend,' Crowley continued with a wry grin, watching it swim away. 'That in 210 BC the first emperor of China, Qin Shi Huang, was so obsessed with finding a way to extend his life that he sent decrees across his empire demanding they search for an elixir. Agents travelled to the far corners of his domain, bringing back theories on everything from wild herbs, minerals and even a mountainous island in the Bohai Sea where immortals were supposed to live. Their searches revealed nothing but charlatans and fakers, until the day a fisherman arrived at his court with the egg of the Yaoguai. '

'A fisherman?' said Lyra.

Crowley nodded. 'With a very unusual egg, one that was said to be cursed.'

Lyra watched the creature glide through the water. 'There are some that would say immortality was a curse.'

The doctor placed his hands together in prayer and bowed. 'The Emperor died soon after, as did most of his court.'

'And so how did you come to possess it?'

'One man survived. I found him, and he told me where it was buried.'

Lind chuckled to himself as he wandered off into another room. 'The shell kept the foetus in stasis. I was able to deliver it intact.'

'Then why do you need me?'

Crowley turned towards her, a fiery gleam in his eyes. 'This is a unique creature, the last of its kind. I wish to learn its secrets. You will help me to join with it.'

39

ROGUE PREDATOR

Northern China. Cretaceous.

Alixia was in deep discussions with Rufius when Josh and Caitlin entered the tent.

Their grave expressions matched those of Methuselah and Benoir who were studying a map of the area.

'What's the plan?' asked Josh, walking up to stand beside Benoir.

The Frenchman folded his arms and shrugged. 'There's something wrong with the almanacs. We've lost the sympathetic connection. We have to leave.'

Methuselah shook his head. 'No, we stay. It's not safe out there. We can't be sure it won't strike on the way back to the gate. We call for backup, there's a Draconian garrison stationed six million years from here.'

Rufius scoffed. 'And how are you going to alert them with our almanacs out of action?'

'When we don't report in they will send a search party,' added Alixia. 'Although that may take more than a week or so.'

'By which time we could all be dead,' said Rufius. 'We have

weapons. We travel at night, the creature's cold blooded, it won't attack us once the sun goes down.'

'That may not be strictly correct,' added Alixia. 'This is an avian predator, we know that they have a higher metabolism, just like birds.'

Rufius scowled, reminding Josh of a schoolboy who had just been disciplined by his teacher.

'Then we must hunt it down!' he growled. 'Before it decides we are prey.'

'No!' Alixia exclaimed, shaking her head. 'What about the prime directive? There must be another way!'

Rufius stood up, his cheeks flushed. 'This is not one of your conservation projects! This is their world, their domain. Our ancestors are scurrying around in the bush trying not to get eaten. We don't have the luxury of protecting a species when they're trying to eat us.'

Alixia put her hands on her hips, her face setting like stone. 'Rufius, we've been friends for longer than I care to remember. You know how important this is to me. How hard I've worked to understand what happened to these creatures. I cannot condone the killing of one just to save us. We are the ones that don't belong here!'

'Noted,' said Rufius before turning to Benoir and Josh. 'Gentlemen, I will be needing your assistance, assuming that you have no objections to my plan?' he added, raising an eyebrow at Josh.

'I want to come too,' Caitlin announced, standing next to Josh. 'Assuming you don't have a problem with a girl joining?'

Rufius's grim expression broke into a smile. 'I was hoping you would, but what about Zack?'

'He will be fine,' Caitlin said, looking towards Alixia, 'his grandparents will take care of him.'

Alixia bowed her head. 'Of course.'

The weapons that Rufius mentioned were not quite what Josh was expecting. The bows were standard, but the arrows were fletched with the queerest looking feathers he'd ever seen.

'Not too many geese around here,' Benoir explained, 'we have to make do with what we can get.'

Caitlin picked up one of the axes, its head carved from flint; virtually everything else was sharpened bone on wood.

'So, we're going to take on an apex predator with two-foot talons with sharpened sticks?' she said, swinging the axe.

Rufius winced and stepped back. 'Careful with that, flint is sharper than surgical steel if it's been knapped correctly.'

'Or we could use this?' said Benoir, producing a spear with a black blade strapped to its shaft.

'Obsidian! Now we're talking,' said Rufius, taking hold of the weapon. 'Razor sharp.' He held it up to his beard and sliced off a tuft, holding up the hair to the others. 'Breaks easily though, so best use it as a stabbing weapon. Should penetrate through the hardest of scale.'

Josh examined the tips of the arrows, they too were black and incredibly sharp.

'So, what say you merry men?' Rufius said, putting on a quaint English accent. He slung a bow over his shoulder and picked up a quiver of arrows. 'And my lady, of course,' he added with a bow. 'Shall we?'

40

LEVEL 7

Copernicus Hall. 1580

S im's eyes ached. Putting down his pencil, he leaned back from his desk and rubbed his temples until the pain subsided.

It was the third time he'd gone through the results of his calculations. Having waited four days before he was allowed any processing time, he wanted to make sure they were accurate before he shared them with the Professor.

Following a major deviation in the stochastic variation limiters, Professor Eddington ordered a complete review of the twenty–first century predictors, which meant all of the data Sim needed had been unavailable until yesterday.

He'd used the time to prepare his program on punched cards, saving hours of manual configuration of the engine, and creating a stack that was as tall as himself.

The engineer, Basil Haldane, looked quite impressed when Sim arrived with the entire program already loaded into its brass cassette.

'A little larger than usual,' Basil noted, sliding the long brass block into the machine and setting a series of levers.

'Running a pandemic simulation,' explained Sim, watching the cards disappear inside the clockwork mechanism.

'Plague,' the compter said, sucking air in through his teeth. 'Thought as much, don't get many as big as this lest it is a plague or a war.'

'How long will it take?'

There was another long pause while the man scratched at his pock-marked chin. Sim tried not to stare at his stubby fingers, each one shortened to the same length where they'd been cropped by a misaligned cassette.

'Hard to tell. There are still several levels running at half-speed. We tried to keep the engines ticking over while they were over-hauling the limiters, but you know those greasers and stokers don't need much of an excuse to take a half day.'

The deck was quickly disappearing as the spring-loaded cassette pushed the remaining cards upwards into the bowels of the analytical engine.

Listening carefully, Sim caught the subtle change in pitch as the gearing above his head began to process his code.

Basil wasn't wrong about the speed, it took almost all of the night to get the initial findings: a long scroll of temporal glyphs awaited Sim when he sat down at his desk the next morning.

The results were difficult to interpret. Like most statistical analyses it was a lengthy list of percentages and probabilities which required a great deal of actuarial training and skill to be able to inter-pret. Sim was in the final year of his apprenticeship and, assuming that he didn't do anything ridiculous like acting on the crazy theories of an Outlier, he would take his final examinations in a little over six months.

But Sim wasn't one to shy away from an interesting challenge, and the doctor that accompanied Fred had been rather convincing, as well as being quite pretty.

He picked up the scroll once more and scanned the array of numbers and dates, marking key points with red ink until he began to see the pattern.

After another round of checking, he got up from his desk.

'He's not going to like this,' he whispered to himself, rolling up the results into a scroll. 'Not one little bit.'

Professor Eddington was busy overseeing the recalibration of the stochastic limiters on the ninetieth floor of the building.

A small army of engineers in grease-stained aprons were busy adjusting the intricate gearing, with the professor calmly reading off the calibrations as they worked.

'Master De Freis, this is an unusual interruption.'

Eddington used the word 'unusual' derisively, he was obviously not pleased by Sim's sudden appearance.

Sim bowed his head and offered him the scroll. 'My apologies sir, but I believe we have a potential level seven event.'

Raising his head, Sim could see Eddington's eyes widening as he unrolled the scroll.

'In the twenty-first century,' Sim added, before the professor asked.

'Forty-two million,' Eddington muttered under his breath. 'Have you validated this?'

Sim nodded. 'Using both Mayhew and Valliard scales. The probabilities are within point three of a percent.'

Sim had studied under the professor since he was fourteen and in all those eight years he'd never seen the man look so anxious.

'A level seven?' Eddington muttered, his eyes narrowing behind his spectacles. 'You realise how serious this could be?'

'Yes sir, you'll find my initial forecast at the bottom of section six.'

The professor unravelled the document and read the conclusion. 'What alerted you to this event?'

Sim paused for a moment, considering whether it was wise to mention the involvement of the Outlier department.

'A friend mentioned it in passing and I thought it was worth further investigation.'

Eddington rolled up the scroll and handed it back to him. 'A wise decision Master De Freis. Contact this friend of yours and have them meet us in the Map Room as a matter of urgency.'

41

XENO LAB

Xenobiology lab. Present Day.

Melanie felt the beads of sweat running down her forehead and blinked as they flowed into her eyes. *You can do this*, she said to herself.

'Suction,' she ordered one of the nurses, who glanced nervously towards her boss. Doctor Shika nodded and the woman placed the tube inside Fred's chest.

The wound was small but the internal damage extensive, there were spines embedded in the tissue around his heart and extracting them took a very steady hand.

The forceps felt clumsy, but somehow she managed to remove each of the seven long, thorn-like barbs from his body.

Sighing behind her mask, she dropped the last of them into the metal tray.

Checking his vitals on the monitor, she stepped away and allowed Doctor Shika's team to take over.

. . .

'That was expertly done,' said the small Japanese woman as Melanie took off her gown in the scrub room.

'I'm used to working with parasites,' she explained, 'one of the high points of working in virology.'

Doctor Kaori Shika nodded inscrutably, holding up the dish of black thorns. 'These are rather unusual, not something I've encountered before and I've studied many ancient species.'

'Neither have I,' Melanie agreed. 'The creature was terrifying, like some kind of dinosaur.' She stopped herself from saying *Dragon*. 'I would assume those are a defence mechanism, probably coated with some kind of neurotoxin.'

'I'll have them analysed. The DNA profile may match something we have in our database.'

Melanie was about to ask how they came to have a database of dinosaur DNA when the doors opened and Fred was wheeled out of the operating theatre.

'He will be in intensive care for the next twenty-four hours. I suggest you get some rest,' Doctor Shika added. 'There are beds in the recovery wing that you can use.'

The nurse escorted Melanie to a side ward and left her to get changed into a clean set of scrubs.

Sitting on the bed, she realised how exhausted she was. The last twenty-four hours felt like a dream, or more accurately a nightmare.

Somehow, Fred had managed to operate the tachyon, bringing them to this place. It appeared to be a laboratory, one of the most advanced she'd ever seen, so much so that Melanie wondered if they'd actually travelled into the future.

It was only when she noticed the strange creatures in the glass tanks that she began to worry about where he'd taken them. While the staff lifted Fred onto a gurney, Melanie stared at the monstrous beasts swimming in the vats, each one like something from a horror movie.

'You brought him to the right place,' Doctor Shika assured her while a sabre-tooth cat stood nuzzling her leg. 'We will take good care of him.'

Melanie insisted on doing the operation herself. She wasn't quite sure why at the time, but now, lying on the bed staring at the ceiling fan, she realised how much she had come to like him.

Get a grip, she told herself, trying to ignore the feelings that were clamouring for her attention.

She closed her eyes and focused on the events in the cave. The creature they were transporting was the obvious candidate for the source of the plague, but where it had come from was still a mystery. It killed most of the crew before they sealed it in, but some must have made it back to the ship and infected the others. Trapped inside the cave, it would have died from lack of food and water or the wounds she'd inflicted on it.

The perfect containment facility, she thought, *no access, sub-zero temperatures*.

She felt the pull of sleep and succumbed to it.

'Can I get you a cup of tea dear?' a kindly voice asked in the middle of a dream.

Half-asleep Melanie stifled a yawn and opened her eyes to find an old lady in a white nurse's uniform looming over her.

'Yes, thank you, that would be lovely,' she said, pushing herself up in bed.

The woman smiled and waddled over to her trolley, pulling the curtain aside as she went.

On the opposite side of the ward was another patient, a young Indian woman who was smiling at Melanie. 'Hi, I'm Caspara, ' the woman said, holding up one heavily bandaged hand. 'Managed to get bitten by a monad.'

'Melanie,' she replied, 'I'm just waiting for my friend, he's in ICU.'

Caspara nodded. 'Heard about him. He's Frederick Ross right?'

'Yes, you know him?'

She shook her head. 'No, but every Draconian knows about his dad, Wolfbeard was a hero.'

'Wolfbeard?'

A smile broke across her face. 'He didn't tell you? Randolph Ross was supposed to have had this great mane of hair; snowy grey like a timber wolf. They say he used to tie bones of the creatures he'd slain in his beard, but I think that's just a myth. He saved a lot of Draconians that day, including my father. I wouldn't be here if it wasn't for him.'

She made a sign with the fingers of her good hand, as if she were warding off evil spirits.

'Fred doesn't really speak about it,' replied Melanie, trying to hide the fact she knew little to nothing about his life.

The woman scoffed. 'I'm not surprised. I've heard he's tried three times to follow his father into the guild, but failed every time. His brothers are all senior Dreadnoughts, it's a wonder they haven't disowned him.'

Melanie felt the anger rising. 'It's not his fault. He's one of the bravest men I've ever met.'

Caspara waved her good hand. 'I don't doubt that for a second. He's a Ross after all, but to not be accepted into the Draconian Guild brings shame on his family, and to end up in the Outliers makes it all the more embarrassing.'

Her cheeks were growing warm. 'What's so bad about the Outliers anyway?'

The old nurse returned with a cup of tea and a large biscuit tin.

'You two getting to know each other?' she asked, putting the tea down and offering Melanie the biscuits. 'I'm afraid all the bourbons have gone, Sister Marjorie is rather fond of them.'

Melanie took a couple at random and waited for the nurse to leave, but instead the old woman took one for herself and sat down on the side of the bed.

'I couldn't help overhearing your conversation dear. To be

perfectly honest, and I hope you don't mind if I join in, but the Outliers have not had the best of reputations. They tend to, how can I put this politely —'

'Cock things up,' suggested Caspara.

The old nurse grimaced. 'I would have used a different word, but all the same, they do tend to leap to conclusions — ones that others would never treat seriously.'

Caspara laughed. 'Like Atlantis. Who's ever heard of a time travelling island!'

The nurse giggled too. 'Yes, my Arthur still goes on about that one.'

Melanie bit into her biscuit to stop herself from saying something, it was a ginger nut, possibly her least favourite, but she chewed on it all the same.

'And what about the time they thought the earth was hollow.'

Both of them were laughing hard now.

Melanie couldn't contain it any longer. 'You know his fighting for his life in there? He nearly died trying to save Shackleton's crew!'

They both stopped. Caspara pulled a face and there was a twinkle in the nurse's eyes.

'Well now dear, we didn't mean any harm. I didn't realise you were sweet on him.'

Neither did I, thought Melanie.

42

MONSTER

Boleskine House, Loch Ness, Scotland. 1914

Lyra shook her head, trying to clear the soporific effects of the sedative. Her thoughts were confused, and muddled. It took a moment for her to realise what he was asking.

'You want to intuit with that?' she repeated, pointing at the swimming creature.

Crowley closed his eyes, pressing his hand against the thick glass pane. 'The Emperor's alchemists believed that this creature held the key to immortality, but it was protected by the curse. He died trying to solve the puzzle — I wish to know its secrets.'

Lyra caught her reflection in the tall green windows, she looked like a child standing next to the old, bloated figure of Crowley. Her instincts were telling her to leave, that she needed to report back to Kelly on what the mad man was up to, but she ignored them. This was her only chance to learn how he freed himself of the burden of sight.

The creature wove amongst the swaying fronds of weeds, its scales glinting in the weak rays of sunlight that filtered down from the surface. It moved with ease through the cool waters, long and sleek, like a giant snake.

'Nobody can live forever,' she said, beginning to shake off the malaise. 'It's just a myth.'

Crowley sighed and took his hand away from the glass.

'My studies of the ancient texts have taught me there is more to this life than can be explained by the so-called "scientific method". You of all people know that the laws of the universe are not defined by a series of equations.'

Lyra shook her head. 'Time is a harsh mistress.'

He pointed to the creature. 'But still one that can be mastered.'

Doctor Lind reappeared pulling a large spherical diving bell. It was suspended on chains connected to rails in the ceiling which ran towards a circular door in the glass wall.

'We are ready master,' he said, bowing low.

Lyra stared wide-eyed at the brass contraption and shook her head. 'I'm not getting in that!'

Crowley shrugged. 'It's perfectly safe. The air pressure will hold the water at bay.'

She shook her head. 'You're mad. The creature will eat us.'

Lind opened a door in the side of the spherical capsule and motioned for her to get inside.

'Once you have completed this task, you will be free to go,' said Crowley, ducking his head as he stepped inside. 'I have instructed Lind to release you should I fail to return.'

She closed her eyes, sensing the timelines flowing around her. 'He's going to kill me,' she said, 'I can see it.'

Crowley stepped back out of the capsule and handed her a pistol. 'If he makes any such move against you, you have my permission to shoot him dead. Now can we proceed?'

The weapon was heavy in her hands. Its chronology littered with so much murder and death she nearly dropped it.

'I want something else,' she said, holding the gun made her feel a little braver.

Crowley paused halfway into the craft. 'What now?'

'I want to know how you lost your abilities.'

His eyes widened a little. 'Ah, that is quite a long story. Shall we discuss it inside,' he said, waving to the velvet lined interior.

Lyra agreed and stepped inside the bell.

43

MAP ROOM

Xenobiology Laboratory. Present Day.

Sim was standing at the end of the hospital bed when Melanie came to visit Fred later that day. She'd managed to sleep for a few hours, but her dreams were full of terrible monsters and she woke in a cold sweat, wishing she hadn't bothered.

'What happened to him,' asked Sim while she checked the monitors. His pulse was low and his sats were down.

'He was attacked by something in Antarctica.'

Picking up his report, Melanie studied the results of the blood tests, there was something worryingly familiar about the cell counts.

'Have you told his family?'

'They've been informed,' said Doctor Shika walking into the room, closely followed by her sabre-tooth cat.

Melanie looked up from the notes and pointed at them. 'Have you seen his white blood cell count? It's way too high.'

The doctor nodded. 'As you suspected, there were traces of a toxin on the barbs. We're still analysing it.'

Melanie put down the clipboard. 'I know what it is,' she added solemnly and pulled back the sheet that was covering his upper body. The skin of his forearms and upper chest were already covered in the fractal patterning, just as she'd seen on the other victims.

'I've seen this before. It's the same virus that wiped out the BAS team. We need to get him into quarantine immediately.'

Doctor Shika's expression darkened and she punched a button on the wall. A curved glass screen slid silently around Fred's bed, encasing him in a transparent coffin. The door behind them sealed shut with a hiss and a red light began to flash above it. Outside, Melanie could see members of Shika's team putting on respirators and masks.

'Are we in danger?' asked Sim, stepping back from the bed.

'Potentially,' replied Melanie. 'I have a test that should be able to prove if we're infected. Assuming you have molecular diagnostics here?' she said turning to the doctor.

Shika nodded, taking hazmat suits from a locker and handing them each one. 'Put these on and follow me.'

Melanie was surprised when the doctor didn't bother to wear one herself. Then, as they left the room, she thought she could see the shimmering outline of a creature surrounding her, as if the doctor was wearing some kind of force field.

An hour later, the results of the tests were negative, much to Sim's relief.

'I was instructed to bring Fred to the Map Room,' he said. 'The Professor wishes to meet him. Will you come instead?'

Melanie looked up from the microscope. 'I don't have time. I have a ton of work to do here.'

'I can do that,' said Shika. 'You're running a standard set of cultures, looking at CPE, correct?'

Melanie was impressed. 'Yes, with a monoclonal stain.'

'Listen, if Professor Eddington has requested more information, that means he's taking the threat seriously,' said the doctor, 'and we could certainly use the Copernicans's help to find the source. Once we identify it, we can neutralise the threat before it even becomes a problem.'

Melanie laughed. 'Now there's a radical new approach to pandemics. Simply go back in time and find patient zero.'

'This isn't the first time we've had to deal with this kind of scenario,' added Sim.

It took Sim a few minutes to locate a chaperone who could escort Melanie back to the Copernican headquarters. The man who appeared out of thin air was dressed in a long black cloak, under which she could see leather armour and a variety of unusual weapons. His face was obscured by a helmet covered in dark lenses.

'Protectorate,' whispered Doctor Shika in Melanie's ear as she pretended to hug her goodbye. 'Be careful what you say in front of him.'

Sim spoke to the man who simply nodded, took off one of his gauntlets and offered his hand to Melanie.

'It's okay,' Sim tried to assure her, 'he's not going to hurt you.'

The transition from the Xenobiology Lab to the Copernican Hall took less than a heartbeat.

She felt the lurch in her stomach again, but this time it felt stronger.

'How far was that?' Melanie asked, watching the Protectorate officer reset something on his gauntlet and disappear.

Sim shrugged and checked his watch. 'Four hundred and forty-two years, fifty days and four hours.'

It was further than Fred had ever taken her in one go. 'Doesn't it make you feel sick?' she asked.

He shook his head. 'Temporal kinetosis. You get used to it after a while, your brain learns to compensate for the dilation.'

. . .

The Map Room was high in the upper echelons of the great clockwork building. Melanie was still feeling a little queasy when she stepped out of the elevator and followed Sim along the metal gantry.

'Where exactly are we?' she asked, looking up at the stained glass roof and trying to think of a structure large enough that existed in the sixteenth century that could house this. *A Cathedral perhaps?* she wondered.

Sim waggled his finger. 'Now that is something of a closely guarded secret. We never discuss the whereabouts of Copernicus Hall.'

Looking over the edge of the brass-railed walkway, Melanie felt her knees weaken. Sim caught her by the arm. 'Probably wise to stay away from the edge until you've got your sea legs,' he said, guiding her into a tunnel of rotating gear wheels.

The room was a vast circular space, it reminded Melanie of a planetarium. The planets of the solar system slowly rotated above her head on jointed metal arms.

In the centre of the system was a shining globe, and standing inside it was a thin, dark-haired man in a long black robe.

'Master Simeon, is this the colleague you spoke of?' The man, who Melanie assumed was Professor Eddington, had a sharp, reedy tone, like a housemaster from a prep school.

Sim bowed to his master. 'No sir, he's been infected, but this is his assistant.' He glanced at her as if to quash any protest she might have about being called Fred's sidekick.

'Infected?' The man rolled the word around in his mouth, his long fingers stroking the control levers that sprouted from the console around him. 'Was this foretold in your calculations?'

'There was a sixty-four percent possibility, but the general outcome remains the same once the Americans intervene. Doctor Braithwaite can attest to the severity of the threat — she's a virologist.'

'And a linear?'

Sim lowered his eyes to the floor. 'She's studied the virus first hand.'

'An infected linear?' the pitch in Eddington's voice rose by several degrees.

'I'm not infected,' said Melanie calmly. 'I study viruses. I know what precautions to take.'

Eddington moved a lever and a console beneath him flickered to life. Symbols and glyphs scrolled over his face as he studied the screen.

'You received a first class honours medical degree from Imperial College, followed by a PhD in microbiology. Then a research position to study adenovirus cloning under Professor MacAllister, for which he was awarded the Lasker Award. You appear to have joined the British Antarctic Survey shortly afterwards.'

Stepping down from the glowing sphere, he gave a small bow. 'Pleased to meet you Doctor Braithwaite. I take it you have already applied some statistical modelling to this epidemic?'

Melanie cleared her throat. 'I have, the virus has an R number that is close to two point two, which would make it one of the most virulent strains the human race has ever encountered.'

The professor nodded solemnly. 'Master Simeon has already shared his calculations with me. He expects the death toll to exceed forty-two million — with a ninety-nine point three per cent certainty.'

The estimate was very close to her own results, which was impressive considering their computing power seemed to be based on steam-driven analytical engines.

'Our first task is to identify the source,' said Sim. 'It's our best chance of stopping the spread.'

'There was a monster,' Melanie said, trying to ignore the fact that it sounded crazy. 'The *Endurance* took it to Antarctica and buried it in a cave. I thought it killed everyone, but I guess some of the men must have made it back to the ship.'

'No one returned from the *Endurance*,' Sim added gravely. 'Shackleton's entire crew vanished, the authorities assumed they were lost under the ice.'

Eddington's eyebrows arched. 'What kind of monster?'

'A dinosaur, or something very much like one.'

He scoffed. 'In 1914? Highly unlikely.'

'Fred believed it was transported there from London. He talked about some government department for Psychical Research.'

The professor returned to his console and moved a series of levers. The other planets in the solar system disappeared into the domed ceiling, leaving just the earth, which seemed to grow in size until the southern hemisphere took up most of the space.

'Can you show me exactly where and when the *Endurance* offloaded its cargo?'

44

LOCH NESS

Loch Ness, Scotland. 1914

The diving bell reminded Lyra of something from Jules Verne's *Twenty Thousand Leagues Under the Sea*. Decorated in plush red velvet and panelled in wood and brass, it was a beautiful piece of machinery. In any other situation she would have enjoyed taking a ride inside it, but sitting in an enclosed space opposite the sweating Crowley while they were slowly transported into the freezing green waters of the loch was not her idea of fun.

Below her feet, the floor of the chamber had a large circular hole where the water rippled like a moonlit pool. Lyra assumed the bell had exterior lights illuminating the hatch.

She heard the clunk of the lifting gear releasing them. Suddenly the compartment lurched, throwing her against the bulkhead and knocking the gun from her grip and into the water.

'You said you would tell me how you lost your abilities,' she reminded him, rubbing her arm and watching the weapon sink into the depths.

'All in good time,' he muttered, fiddling with the controls of the bell. 'First I need to ensure we don't drown.'

Lyra looked out through one of the small portholes into the murky green waters. A silence descended on the bell, only punctuated by Crowley's laboured breathing. Taking advantage of the brief moment of calm, she reached out with her mind, searching for the creature.

It was nearby, she could sense its timeline flowing around them, see it circling their little brass bubble.

'It's close,' she whispered.

'Indeed,' said Crowley, mopping his forehead with a handkerchief.

The air was growing warm.

'We don't have long,' she added. 'You promised to tell me how you lost your sight.'

Sighing deeply, he ran his hand over his bald head.

'I've always been fascinated by the idea of immortality. After leaving the Order, I spent many years searching for answers. I consulted with the world's wisest men, venerable sages who dedicated their lives to the pursuit of universal truth. I studied ancient texts in forgotten languages that even the Scriptorians had yet to discover. But the answers eluded me. I was beginning to believe, like you, that it was nothing but a myth. Until, on one occasion in the city of Peking, I was told of a man who was rumoured to be a thousand years old. His name was Song Wuji, he was a Fangshi, a geomancer and thaumaturge — a wizard.'

'A wizard?'

Crowley nodded. 'He was timeless. You of all people should understand what I mean when I say that. He was no longer bound by temporal laws, he left no trace on the continuum.'

There were tears in Crowley's eyes as he spoke.

'He told me of how he served under the First Emperor as Alchemist Royal. How he had been the only member of the court to survive a terrible plague. At the touch of his hand, it was as if the scales fell away. For the first time I could truly understand what it was to be at one with the universe. He told me of the egg and how it blessed him with eternal life. When the meeting was over, I was a mortal man — I will be forever in his debt.'

'He took your sight?'

'He opened my eyes.'

'How?'

Crowley shook his head. 'I cannot explain, but the Fangshi had powers that no linear should possess.'

Lyra wondered for a moment if this wizard could be another manifestation of Abandon.

'Did he give you the egg?'

He shook his head. 'No, but he told me where it was hidden.'

She sensed the timeline of the creature as it approached once more. 'In the tomb.'

He looked genuinely surprised. 'You are a powerful seer indeed. Yes, in the mausoleum of Qin Shi Huang, a veritable mountain of a tomb.'

'And now you wish to meld minds with this creature?'

Crowley ran his tongue along his top lip. 'Once I have its knowledge, then I can release you from your burden.'

Lyra wasn't convinced, whatever had taken Crowley's powers would require more than a little ancient wisdom. She closed her eyes and reached out to the entity with her mind, feeling the creature's timeline stretching back into the distant past.

'How did it survive all of that time?'

He tapped on the brass wall of the diving bell, making a metallic ring. 'The shell was made from some unusual materials. I think the mother must have been born in the Maelstrom, it had a temporal stasis field that Lind was able to break.'

'Her name is Shenlong,' Lyra added, touching the creature's mind.

'Spirit Dragon? Very fitting.'

Shenlong's head broke the surface of the moon pool. Her scales shimmering like opalescent jewels in the light. She was a beautiful creature: part dragon, and part demon, with long tentacle-like feelers reaching out from her face like whiskers. Her large eyes burned with a blue fire as she scanned the chamber, turning until she faced Lyra.

Hello my troubled one, her voice rang in Lyra's head. *You are an interesting child.*

Lyra blinked, trying not to react, but Crowley smiled knowingly. 'She speaks to you?'

Shenlong's snout was less than an inch from Lyra's face, she could feel her warm breath on her skin.

Lyra nodded.

'Perfect,' he said, clapping his hands together. 'Now we can begin.'

Whilst the creature was distracted, he attached two electrodes to her long ears. She hardly seemed to notice.

You seek someone, the dragon continued, its head tilting slightly. *A traveller from another realm?*

Lyra nodded, inadvertently sharing the memory of her meeting with Abandon.

Ah, yes, Shenlong thought, turning the moment over in Lyra's mind. *We have encountered the wanderer.*

How? Thought Lyra, *you've been asleep for so long.*

We remember our other lives.

Shenlong shared her memories; thousands of moments stretching back into the deep past, and Lyra realised these were genetic recollections, passed down from her mother and grand-mother, stretching back to the birth of the universe. These were crea-tures who had witnessed the beginning, who had watched the sun rise on the first day. Beings from the Maelstrom who had chosen to remain in the Continuum.

On the other side of the diving bell, Crowley was attaching the ends of the wires to a metal helmet which he proceeded to strap to his head.

'If you would be so kind,' he said, waving at a similar device hanging on the wall behind her.

Do you know where he is? asked Lyra, taking the headgear off the wall.

The dragon rose slightly out of the water. *I have seen what is to come daughter of time, it is not where but when.*

Lyra hesitated before placing the helmet on her head, unsure of what would happen next. To allow Crowley into the mind of such a wealth of knowledge was a dangerous thing, but without him, she may never be able to free herself of Abandon's gift.

'Now!' he commanded.

Suddenly, she felt the electricity course though her skull as Crowley closed the circuit breaker, severing the psychic connection between her and the creature.

'Bring us together,' he demanded.

The light in the dragon's eyes dimmed as Lyra stared into them.

She reached out with her mind.

Shenlong was like a bright shining sun compared to the meagre candle-flicker of Crowley. She felt the guilt overwhelm her as she insinuated his consciousness with the dragon's. The intuit was seldom performed on two living beings, meant as a way to impart knowledge from the preserved brain of a departed elder to a novice. Lyra wove them together, until there were no longer two lines but only one.

When she looked up from the dragon, Crowley's body was limp. His face pale, slack-jawed, his mouth hanging open like a gibbering fool.

What have you done? came the voice in her head once more, but this was no longer the gentle tones of Shenlong, but the insane ravings of Crowley.

The dragon's head shook, shedding itself of the cables he'd attached.

The force of its departure shook the bell, spinning end over end into the deep waters of the loch.

Lyra braced herself as the water poured in through the opening.

45

THE HUNT

Northern China. Cretaceous.

The jungle was thick and hard going. The air was filled with clouds of insects. It became so bad that they had to tie cloths over their faces, making it hard to breathe.

After three hours, Josh was finding it increasingly difficult to keep up with Benoir and especially Rufius, who was moving swiftly between the giant tree roots like a man half his age. *So much for him retiring,* he thought, ducking under another low hanging branch covered in vicious-looking thorns.

Everything seemed to be going out of its way to trip or hamper his progress, and Caitlin had already stopped him falling on his backside more times than he cared to admit.

'Do you want to take a break?' she asked, as he stumbled again.

'No! I'm fine,' he insisted, getting back to his feet.

She retrieved his bow from a nearby bush and handed it to him. 'Try not to look down, you're focusing too much on the ground.'

Josh laughed, pulling down his mask. 'If I don't, I'll definitely fall over.'

Caitlin took her own mask down and kissed him. She knelt down to untie the leather thongs on his sandals. 'You're trying too hard. Take your shoes off.'

'Why?'

'It's easier to feel the floor.'

'And all the creepy crawlies,' he said, pulling his foot out of her hands. In any other time it wouldn't have bothered him, but the bugs here looked as if they could take a toe off.

'They're mostly harmless.'

'Hah, that's like saying they're slightly deadly. Did you see the size of that wasp this morning?'

She sighed and stood up. 'It was a hymenoptera and that only proves what I'm saying, you're more likely to trip over one than tread on it.'

He grunted and took off his other sandal, wriggling his toes in the leaf litter that carpeted the jungle floor. 'You forget I'm from South London, the only time we went bare foot was when we forgot our plimsolls in PE. The ground feels weird — like it's alive.'

Benoir's head suddenly appeared out of a thicket of giant ferns. 'You guys okay?'

'Yes,' confirmed Caitlin. 'Just taking a breather.'

'We've found something up ahead — could be a roost.'

'Great,' said Josh, slightly sarcastically, hanging the sandals around his neck and pulling his mask back up.

Caitlin watched him go, his feet planting themselves perfectly between the hazardous roots, knowing that he would never admit she was right.

Rufius crept carefully through the thicket, motioning to them to do the same. For such a big man, he moved without a sound between the trees.

The roost was nothing more than a clearing; trees and long grasses crushed flat by the beast to create a crude landing pad in the middle of the forest.

Drawing closer, Josh noticed the bleached bones of long-dead creatures scattered around the edge of the nest. Horned skulls the size of an armchair lay discarded beside the white cages of ribs that he could have easily stood inside.

'It's been here recently,' said Benoir, taking his hand out of a large pile of dung and wiping it on a broad leaf of a fern. 'Less than six hours ago.'

Rufius nodded and scanned the surrounding bush for a suitable hiding place. 'There,' he said, pointing towards a dense screen of foliage. 'Downwind.'

'Have you ever killed a dinosaur before?' Caitlin asked Benoir as they settled behind a screen of giant ferns.

'Only out of mercy,' he replied, 'when there is nothing else that can be done.'

'Law of the jungle out here,' said Rufius, slapping his cheek and inspecting the bug that lay flattened in his hand. 'If it doesn't come soon we'll be eaten alive.'

'Try this,' said Caitlin, handing him a cake of foul-smelling soap wrapped in cloth.

Rufius's nose wrinkled as he sniffed at it. 'Another of Crooke's creations I assume?'

She laughed. 'No, mine actually, I got it from a book on natural remedies.'

He rubbed the soap between his hands and then worked the oils into his face and beard. 'I've never understood why every "natural" medicine has to smell like it's been dug out of the bottom of a bog.'

'Probably because we all used to smell like that,' said Caitlin.

'Speak for yourself,' he replied, handing her back the bar. 'I had a bath last Wednesday.'

Rufius went to cut down some saplings to make into spears and Benoir fell asleep against a tree.

Josh opened up his pack and handed her a small lump of bread and some cheese.

'So, did you spend a lot of time back here?' he asked, taking a bite out of a misshapen apple.

Caitlin nodded. 'It seemed like most of my childhood, but I guess it was just me remembering the good times. There were so many amazing adventures, it made going to school seem very boring, I think I just blotted it out.'

'Slightly different from mine,' he said with a sigh. 'I used to dream of dinosaurs. I didn't actually see one until we went to the Natural History Museum on a school trip, by then I was more into girls than piles of old bones.'

She frowned at him. 'You went to the museum? How old were you?'

'Thirteen. Why? Is it so hard to believe?'

Caitlin shook her head. 'No, it's not that, but you should have been noticed. The museums and libraries keep a watch for anyone with latent talents, and yours are pretty hard to miss.'

Josh took her hand. 'I'm glad they didn't. I like the way I got found.'

She blushed a little. 'Well, that wasn't just down to me. He had a lot to do with it.' She nodded towards Rufius.

'I know, but you're the reason I stayed.'

She kissed him gently. 'You're the reason we're all still here.'

Josh shrugged and took another bite from his apple. 'You would have done the same.'

Caitlin shook her head. 'I don't think so. I don't have your talents, no one does.'

He paused, his eyes growing distant, as though trying to remember something.

'Do you ever wonder what Zack will be? Sometimes I dream that I've seen him as a man.'

She laughed. 'With us for parents? Either a wild, unstoppable, inquisitive trouble-maker or an introverted bookworm.'

Josh put his arm around her and pulled her in for a kiss. 'Is that how you see me? A trouble-maker?'

Caitlin smiled. 'Who said I was talking about you?'

The sound of wings beating above the canopy snapped them out of their embrace and sent them scrabbling for their weapons.

Rufius appeared from the woods carrying a bushel of sharpened sticks, his hair threaded with leaves and twigs.

Benoir woke and rose to his feet.

Quietly they moved to the edge of the clearing.

The creature was enormous. Its long, serpent-like body covered in the most beautiful, shimmering scales that reflected every colour of the rainbow. Leathery wings beat slowly as it came into land, whipping the trees into a frenzy, creating a miniature cyclone of leaves and branches.

Between its claws squirmed a young mastodon, which must have weighed at least a tonne.

They all stood, transfixed by the sight of the creature, the nearest thing Josh had ever seen to a real dragon.

Its head was the size of a small car, with the long snout of a dragon and vicious horns that swept back away from its skull ending in sharp blood-stained points. Trailing from its jaws were tentacle-like feelers that probed its prey, wrapping themselves around its throat to strangle the sounds of struggle.

It settled down into the flattened grass and began to devour its prey. Rufius hefted an obsidian spear and motioned to the others to spread out. Josh notched an arrow and kept low, creeping through the bushes until he had a clear shot at the creature.

46

RESCUE

Loch Ness, Scotland. 1914

Floating inside the dark diving bell as it sank, Lyra could feel the cold water leeching the heat from her body. Her legs and arms were growing numb, soon she wouldn't have the strength to swim to the surface.

Outside, she could sense the chaotic mind of Shenlong thrashing around trying to rid herself of the unwelcome guest. The intuit had gone so badly wrong, somehow Crowley's mind had become meshed with the creature, and now his physical body was somewhere at the bottom of the loch.

The air pocket was growing smaller with every second. Her face pressed to the brass wall, Lyra closed her eyes and calmed her breathing. What little oxygen she had left would have to last a little longer if the people in the boat were going to reach her.

There were three men approaching on a motorised ketch. In her mind, Lyra could see their glowing figures on the surface, as though looking up through the wrong side of a mirror.

At first, she'd assumed they were fishermen, but their timelines told a different story; they were government men, from a mysterious department known as "Psychical Research". They travelled all the way from London because someone had reported seeing a strange serpent-like creature in the loch.

One of them was dressed in a deep-sea diver's suit. His ball-shaped head and lumpy boots made Lyra wonder if he had ever worn them before as he waddled around in the boat, nearly capsizing the small craft.

She felt the water touch her chin and clamped her lips together.

A minute later he launched himself into the water and sank like a stone.

His timeline unspooled like a roll of film. His name was James Murray, and he was once a Lieutenant in the British Navy, stationed in China during the Boxer rebellion.

And he'd died, more than once.

There was an unusual darkness to his aura, one that Lyra had only observed in a few. Those who returned from beyond the veil carried a taint. She hesitated, her mind pulling back from going deeper into his time-line.

The water touched the tip of her nose and she tilted her head into the last inch of air.

As Lieutenant Murray shuffled slowly across the lake bed towards her, Lyra wondered if she mightn't have had a better chance with the dragon who was at the other end of the loch.

The sound of a hook being attached to the top of the bell shook her out of her reverie, and seconds later the metal chamber shuddered and began to rise upwards.

Nearing the surface, Lyra took one last breath and swam out of the hatch into the fresh air of the morning.

The ruddy, smiling face of Michael Davey greeted her over the gunwale, his thick hand extended to help her out of the water.

'There we go,' he said, effortlessly lifting her up and onto the deck. He was a big man, over six-feet tall with broad shoulders beneath a rather tight fitting jacket.

Lyra felt a strange sensation at his touch, but restrained from reading his timeline, letting go of his hand.

'You'll catch your death,' he said in a Geordie accent, wrapping a blanket around her shoulders.

The other man, who she knew was called Tyler Cobham was helping Lieutenant Murray remove the brass diving helmet.

'Davey, give her a drop of brandy. She'll be in shock before you know it!' snapped Murray.

The big man nodded, taking out his hip flask. 'Here girl, have a nip of this.'

Lyra took a drink, it wasn't the finest brandy she'd ever tasted, but it washed away the brackish taste of the loch water and warmed her chest a little.

'Thank you,' she said, handing it back.

'Now to more important matters,' said Murray, pulling off his gloves. 'What can you tell us of the beast?' He pointed out across the water, where its sinuous curves could be seen arcing like a giant snake.

'Her name is Shenlong, and she's the last of her kind.'

Murray failed to hide his surprise. 'And how in all things that are holy do you know that?'

Lyra thought it was probably wiser not to mention Crowley, explaining his involvement would only lead to questions she'd rather not answer.

'There's a doctor, his name is Lind.' She nodded towards the old Manor House on the shores of the lake. 'He resurrected it.'

'Sir! She's turned!' exclaimed Davey, pointing at the dark sinuous shape which was now heading towards their boat. He scrambled to one of the lockers on the deck and took out a large net.

Cobham ran to the wheelhouse and reappeared with a long rifle.

'Wait!' screamed Lyra, stepping in front of him. 'You can't kill it!'

The man ignored her, cocking the weapon and raising it to his shoulder.

Lyra turned towards Davey hoping he would help her, but he was busy untangling the net.

Leaning against the gunwale, she closed her eyes and stretched her hand out towards the approaching creature. Its mind was still in turmoil as it wrestled for control of its body with Crowley's consciousness.

You must leave this place, she broadcast to it, hoping that some part of its conflicted mind would take notice. *They will kill you.*

She opened her eyes when she heard the men draw in a sharp breath. The head of the serpent broke the surface and the force of the approaching bow wave rocked the boat.

The serpent rose still further, lifting itself out of the water. Lyra felt a sudden gust of wind against her face and Shenlong's silvered body glided effortlessly over the masts of the boat. The force of her beating wings threw Davey and Murray to the deck.

Cobham braced himself and took careful aim, firing into her underbelly.

Lyra screamed.

47

PRESIDENT

Washington DC. Present day.

Sitting on the balcony of his hotel sipping his third cup of coffee, Colonel Cooper skimmed through the presentation on his laptop.

His overactive brain devoured caffeine like a junkie mainlining heroin. The tremors in his hands gradually mellowing as the dark-roasted robusta flowed into his veins. His men used to joke that if you cut him, his blood would be espresso.

Numerous bottles of pills sat on the table beside his untouched breakfast. Cooper hated taking them; the painkillers made it hard to think, clouding his judgement, and the PCV chemo combination made him physically sick.

The doctor warned him that without them the tumour could cause a seizure or a stroke. The thought of spending the rest of his limited time on the earth as a dribbling vegetable was the only thing that made him take them.

. . .

The numbers in his presentation read like something from a war game simulation. Predicted death-tolls in the millions was a staggering amount of people — a difficult scenario to visualise for any normal citizen, let alone the idiot that was currently occupying the White House.

Cooper was to attend a presidential briefing that morning. The development of the vaccine needed a significant amount of additional funding and going through a senate oversight committee was going to take way too long. He had to find a way to put it in terms that the President would be able to comprehend. Historians estimated that between forty and fifty-million people died in World War Two, a number that was no match for the hundred million who died during the Bubonic Plague in the fourteenth century, but something more contemporary for the man with the power to sign-off on emergency funding.

The figures were conservative, Cooper knew it could be a whole lot worse if the vaccine wasn't effective or distribution was limited.

The depopulation of the country was a real possibility.

He made some changes to the last slide. The President had a limited concentration span and the rule of three was the best strategy when it came to a man with more Twitter followers than brain cells.

'Mr President, this is a matter of national security,' Cooper insisted, wondering how many times that line had been used in the Oval Office.

The white-haired man sitting behind the Resolute Desk stared at him with his usual smug grin creasing his over-tanned face.

'Thank you for the briefing, Colonel Cooper,' the President replied in his strong Texan drawl, 'but as far as I can see you've already dealt with the threat. What possible reason would I have for throwing millions of taxpayer's dollars into researching a vaccine when the only real danger is contained?'

Cooper bit his tongue, holding back the urge to berate one of the most powerful men in the northern hemisphere. *How the hell did it come to this?*

He pointed at the numbers on the screen. 'Because, sir, our models suggest that if this strain were to get out into the general population it would be devastating. Millions would die.'

The President grinned, turning to one of his aides. 'Could we localise it to the Western States? I hear I'm not scoring well in Nevada these days.'

'It could wipe out Nevada, Oregon, Utah in under a week,' Cooper said under his breath.

'What does Wilks say?'

Professor Wilks was the Director of the Center for Disease Control, someone that Cooper had come to despise for his complete lack of action over Ebola and Zika viruses.

'We haven't shared this with the CDC. We've been operating on a strict need-to-know basis.'

The President's face lost its smugness. 'So you've got a potential pandemic, safely stored in some vault in Fort Detrick along with countless other deadly viruses. Which already has one of the largest budgets of any defence project and now you're asking for an additional fifty-million dollars to ensure we're prepared in case it gets out?'

Cooper took some of the photographs of the *Endurance* from his briefcase and placed them on the desk. 'This virus has lain dormant for centuries, like a sleeping monster. What I witnessed in Antarctica was like nothing I've ever seen, and I've seen a lot of bad shit done to good people. This is your one chance to do the right thing. Do you want to be remembered as the President who could have saved the world but didn't?'

For a moment, Cooper saw a flicker of realisation in the President's eyes. It was the one area that the man understood very well, the headlines in tomorrow's media were the only thing he cared about.

His aide's phone buzzed. 'Your next meeting is here Mr President,' he said, scrolling down the long list of messages.

In a second the moment was gone.

'I'll think about it,' was all he would say, dismissing Cooper with a wave of his hand.

Walking out of the White House, Cooper took out his sat phone and dialled an encrypted number.

'This is Cooper. Initiate Project Contagion on my authority. Kilo-Zulu-Six-Sixty-Alpha-Five.'

The order was repeated back to him.

'Confirm. Deploy.'

At Fort Detrick, Lieutenant Miller signalled to two of his men to follow him towards Hangar Seven. They fell in behind him without question.

48

THE FLYING SCOTSMAN

Flying Scotsman, United Kingdom. 1914

Woken from a dreamless sleep by the sound of a locomotive's whistle, Lyra realised she was in the sleeper compartment of a train carriage. The warm bed and the gentle rhythm of steel wheels on the rails were lulling her back towards sleep.

Shaking off the torpor, she drew back the curtains, blinking at the early morning light. The train was slipping through a beautiful, pastoral countryside at speed. *East Coast Main Line*, she thought, *The Flying Scotsman*. This was the golden age, when sleek, powerful steam engines could transport you from Edinburgh to London in less than eight hours.

In the past, she'd always felt at peace on trains, for some unknown reason the motion calmed her mind, stopping the constant interference from other people's lives. But that was before Abandon's gift, now she could sense every passenger, including the three men from the boat in the next compartment.

Pinching herself to check that it wasn't all a dream, she wondered if Crowley's drugs might have caused her to hallucinate the whole thing. *Unlikely,* she told herself, the events of the last twenty-four hours were far too surreal to imagine, even for a seer.

The wooden doors slid apart and Davey's pudgy face appeared, confirming yesterday was definitely not a figment of her imagination.

'Morning,' he said with an inane grin. 'Feeling better?'

'Do you ever knock?' she said, pulling the bedsheets up to her shoulders, before wondering who exactly had undressed her the night before.

'She's awake,' he shouted, disappearing back into the corridor.

Lyra found her clothes dried and neatly folded on the seat opposite. Dressing quickly, she considered her options.

The last thing she could remember was Cobham shooting at Shenlong's silvered underbelly as she passed over her head. The force of her wings nearly overturned the boat and Lyra was thrown across the deck, where she must have hit her head, because there was a lump on the back of her skull the size of an orange.

Her plan to investigate Crowley hadn't gone as planned. The man was now lying drowned at the bottom of Loch Ness, his mind trapped in the resurrected body of a Chinese spirit dragon. That was not going to be the easiest thing to explain, and she could picture the displeasure on the Grand Seer's face when she told him.

She wouldn't be surprised to hear that the Protectorate were already investigating it.

Except Crowley wasn't entirely dead.

And he was an exile after all. A rogue who had been thrown out of the Order for abusing his powers.

Even if they didn't arrest her for that, she was still no closer to relieving herself of Abandon's gift. With Crowley gone and the creature missing, her only chance now was to find the wizard, Song Wuji and hope he held the answers.

Now might be the right time to make a quick exit, she thought, examining the small mirror screwed to the wall as she tied her hair back into a pony tail.

Davey reappeared with a breakfast tray and another beaming smile.

'Sorry about before,' he stuttered, trying to place the tray on the side table without looking at her.

She grabbed the teacup before he spilt it.

'It's fine,' she said. 'You just surprised me.'

He stepped back, stuffing his hands into his pockets and keeping his eyes to the floor.

'We'll be in London within the hour. Lieutenant Murray requests that you be ready to leave when we arrive.'

Lyra feigned a look of shock. 'Does he now? Am I your prisoner?'

Davey blushed. 'Well, I wouldn't put it quite like that.'

'Who are you?' Lyra demanded, careful not to admit that she already knew, but it was the appropriate question that any normal person would ask.

'The Department of Psychical Research,' he said proudly, his chest swelling. 'We investigate the strange and unnatural.'

Lyra pretended to be impressed. 'And you think that includes me?'

'Well, not exactly, but the Loch Ness monster.'

'Shenlong,' she corrected him, putting down her teacup and picking up a piece of toast to slather with strawberry jam. She hadn't eaten anything since leaving Benoir in the Cretaceous.

'There were reports you see. Of a serpent in the loch, and that is what we do, follow up on unusual sightings.'

'And kill them?'

'We don't kill things, we capture and study them.'

Like the Xeno's, thought Lyra, intrigued to know why she had never heard of this department before. Whoever they were, they weren't from the Order, but there was something unusual about them and Davey's timeline also showed signs of unnatural activity.

'I saw you try and shoot her!'

Davey chuckled and went over to look out of the window. 'That was a tracker. We're following her flight path right now. She's heading directly for London.'

Realising that Lyra may have misjudged them, assuming that they were simple hunters, she gave up on the pretence of anger.

'And where exactly do you keep these strange creatures?'

Davey looked a little coy, wringing his hands as if the where-abouts were supposed to be a secret.

'You might as well tell me, as I assume that's where you're taking me,' she added, taking a bite of the last piece of toast.

He sighed. 'Beneath the Tower of London.'

'Really?' exclaimed Lyra, nearly choking. 'I always wondered what went on under there!'

'Davey!' Lieutenant Murray shouted from down the corridor. 'Where are you man?'

Davey's eyes flicked to the door, his face paling. 'Don't tell him I told you,' he whispered. 'I'm in enough trouble as it is.'

With that he left.

Lyra picked up her tea and sipped it watching another quaint little village slip by the window.

Maybe I'll stick around a little longer, she thought, *just to find out what these guys are up to.*

49

CRYOSTASIS

Xenobiology Laboratory. Present day.

When Melanie returned to the lab, she found Fred's room was empty. A cold shiver ran down her spine and her mouth went suddenly dry. With her heart hammering in her chest, she ran out onto the ward, looking around for someone to ask, but there was no one.

She tried to convince herself that they would have come to find her if he'd died, that Doctor Shika would have sent someone to wake her.

Her eyes stung where she tried to hold back the tears.

'They moved him,' came a familiar voice, it was the old nurse. 'He's in cryo.'

Trying to stay calm and not bombard the woman with a thousand questions, Melanie followed the nurse through a maze of corridors until they reached a door protected by two armoured guards.

Inside stood what appeared to be a large hyperbaric chamber, the kind that deep sea divers used for decompression, except this one was surrounded by giant magnetic coils.

Doctor Shika was checking the readouts on a series of displays attached to one side of the cylinder. Her cat padded over to greet Melanie, nuzzling his head into her leg.

'Induced temporal stasis,' the doctor explained, rapping on the side of the chamber with her knuckle. 'We're keeping him on a tight three-millisecond loop.'

Confused, Melanie looked through one of the portholes. Fred's face was ghostly pale, like a porcelain effigy. She touched the glass, her fingers melting the thin layer of ice that had formed there.

'Don't worry, he's safe. The chamber stops the disease progressing.'

'For how long?'

'Indefinitely, or at least until we find a cure.'

Melanie turned to face the doctor. 'So you can stop time?'

Kaori tilted her head from side to side. 'Not exactly, just reduces it to near-zero. In the same way that freezing slows down the molecules in food.'

The scientist in her wanted to know more, this world he'd dragged her into broke every universal law she'd ever been taught, but that would have to wait until Fred was back on his feet.

'I want to work on the cure,' Melanie demanded through gritted teeth. 'You're not sending me back.'

Kaori smiled. 'I assumed you would. Come with me.'

The doctor led her through a series of metal airlock doors until they reached a long glass tunnel that seemed to stretch out over a void of dead space.

'You will need to wear this,' she said, handing Melanie a digital watch. 'It will monitor your vitals, and track your exposure levels.'

Strapping it to her wrist, Melanie gasped as the entire band came to life, displaying her ECG, temperature, SpO_2, respiratory rate and other vital statistics.

The doctor knelt down and stroked her sabre-tooth cat, whispering in his ear. The cat responded with a wide yawn and settled down in a corner. Kaori got to her feet and keyed a code into the security panel on the door and it slid back with a slight hiss.

'We keep the most dangerous pathogens in a bifurcation chamber,' she said, stepping into the glass tube. 'You'll feel a little disorientated crossing the boundary, but don't worry, it will soon pass.'

The walk across the void seemed to take forever, every step taking significantly longer than the one before. Melanie could feel her heart beat slowing, her breathing getting heavy. As if in slow motion, Doctor Shika turned and took her hand.

It became harder to see clearly, her vision blurred as light particles swarmed around her and she had to close her eyes to stop the motion sickness.

Holding tightly onto Kaori's hand, she focused on putting one foot in front of the other.

Minutes seemed to pass between each step until it was finally over.

'Are you okay?' the doctor asked, shining a pen light into each eye.

Melanie blinked. 'Yes, what the hell was that?'

'Temporal dilation. We're now in a separate branch of time, specifically created to protect the continuum from any potential outbreak. When you return to it you'll find that no time has passed whatsoever.'

They walked through into a white room filled with technicians in lab coats sitting at their workstations scrutinising slides under microscopes. It was a very familiar sight, one that Melanie hadn't realised how much she'd missed.

'Shouldn't they be wearing protection?' she said, her voice sounding slightly strange at normal speed.

Doctor Shika clicked her fingers. 'Ah, yes, thanks for the reminder — George, do you have the Kool Aid?'

Melanie was about to ask about their safety protocols when a small man approached them holding a tray of drinks.

'One last precaution,' said Kaori, passing her a glass of dark red liquid and taking one for herself. 'Just a safety measure really.'

Holding up the glass to the light, Melanie inspected the contents. 'What is it?'

'A cocktail of anti-virals and a bunch of nanobots, mostly for monitoring. We find they come in useful in the event of any accidental infections.'

Melanie sniffed the drink, wrinkling her nose at the smell of alcohol. 'And rum?'

Shika shrugged and knocked the whole drink back in one go. 'Got to have something to steady the nerves after what you've just been through.' She put the empty glass back on the tray and smiled. 'George makes a mean Cosmopolitan by the way.'

Following her lead, Melanie drank the concoction, feeling the warmth of the rum spreading soothingly across her chest.

Kaori put down the glass and clapped her hands together. 'Right, that's the formalities out of the way, where do you want to start?'

'Have you managed to map the genome?'

The doctor nodded and motioned towards the far end of the lab. 'Right this way.'

50

THE KING

Tower of London. 1914

I t was raining when the coach pulled up to the rear entrance of the castle. Without a word Murray threw a blanket over her head and bundled her out of the carriage. Davey and Cobham took hold of her arms and virtually carried her towards the gates while the Lieutenant strode on ahead.

They came to a stop and relaxed their grip. She pulled up the edge of the blanket to find a stony-faced yeoman standing to attention. Behind him stood a pair of tall, iron-bound doors, reminding Lyra that the Tower had always been more of a prison than a fortress. The man kept his eyes forward, with a practised, impassive stare while they waited for the bolts to be drawn back on the other side.

Lyra took a moment to sample his timeline.

His name was Arthur Tibbs, an ex-police constable with a penchant for large women, strong beer and pork pies. Thanks to his vices, his would be a short, uncomplicated life — one that most of her guild would consider inane and dull, but somehow Lyra couldn't help but feel a little envious of its simplicity.

. . .

With the low groan of ancient hinges, the massive doors swung apart and they marched her into a courtyard of sheer stone walls.

Lyra shivered in the cold shadow of the keep, the blanket was sodden and she shrugged it off. Above the battlements, the rain was slowing as the storm clouds passed, revealing a slate grey sky.

Wooden crates were stacked in one corner, their sides branded with a Royal insignia. Straw lay scattered across the cobbles and Lyra could smell the sharp tang of horse dung beneath it. Sweating porters in white shirts and leather aprons stopped their work and stared over curiously as they passed. A squat foreman appeared from a side door and chided them to 'mind their business'. Reluctantly, they returned to unloading hessian-wrapped artefacts from the cases, moaning under their breath as they carried them into the main building.

She was taken through a series of narrow passages, some no more than gaps between two walls, their cobblestones half submerged in puddles of oily water. Finally, they reached a small studded oak door in the side of one of the towers.

'Open up,' barked Murray, rapping on the door.

A grille slid open revealing a large blue eye blinking at the light. 'Who goes there?' asked a gruff voice.

'The King's men.'

'And which king would that be?'

'Richard, Cœur de Lion,' replied Murray.

Lyra made a note of the watchword as long iron bolts were drawn back behind the door.

'Enter,' said the guard opening the door. He was wearing chain mail beneath a tabard in the style of a knight from the Norman Conquest and the strangest helmet she'd ever seen. It covered his head with what appeared to be a magnifying lens welded into the face plate.

'Mortimer,' Davey greeted the man as they entered. 'Nice hat.'

It was only once they were inside that Lyra realised the room was actually an elevator.

'Where to?' Mortimer asked, the helmet distorting his voice.

'Basilisk Vault,' Murray replied as the man pulled the security shutters across the door.

'Basilisk Vault,' Mortimer repeated, moving a brass lever to the symbol of a snake-like creature on his control panel.

The elevator descended rapidly and Lyra experienced a slight sense of weightless as they dropped.

Mortimer was over six feet tall and had to stoop to look at her, the lens enlarging one of his eyes like a cyclops.

'Who is she?' he hissed, tilting his head from side to side like a dog.

'A witness,' the lieutenant replied, 'no need to concern yourself.'

'My job,' the man growled, 'is to examine all who enter. No exceptions.'

Lyra could feel the man's mind probing hers. She smiled nervously, batting her eyelids at the giant lens. 'I don't mind. I've nothing to hide.'

'Not necessary,' said Murray holding up a gloved hand and stepping between them. 'She's my responsibility.'

Mortimer moved back, but his mental probing continued. He was good, not as skilful as Kelly but still quite an adept redactor. Her psychic defences kicked in automatically, closing off the more unusual areas of her memory, allowing him into a sanitised version of her life, one that the Grand Seer had taught her to share many years ago.

'She's hiding something,' muttered Mortimer under his breath. 'I can feel it. Locked doors and hidden paths. She's trouble, mark my words.' He tapped the side of his helmet, making it ring like a bell.

Murray ignored him and turned to Davey. 'Go down to signals and see if they can reconnect with the tracking device. Now we know it can fly, it's going to be hard to hide it from the general population. Cobham, send a message to Air Command, their Zeppelin fleet is anchored at Greenwich, we may have need of them.'

'Will it come for her?' Davey asked in his simple, childish way.

Lyra caught her breath, she hadn't considered that Crowley might try and find her.

'Just keep your eyes and ears peeled, both of you,' snapped Murray as the elevator began to slow down. 'I want to know the minute it rears its ugly head.'

Mortimer pulled back the security grille and Davey and Cobham walked off in different directions.

They must have travelled over half a mile below ground, Lyra estimated, walking along the tunnel. The walls were brick-lined like a sewer, but it was dry and with no hint of water. Electric lights were strung along the length of it, glowing warmly with Mr Edison's carbon filament.

'Where are you taking me?' she demanded, trying to act the part of the victim, ignoring the lines of fate that were weaving out ahead of her.

'To meet the King,' snapped Murray.

The Basilisk Vault was not quite what Lyra expected.

Unlike the Xenobiology department, there were no mythical creatures preserved in glass display cases, as one might expect from the name, nor indeed were there any Basilisks. It appeared to be a library filled with rare books and ledgers of the department.

'The Department of Psychical Research was created by His Majesty James II,' said the King, rising from a wing-backed chair. Immaculately dressed as a gentleman in a houndstooth three-piece suit, his hair was slicked back, with a full moustache and beard peppered with the early signs of grey. He carried himself with an imperial bearing as he walked towards her. 'Of course in those days it went by a more grandiose title: The Royal Society for Demagoguery and Witchcraft.'

This was King George V, whom Lyra had met once when he was a young boy. The Grand Seer had taken her to meet his grandmother, Queen Victoria, at Osbourne House, but that was another story and she was sure he wouldn't remember a brief encounter over forty years ago.

'Lieutenant Murray tells me that you were found at the bottom of Loch Ness,' the King said, tapping the ash from his cigarette into an ancient-looking metal bowl. 'How the deuce did you find yourself down there?'

'I was helping someone.'

The King's eyebrows arched slightly. 'And who might this someone be?'

'Crowley, my Lord,' interrupted Murray, 'the occultist.'

Lyra was a little surprised at the mention of his name, she'd assumed they believed the lie about Doctor Lind.

'Ah yes, Aleister Crowley. We've been watching him for some time have we not?'

'Sixteen years, Your Highness. Since he joined the Hermetic Order of the Golden Dawn.'

The King nodded grimly. 'And now he's drowned?'

Murray turned to Lyra. 'We know he was with you in the diving bell.'

She glanced down at her feet. 'He was.'

'And what exactly was he hoping to achieve with this ill-fated experiment?' asked the King, putting out his cigarette and lighting another.

Lyra wondered whether there was a suitable lie that wouldn't sound more insane that what actually occurred.

'He was trying to read the mind of the creature.'

Again the King's eyebrows arched, and he nearly choked, blowing out great gouts of smoke. 'You witnessed this?'

'I assisted.'

'Are you some kind of mentalist madam?'

'Of sorts, Your Highness,' she replied. There were many words to describe her talents, she chose the one that suited the era. 'I'm a clairvoyant.'

His eyes widened. 'And did he achieve his goal?'

She shook her head. 'We failed. His consciousness interfered with the creature, I think it has driven it mad.'

The King cast a sideways glance at his lieutenant. 'Do we know where this half-crazed monster is at this moment?'

Murray sighed. 'No Sire, the radio tracker seems to have malfunctioned. Cobham thinks it may have shaken free. We weren't expecting it to be able to fly.'

'I think I know where it's going,' interrupted Lyra.

51

APEX PREDATOR

Northern China. Cretaceous.

Josh loosed the third arrow, this time hitting the creature squarely in the chest and watched it bounce off as if it were made of solid steel.

Same as the first two, thought Josh, notching another and taking aim. 'The scales are too thick,' he shouted to Rufius.

The old watchman was standing in front of the beast, thrusting his obsidian spear at its head. 'Try for the throat,' he replied. 'Or its eyes.'

Rufius had to duck and roll as the snake-like tentacles wrenched the spear out of his hands and lunged at him.

Josh took careful aim at the head of the dragon, closing his left eye to aim along the shaft of the arrow. He slowed his breathing, like Caitlin had taught him, feeling the tension in his left arm as he drew the string back to his cheek.

The creature reared, opening its wings and blocking out the sun.

Josh released the arrow and it flew straight, sinking between the iridescent scales below its jaw and the beast wailed with pain.

Light burst from the wound, ribbons of energy flowing out where blood should have been. Josh watched open-mouthed as the arrow was slowly forced out like a splinter.

Lifting its head, the beast opened its large jaws and let out a long, mournful sound, as if calling for help.

They all stopped, listening intently for the response, scanning the horizon for another pair of wings.

But nothing came.

Rufius ran back to Josh and Caitlin.

'This is no ordinary beast,' he said, picking up another spear. 'If I didn't know better I would say it had the scent of the Maelstrom about it. I'd give my right arm for a squad of Dreadnoughts right now.'

He was breathing heavily and there was blood flowing from a gash over his right eye.

'There's no sign of a breach, if there had the Dreadnoughts would be here,' Caitlin said, looking for another stone for her slingshot.

'None that we know of,' added Rufius, hefting the spear. 'What we really need is a ship like the *Nautilus*. Those forward cannons would do just nicely.'

'It's too powerful,' said Benoir, stepping out of the thicket. 'I agree with Rufius, we need support, we should retreat and wait for backup.'

'And how long do we wait?' snapped Caitlin. 'We're six million years from the nearest garrison and there's no way to reach them.'

'Looks like it's down to us then,' Rufius said, picking up another spear and turning back to the creature.

To Josh, it seemed to have grown in size.

Running back into the clearing, Rufius narrowly avoided the arc of the long tail as it swung around, slicing through the nearest trees.

'Benoir, a little assistance would be good!' he shouted, getting back to his feet.

The Frenchman picked up a spear and ran to join him.

'Do you think you can hit it in the eye with that?' Josh asked Caitlin as she placed a sharp piece of flint into her sling.

'I'm not sure. It's a small target, and its protecting its head pretty well.'

'I'll give it something to think about,' he said, raising his bow.

They moved towards it, until they were close enough to get a clear shot. Josh fired his next arrow into one of its wings, causing the same effect as before; the leathery skin began to glow and the tear rippled with energy.

While it was preoccupied by the wound, Caitlin let her shot fly.

The stone hit the creature's eye and it howled in agony. Tentacles swarmed over the damage as it rocked its head from side to side. Ribbons of light bled out from between the feelers as they were frantically woven together to stem the flow.

'Move,' screamed Josh as a barbed tail came crashing through the undergrowth towards them.

Josh pushed Caitlin hard, and she fell backwards into a thorny bush while he took the full force of the impact, knocking him thirty feet into the air and into a nearby tree.

Now the creature was half-blinded, Benoir and Rufius saw their chance and launched a joint attack, thrusting their spears into its upper body. The obsidian blades slipping easily beneath its scales and into the flesh, causing another long howl of pain.

This time, something reciprocated.

Their long spears were ripped out of their hands. Knocked aside by the beast's wings as they wrapped themselves protectively around its body, creating a field of shimmering energy.

Shrouded inside its wings, the beast began to pulsate with light, a throbbing that resonated like a heart beat.

Rufius and Benoir stumbled away, forced back by the fields of energy it was producing.

In the darkening sky above the clearing, a ring of light appeared. Expanding quickly until it created a window into a chaotic universe beyond.

'Breach!' bellowed Rufius, grabbing Benoir's arm and pulling him away towards the forest.

Winds rose quickly, lifting up the bones of the dead and twisting them into a spiralling vortex. The branches of the trees bent and snapped like twigs at the edge of the tornado.

Slowly, behind the spinning wall of debris, the creature unwrapped itself. Shedding its physical body like a snake sloughing off its skin, an ethereal, ghost-like version of the beast rose up into the chaos of the Maelstrom above.

From his perch in the treetop, Josh could see other creatures swarming around it as it ascended, singing to it in a strange, haunting language.

As quickly as it had appeared, the portal closed around them and its remains crashed to the floor.

Caitlin crawled out of the undergrowth, her hair wild like a feral child. 'You okay?' she called up to Josh, rubbing her forehead and realising that it was bleeding.

'Yeah,' he replied, climbing down out of the tree. 'Sorry, think I might have pushed you a little harder than I thought.'

'Probably saved my life,' she said, trying to hug him.

He winced in pain. 'Think I might have cracked a rib or two.'

Caitlin took a couple of small leaves from a pouch on her waist and handed them to him. 'Chew these. They're a member of the coca family.'

Josh stared at them. 'Isn't this what they make cocaine from?'

'The Peruvians have been using it for pain relief since before the Incas.'

He smiled, putting them into his mouth. 'I love how much you know about history.'

She kissed him. 'Might save your life one day.'

. . .

They found Rufius and Benoir in the clearing examining the ruined carcass of the creature.

'What was it?' asked Caitlin.

The old man scratched his beard where the blood had matted it. 'Creature of chaos or at least the offspring of one. They must have mated with a local species. Never seen anything like it.'

Walking around the body, Caitlin noticed how the scales had dulled, losing all of their iridescence so that it now resembled the skin of any other dinosaur.

The head, however, was magnificent, bearing all the hallmarks of a Chinese dragon.

'It's not from any species that I recognise,' she said. 'Alixia would know.'

'She was protecting her young,' said Josh, standing a few yards away, staring at something into the long grass.

The nest was surrounded by a ridge of earth and stone. Inside, a clutch of eggs, each one the size of a human head. They had all been destroyed by the storm, leaving shattered shells and the tiny bodies of dead dragons scattered over the ground.

Benoir went back to fetch Alixia.

By the time they arrived, Josh and Caitlin had built a temporary shelter over the creature and Rufius was roasting a small mammal over a fire.

'Assumed you'd be wanting to stay the night,' said the old man to Alixia. 'This is going to take a few days to unravel.'

She nodded demurely, examining the remains of the creature. 'More like a week.'

While the rest of her team unpacked their gear, Alixia came over to see Caitlin.

'You're injured,' she said, touching the fresh cut on Caitlin's forehead.

'That was me,' explained Josh.

Caitlin laughed. 'He was trying to save my life.'

Alixia sighed. 'I should never have allowed you to do this. Rufius believes this was a hybrid — he says that it opened a portal into the Maelstrom.'

'Something did,' agreed Josh. 'It was as if it called for help.'

'We found this,' added Caitlin, holding up a large piece of crystalline egg. 'There are more in the nest.'

Alixia took the shard in both hands and held it up to the fire. The shell refracted with a thousand tiny pinpricks of light. 'Looks like diamond.'

52

SAMADHI

St James's Palace, London 1914.

'Why do you believe he will attack the palace?' asked Murray, stepping down from the carriage onto Cleveland Row. The North Gatehouse of St James's Palace loomed behind him like the entrance to a red-brick fairy castle in the middle of a London Street.

'Not the palace itself, but the headquarters of the Golden Dawn,' Lyra said, turning and pointing to a yellow-stuccoed building on St. James's Street. 'A few years ago, they refused to initiate him into the higher orders, and they've been mortal enemies ever since. Crowley will want to show them what he's become. In his mind, he's attained *samadhi* — the union with a god.'

Night was falling, and the lamplighters were moving along the street, climbing wooden ladders to ignite the gas lamps.

'We should warn them,' insisted Lyra, pulling up the collar on the coat Davey had given her. Something about this evening was making her shiver, and it wasn't the inclement weather.

'I don't think that will be necessary,' muttered Murray, consulting a device that Cobham was holding and then looking down Cleveland Row. She realised they must have got the tracker working again.

Seconds later, a convoy of large wagons clattered into the street pulled by teams of massive shire horses. At first Lyra thought they were some kind of travelling circus, but when she saw the uniforms of the men driving the wagons, she realised this was all part of Murray's plan.

'You're going to try and catch her?' she exclaimed, watching the men dismount and begin to unpack equipment. With a regimented efficiency the soldiers took long rolls of netting and rope from the backs of the carts and laid them out on the floor.

'We are,' Murray replied, removing a large gun from a case on the back of his carriage. It was a beautifully ornate weapon, with an engraved brass stock. The barrel was wider than usual, making it more like a small cannon than a rifle. 'I suggest you wait inside the palace until this is over.'

Suddenly, Lyra sensed the chaos approaching, timelines around her were converging. Men were about to lose their lives and she knew there was little she could do to stop it.

'She's coming,' she whispered. 'You're all going to die.'

'Davey!' Murray barked, 'get this bloody woman out of here!'

'Yes, boss,' said the big man, appearing from behind a team of horses, his face covered in oil. Lyra suddenly realised what was causing her so much anxiety. On the back of the largest wagon was a steam-powered generator, blue arcs of energy flickered over its cylindrical body as men hastily attached cables to it.

Electricity.

The nets crackled with power as Murray's team, wearing long gauntlets and rubber-soled boots, spread them out across the street.

Shenlong's roar drowned out the cries of the horses which scattered before the great serpent as it dropped from the sky, swooping down Cleveland Row.

Carriages careered into each other, splintering into matchwood as the drivers lost control of their teams. The beast swooped low, its wings spanning the width of the street, the force of the wind knocking people to the ground.

Murray barked orders to his men, who turned towards the approaching beast and calmly raised their weapons.

Davey grabbed Lyra and threw her over his shoulder, running back towards the relative safety of the gatehouse of the palace. She tried to struggle but it was no use, he was far too strong.

Looking back, she saw Cobham climb up onto one of the wagons and pull back a tarpaulin to reveal a giant harpoon gun. Others joined him and proceeded to attach the cables from the nets.

Lyra closed her eyes for a moment, trying to make sense of what was to come, but there were too many lines, too many routes to follow.

Shenlong roared once more and rose into the air.

Cobham and Murray fired what appeared to be rockets into the air. Their missiles towing ropes that spooled out, pulling the giant net into the air and over the oncoming serpent.

Lyra held her breath as the creature seemed to fold under the weight of the net, falling from the sky and crashing onto the street below.

The mesh glowed with an iridescent blue light as it enveloped the dragon, electricity arcing over its writhing body. Murray's men cheered and ran to secure their captive with heavy iron stakes, hammering them into the pavements with sledgehammers.

But before they could finish, Shenlong's tail broke free, thrashing violently against those nearest to it. Smashing them into railings and through the windows of nearby buildings, breaking them like children's puppets.

The generator stuttered and went out, the power faded from the net and Shenlong seemed to regain her strength, her tentacles snapping the mesh around her head and freeing her jaws.

She roared, pulling herself up to her full height, and although her wings were still entangled in the netting, she snatched up one of the nearest wagons and tore it to pieces as though it were made of paper.

Turning his back on the creature, Murray barked his orders at his men. They were more concerned with keeping clear of the beast's jaws than what their commanding officer was telling them to do. Momentarily distracted, Murray was oblivious to the sweeping arc of its tail, which hit him squarely in the back and threw him across the street.

Cursing under his breath, Davey placed Lyra gently in an alcove inside the gatehouse and ran back into the fray.

As he ran, Lyra noticed a change in Davey's gait and suddenly his clothes no longer fitted as well as they had; the sleeves of his jacket were splitting — coarse, fur-covered arms appearing from beneath the torn cloth.

Murray lay amongst the carnage unmoving.

Shenlong slid along the street, fire in her eyes, the nets dragging her wings behind her, crawling ever closer to the prone lieutenant.

Davey, now more wolf than man, leapt sixty feet into the air, landing on Shenlong's back.

Cobham rushed to Murray. Slicing through his palm with a blade, he held it to Murray's mouth and let him drink from it.

The creature roared at Davey, twisting its head to snap at the wolf man as he gathered the ropes of the net tightly around its neck, pulling its head up as though reining in a horse.

Murray stirred, his broken bones seeming to heal instantly as Cobham helped him to his feet.

Shenlong lunged at the two men, breaking Davey's makeshift harness and throwing him off its back. Cobham leapt into the air, landing easily on the roof of a nearby building, while Murray's physical form simply turned to smoke and disappeared.

Lyra ran towards them, trying desperately to understand who

these men were and why had she not seen this. Her mind reached out to the tormented creature, hoping that she could soothe its troubled soul, but it was all too confusing, the electrical current was disrupting her ability to read the scene.

As she approached, Davey appeared from under the wreckage of a wagon and shook himself like a dog before running to help his friends.

Lyra stood before Shenlong, holding her hands up towards the dragon, grasping at the invisible strands of fate that swarmed around her. *Be calm*, she whispered gently with her mind. *We mean you no harm.*

You! Crowley's voice thundered through her brain, forcing her to her knees. *You did this to me!*

Shenlong lowered its head towards her, its jaws opening wide to reveal rows of crystalline teeth.

Lyra could feel the hot breath on her head, tentacles writhing through her hair.

I want to help you! She thought, lifting her head to meet Shenlong's gaze. Its eyes were dark and filled with malice. Lyra fought back the terror, holding her ground, hoping that the spirit dragon would find an opportunity to take control of its body while Crowley was distracted.

You help me? You are nothing but a mere worm! I have become a god!

There was an insanity to his thoughts that was far worse than anything she'd experienced in Bedlam, but she knew whilst he was focused on her, it would give the others time to regroup.

You promised to take away my burden!

And indeed I shall!

A searing pain sliced through her mind and she felt her body go numb as tentacles wrapped themselves around her, lifting her from the ground.

As her vision faded, she glimpsed men below her running cables from the now working generator to the net wrapped around Shenlong's body.

Crowley was deep inside her subconscious, his mind ripping

open the most secret of places, and she screamed as he tore into the deepest memories.

She tried to leave her body, to shift her consciousness into the astral plane, but Crowley's psychic force bound Lyra to him, keeping her within the physical realm. She tried desperately to fight back, but it was no use, he was too powerful. Enhanced by Shenlong's abilities, there was little she could do but surrender as he exorcised her gift.

Suddenly the electrical current surged through her body and everything went dark.

53

CAMP FIFTEEN

Base Camp 15, Northern China, Cretaceous.

S im appeared within the ring of standing stones, and fell to his knees. Travelling over sixty-six million years in one leap was not something he attempted very often. The temporal dilation effects of a prolonged jump made him dizzy. As a member of the Copernican Guild, he hardly ever went into the field, preferring to leave that to more capable watchmen, like Rufius and Josh.

The last time he'd visited this epoch was with his mother over ten years ago.

He took a long, deep breath, giving his lungs time to acclimatise to the richer oxygen levels, then slowly got to his feet and brushed the dirt from his knees.

Without consciously trying, Sim's logical mind assessed the surroundings: the temperature was at least ten degrees warmer than he'd expected and the humidity significantly higher.

The sun was high in the cloudless sky, close to noon.

There were no immediate threats, nor any sign of a welcoming committee.

I am safe, he reassured himself. Although that was an entirely relative term. There were thousands of ways he could die the moment he stepped out of the landing zone. He knew this because he'd read the last risk assessment his mother's team filed before they left.

Sim took another deep breath and counted backwards from ten. *You can do this*, he told himself.

There was probably a word for the anxiety he felt whenever he had to travel outside of his designated era, like a form of agoraphobia.

Professor Eddington had insisted he pursue this investigation personally, probably as a form of punishment for bringing a linear into the heart of the Copernican headquarters. Sim had tried to message his parents using his almanac, but it failed to deliver. According to his friend in the Registry the sympathetic links to the Cretaceous were failing, which was unusual, but not unheard of when separated by such a vast distance.

Sim wasn't convinced, and he needed to speak to his mother.

From Melanie's description of the creature, he was ninety-three per cent certain it was a prehistoric reptile. Sim's working hypothesis was based on a long lost creature captured during an expedition into some unexplored region of Africa.

His mother had dedicated most of her life to the study of extinct species. Sim was raised in a house filled with her prehistoric conservation experiments, especially in the basement; a flooded Byzantine cavern which she would regularly use to breed plesiosaurs and other aquatic dinosaurs.

If anyone would know what it was, she would.

Making his way down the steep side of the valley, he spotted the fortified encampment sitting beside the shimmering river, just as he remembered it.

His mother had organised numerous research stations

throughout the Cretaceous period. Setting them up became a regular event during their summer holidays. In the beginning, when they were younger, it was a marvellous adventure with weeks of playing amongst the giant coniferous trees and going on safari to watch lumbering dinosaurs roaming across the plains of Eurasia. But as they grew older it turned into something of a chore. As soon as Sim was able to swing an axe or pull a saw, he was drafted into the construction crew and quickly learned that manual labour was not for him.

His older brother, Phileas, on the other hand, excelled at it, the hours of hard work hardening his muscles and honing his physique. Girls began to hang around where they were working, especially when Phileas took off his shirt. Sim's twelve-year-old brain found it hard to understand what the fascination was with the sweaty, smelly, lump of a brother, but was happy to tag along when they went down to the river for a swim.

He was always much skinnier than Phileas, who was now a senior analyst in the Copernicans, and captain of the *Heliocentrics*, the guild's rugby team.

A year ago, Phileas met a Scriptorian called Myra, and moved in with her, much to the chagrin of their mother whose seventeenth-century Catholic upbringing meant she held rather strong views on sex before marriage.

Sim wanted to point out that Phileas had broken that particular rule a long time ago, something that he'd inadvertently witnessed after one particular skinny dipping evening eight years ago, but he held his tongue. He was no snitch.

This was Camp Fifteen, Sim recalled, walking down the switchback stairways. He recognised the markings on the posts, carvings that he'd made with the knife his father gave him on his thirteenth birthday. It was an obsidian blade, 'Dragon glass', Methuselah called it, holding the knife up to the light, 'from the heart of a volcano.'

The 'S' insignia sat proudly on each of the posts, surrounded by a shield in the same design as the Superman emblem, something that still made Sim smile even now — to think that the crest of the House of El adorned a piece of timber sixty-six million years before it had even been dreamt of by Siegel and Shuster.

He could still remember thinking as he did it, how intriguing it would have been to see the look on an archeologist's face when he discovered the petrified remains millions of years later.

Although that would never happen, of course, every minute particle of evidence of there ever having been an outpost here would be removed by a Draconian clear-up crew the moment the site was abandoned.

Tread lightly on the past, his mother used to say, *leave no mark on history.*

'Simeon!' the guard on watch called down from the gate as he walked up towards it.

'Hi,' Sim replied, holding up one hand to shade his eyes from the bright sun.

He recognised the awkward, slightly hunched figure of Vernon immediately. He'd worked for his mother for as long as Sim could remember, like an old retainer in the horror movies his father loved to watch.

Sim and his friends used to call him Igor, but never to his face.

It took a few minutes for Vernon to get down the ladder and open the gate. His legs were never that steady and they had only worsened with age.

With a beaming smile, he gathered Sim into his arms like a long lost child. 'So good to see you,' he said, standing back to examine him. 'My! Haven't you grown!'

Sim realised that it was probably ten years since he'd seen Vernon and suddenly felt a little guilty for not making the effort to come and visit.

'Yeah,' he replied awkwardly. 'Been very busy with work.'

Vernon's eyes lit up. 'Yes, your mother told me, it sounds incredible, you must tell me all about it. We hardly get any news back here.'

The old man put his arm around Sim's shoulder and they walked through the gate together.

54

PATIENT ZERO

Charles Town, West Virginia, Present Day.

Chief William Fogarty was never one to complain. With just two months to go until retirement and a boat in Gills Creek waiting for him, things were looking pretty good.

In his thirty years with the Charles Town Police Department he'd never had to take a life. In fact he'd only drawn his firearm on three occasions. The violent crime in his district was one of the lowest in the US, for which he took at least some of the credit and a great deal of pride.

Driving east towards Harper's Ferry, he waved to Sarah Mallory and her kids as they cycled into town. She was a good woman, a local primary school teacher with a drunk for a husband. Last month he'd fallen asleep at the wheel and their SUV had ended up in the Potomac, so he was currently in rehab as part of his restitution.

The sun was climbing over the trees, and the Chief reached for his sunglasses, taking his eye off the road for a split second.

When he looked back, he slammed on the brakes, but it was too late to stop from hitting the shambling figure walking down the middle of the road.

There was a sickening thud and the squeal of rubber as his cruiser swerved off the road and into a ditch, followed by the rapid deployment of his airbag.

He was out for less than a minute. Head still swimming from the impact, the Chief instinctively reached for the radio and called it in. Cathy on despatch was her usual calm self as Fogarty described what happened. *She would've only just come on her shift*, he thought randomly, extracting himself from the airbag and getting out of the patrol car. *She'll send a crew from Jefferson in Charles Town, that's a fifteen minute drive.*

Climbing out of the ditch, he saw the body of the pedestrian laying crumpled on the road twenty feet away.

Like a rag doll, he thought, walking towards it, trying desperately to remember how fast he was going. His head was a little fuzzy, the impact of the bag was like getting punched by Mike Tyson, but it didn't really matter, the dash cam would have recorded everything.

The Chief checked for a pulse and was relieved to find the man still had one. He was dressed in old thrift store clothes that looked like he'd slept rough in them for weeks. Yet his skin was clean and he smelled like he'd had a bath. Fogarty checked his pockets for ID but found nothing but a bus ticket. The man groaned and the Chief took off his jacket and carefully tucked it under the man's head, putting him into the recovery position.

As he did so, he noticed the strange scarring on the skin of his forearms, where maybe a tattoo had been removed. It was an intricate pattern, one that looked a little like a hoar frost on a window pane.

Fractal.

'Hey buddy, don't move, the ambulance is on its way,' Fogarty reassured him, looking towards the town.

Should be ten minutes, assuming we're the only RTA this morning.

The radio squawked, and he went back to the car.

'Hey Chief, ambulance five minutes away. Del wants to know if you need him to shut the road?'

'Affirmative, and get Del to bring the truck down here. I think my car's going to need a tow.'

Switching on the lights, he took the traffic cones out of the boot and created a roadblock ten yards in both directions.

The injured man groaned again. Fogarty grabbed a bottle of water and went over to him.

'Billy junior shouldn't take the I60 today — tell him,' the man whispered.

'Sure,' said Fogarty, tipping the water slowly into the man's mouth. The man was obviously delirious — it happened sometimes with head injuries. The fact he was conscious was a good sign, although it was a little odd that he seemed to know his grandson's name and what route he took to work. 'What's your name boy?'

'It's important!' the man insisted, grabbing the Chief's arm. 'Call him now.'

There was a real look of concern in the man's eyes.

The fractal patterning was spreading up his neck now and Fogarty was relieved to see the blue lights of the ambulance on the horizon.

'Billy, it's your grandpa,' said the Chief, watching the medics go to work. 'Have you left home yet? No? Good. Look, this is going to sound crazy, but maybe don't take the I60 today, I heard there was some trouble up there.'

The medics worked quickly and got the man stable and onto a gurney, then headed back to Jefferson Medical Centre.

Del turned up with the tow truck ten minutes later.

'Hey Chief,' he said, pulling the winching chain down and hooking it to the fender of the crumpled cruiser. 'You hear what happened up on I60?'

A cold shiver ran down Fogarty's spine. 'No Del, I've been a little tied up.'

Del sucked air in through his teeth. 'Sheesh, it's a mess and no mistake. Had a petrol tanker jackknife across three lanes, multiple casualties, the entire underpass is on fire.'

Fogarty redialed his grandson's number, holding his breath until he answered.

'Hi Grandpa. Wassup?'

55

MOTHER

Base Camp 15, Northern China, Cretaceous.

Benoir used a team of mastodons to haul the remains of the predator back to the camp and deposited it in one of the larger storage tents.

'It's some kind of hybrid,' Alixia explained, 'part dracorex, part pterosaur and something else I can't even begin to identify from the Maelstrom.'

Sim knelt beside the body, fascinated by the creature's horned skull. 'From the Maelstrom?'

She nodded. 'It's certainly a first. I've never seen a successful mating of a non-linear species. Rufius said others of its kind created a breach to rescue it.'

Sim walked along the carcass which was over fifty feet long.

'Don't get too close, dear. I suspect those barbs may be coated with a toxin,' his mother said, pointing to the vicious looking points on its flail-like tail.

'We've had reports of a similar creature in 1915,' he said, kneeling down and using a stick to lift some of the tentacles around its jaws. 'We think Shackleton may have transported something like this on his expedition to Antarctica. It could explain the disappearance of his entire crew.'

His mother folded her arms and pursed her lips together in the way she did when she was thinking deeply about something important.

'Unlikely, we've not found any evidence of its offspring surviving, at least not in this continuum.'

'Could there have been another breach?' Sim continued. 'One that went undetected?'

Alixia frowned. 'Potentially, but I doubt it.'

Sim walked down to the tail and examined the barbs. 'There has to be a link. When the *Endurance* was rediscovered by a salvage team at the Frontier they became infected with an unknown virus — now there's a high probability of a global pandemic. Professor Eddington has declared a level seven event.'

'Level seven,' Alixia repeated under her breath. 'And you think these creatures could be connected? Who reported this?'

Sim got up to his feet. 'Do you remember Frederick Ross?'

'The Outlier?'

'Yes, he was investigating Shackleton's expedition in 1915 when he was attacked by a prehistoric monster. He's currently in stasis while the Xenos try and find a cure.'

Alixia knelt down carefully beside the creature's tail. 'Then you'll need to take some samples back to Doctor Shika. It may help her to identify the toxin.' She put on a pair of gloves and carefully cut off some of the barbs with an obsidian knife.

Leaving the tent carrying a small clay jar, Sim found Josh and Caitlin waiting for him.

'Hey,' Caitlin said, wrapping her arms around him and giving him a hug. 'How've you been?'

'Okay,' he said awkwardly, he was never that comfortable with physical signs of affection.

'What's in the jar?' asked Josh.

Sim took the stopper out of the jar and held it so that they could see the section of tail inside. 'Mum wants me to take this back to the Xenos. She wants it analysed.'

Josh sneered at the smell. 'I came very close to taking a hit from that yesterday. Is it dangerous?'

'Toxic. Potentially highly toxic,' Sim warned, putting the stopper back in place. 'I think this might be linked to a virus outbreak at the Frontier. Eddington's escalated it to a seven.'

Caitlin frowned. 'Lyra had a vision about a plague the other day. She went to talk to the Grand Seer. Benoir hasn't heard from her since, he's very worried. Have you seen her?'

Sim shook his head. 'No, not for a while. What kind of plague?'

'Some kind of global pandemic I think. He wasn't really sure. Apparently she just woke up and said she had to go.'

'Should I get checked?' said Josh, taking the jar from Sim.

Sim shook his head and took it back. 'You'd be dead by now.'

Caitlin's expression hardened. 'We need to find Lyra.' She turned to Josh. 'Go and get Benoir and Rufius.'

'I'm sure she's fine,' said Sim, as if to reassure himself. 'She knows how to look after herself.'

Caitlin didn't look convinced. 'You know what she's like when she gets an idea in her head.'

'True,' Sim agreed.

A few minutes later, Josh returned with Benoir and Rufius, both looked as if they'd been dragged through a hedge backwards.

'Benoir was teaching me to ride a mastodon,' Rufius said in way of an explanation.

Caitlin made Sim repeat what he had told them. Benoir grew more agitated as he described what Frederick Ross had discovered.

'And he's in stasis now?' asked Rufius.

Sim nodded. 'Doctor Shika and Doctor Braithwaite are working on a cure.'

Rufius sighed. 'I knew his father, one of the bravest men I ever met.'

'How did this thing end up in Antarctica?' asked Benoir.

Sim shrugged. 'You know what Outliers are like. He says he was investigating Shackleton's voyage to the South Pole. Doctor Braithwaite is convinced the virus is connected to the discovery of the *Endurance*.'

'Ridiculous expedition,' growled Rufius, 'doomed from the beginning.'

Alixia walked out of the tent holding her almanac, her expression grave.

'The Registry has finally resolved the connection issue. I've received a message from the Founder, we're to return to the Chapter House immediately. They going to quarantine the Frontier and they need our help.'

Benoir shook his head stubbornly. 'No, I need to find Lyra.'

Rufius slapped him on the shoulder. 'I'll come with you. Kelly will know where she's gone.'

'You should go too,' Caitlin said to Josh. 'I'll take Zachary back with Alixia.'

56

VIRUS

Xenobiology Department. Present Day.

Professor Eddington and Doctor Shika were already in the boardroom when Melanie arrived. Sitting between them at the head of the table was an older man with close-cropped grey hair, a white beard and the most stunning pair of blue eyes.

'Doctor Braithwaite,' Shika said, standing as she entered the room. 'This is Lord Dee, the founder of our Order.'

The founder stood and bowed formally. 'I am honoured to meet you. Although I wish it were under better circumstances,' he said gravely.

'I have some good news, I hope,' replied Melanie, sitting down next to Doctor Shika and handing her a dossier of notes. 'I've sequenced the genome and identified the attachment proteins. It's a strange one, the structure appears to change when observed, it's as if it exists in some kind of superposition, in a quantum state.'

'Interesting,' said Kaori, studying the results.

Melanie continued. 'It looks as though it's preternaturally ageing the host cells.'

Eddington scoffed. 'A temporal virus? That's ludicrous, yet another Outlier theory!'

The founder ignored him. 'Doctor Braithwaite, we're beginning to receive reports that the virus may have entered the general population. Professor Eddington tells me that you had already done some work on modelling the epidemiology.'

Melanie sighed. 'I had started, but the American took all of my data.'

The old man raised one eyebrow. 'The American?'

'His name was Cooper. He told me he was with the CDC, but I think he was military.'

Eddington cleared his throat. 'My department has been developing a prediction model, my Lord. There is little doubt that this is a very serious threat to the continuum.'

'Where was the outbreak?' asked Melanie.

'West Virginia,' said Doctor Shika, tapping on her tablet. A three-dimensional map of the United States appeared above the boardroom table, then zoomed into the state. 'A small town called Harper's Ferry. There was a traffic accident involving patient zero. The first responders have all contracted the virus as has the Chief of Police. I've sent a team to monitor the situation.'

Melanie squinted at the holographic map. 'How did it get out there?'

'I have initiated an investigation into the source,' said Eddington, clearly uncomfortable with the display of modern technology. Kaori told Melanie that most Copernicans had a disliking for electricity.

The founder nodded. 'Doctor Shika, how long will you need to develop a vaccine?'

Kaori scratched her head. 'I'm not sure, ten, maybe twenty years.'

Melanie scoffed. 'We'll be lucky if we have twenty weeks, let alone years.'

They all laughed.

The founder raised his hand to silence them. 'I'm sorry doctor, you must excuse us. We forget you're unused to our ways. It's hard for you to appreciate a non-linear perspective.'

'We don't develop the vaccine over the next twenty years,' explained Kaori. 'We go back twenty and start working on it. Once we begin, it will have already been developed and tested by the time the outbreak occurs.'

Feeling a tension headache building behind her eyes, Melanie rubbed her temples and took a deep breath. 'I don't think I'm ever going to get used to this.'

'Well, fortunately you never will,' said Eddington, it was a thinly-veiled threat, reminding her that at some point she would have her memory redacted.

'What about Fred?' she asked Doctor Shika. 'Can you go back and vaccinate him?'

The founder gave a deep sigh as he got up from the table. 'Unfortunately, we cannot benefit from a retroactive intervention, our timelines do not allow for such adjustments.'

Melanie frowned. 'So how are you going to cure him?'

'There are other ways,' said Kaori, putting a reassuring hand on her shoulder. 'We've analysed the toxins from the barbs, we can work on an antivirus.'

'Thank you Doctor Shika, Doctor Braithwaite,' the founder began, 'please keep me updated on your progress. Professor Eddington, I believe it would be wise to appraise the Draconians of the situation?'

The Professor nodded stoically. 'I will inform Grandmaster Derado.'

Back at the Xeno's laboratory, they found Fred's brothers sitting beside his stasis chamber. Dressed in leather combat gear, they each had cuts and bruises on their hands and faces as if they'd just come back from a battle.

'We got here as soon as we could,' said the youngest, who Melanie thought was called Henry.

'What's the verdict?' asked the eldest, William, the tallest and stockiest of the three red-headed men.

Doctor Shika checked the display. 'He's stable, the disease hasn't progressed any further, thanks to Doctor Braithwaite, we were able to catch it before it overwhelmed his system.'

They nodded to Melanie in appreciation.

'And you're working on a cure?' said Edward, who could have been his sick brother's twin.

'We are. He's in good hands.'

Melanie could see why Fred would be so intimidated by them when they stood up. None of them were under six feet tall.

'Thank you doctor,' said William. 'Is there anything we can do?'

Kaori thought for a moment. 'I might have something for you. I'll be in touch.'

They nodded and simply disappeared into thin air.

57

CAGES

Tower of London. 1914

Lyra woke slowly as if from a deep sleep. Her senses gradually returned to her body, feeling the soreness in her muscles from the electric shock.

The memories of the night before flooded back into her mind; images of the dragon caught in the net, the screams of the horses, Davey transforming into a giant wolf and Murray turning on the power.

At the moment the current hit her, Crowley had been deep inside her subconscious. Echoes of his life were still embedded in her brain like misplaced frames of a film; his time in the Golden Dawn, of masonic halls draped in ritualistic banners and of an old Chinese man with a star tattooed onto his bald head.

Song Wuji. The Fangshi.

Crowley's memory of the wizard was incomplete, but Lyra was sure that this was the man from her vision. This was the man that told him about Shenlong.

Instinctively, she tried to reach out with her mind, searching the timelines around her.

But there was nothing.

She cried out. The world around her felt strange and unnatural, as though she'd lost one of her senses. Her sight was gone.

'Are you all right?' asked Davey, putting his head around the door and holding up a lamp.

Lyra opened her eyes and found herself on a small cot in a store room, surrounded by empty glass jars and broken equipment.

Blinking at the light, she sat up on the bed and stared at him. His face was physically human once more, but there was a glint in his eyes, a hint of gold in his irises that she hadn't noticed before.

And he had no aura.

Lyra jumped out of her bed and took hold of one of his hands. Feeling the rough skin with her fingers, but nothing else.

Her ability to read his fate was gone.

Tears welled in her eyes.

'Are you sure you're all right?' he repeated.

She nodded. 'It's gone,' she whispered, her throat tight with emotion.

Davey shook his head. 'No, the boss has the dragon in one of the holding pens downstairs. Took twenty of us to get it onto the wagon.'

Lyra wasn't really listening. She looked at her small hand in his, relishing the feel of purely physical contact. It was such an odd sensation to touch another human being and not be instantly overwhelmed by their destiny.

'What's the matter?' he asked gently, noticing the tears in her eyes.

She took back her hand and wiped them away. 'Did you hurt her?'

He shook his head. 'No, she's fine, but a little crazy.' He waggled his finger around his temple. 'Lieutenant Murray had to drug her.'

'Can I see her?'

Davey grimaced and scratched his ear, it was clear he'd been given orders that she wasn't supposed to leave the room.

'Well—'

'Am I a prisoner?' she demanded, crossing her arms.

'No, not exactly.'

. . .

The holding pens were huge iron cages in a vast cavern-like basement deep under the Tower. Davey took Lyra down in a brass elevator, which quickly descended twenty levels before it came to a sudden stop.

Electric lights hung in looping lines around the vaulted brick arches, glowing with a warm orange incandescence that reminded Lyra of Christmas at Benoir's parents' house in Paris. She felt a sudden pang of longing, wondering where he was, wishing she could tell him what was going on, wishing she could hold him.

That would have to wait, she chided herself, *first I need to save Shenlong.*

Walking between the empty cages, Lyra ran her hands along the dull, rusting bars. Finding nothing beneath their pitted surfaces, she tried to imagine what strange and unusual beasts had been kept inside them. She knew what it was like to be treated like a misfit and a freak. Growing up with her gift meant spending most of her days hiding from the rest of the world. The memories made her shiver, but that was over now, now she was normal.

Before they turned the corner, she heard the roar of the dragon, its soulful cry chilling her to the bone.

In the shadows of the largest cage, a sinuous body uncurled itself and rose to its full height. Its eyes were filled with pure hatred, hissing at her and spreading its wings wide until they touched both sides of the cage.

Some part of Crowley is still in there, she thought, stepping back from the bars.

'What's the matter?' asked Davey, noticing her discomfort.

Lyra wanted to trust him, to share what she knew about the poor creature, but over the years she learned that people were generally narrow-minded when it came to appreciating her talents. In earlier times she would have been burned as a witch, and nearly had been on more than one occasion.

'Nothing.'

Davey came to stand beside her. 'She's a beauty isn't she?' he said with all the wonder of a child at the zoo.

'She doesn't belong here,' Lyra insisted, watching the beast's head sway from side to side. 'What are you going to do with her?'

'We're considering our options,' said Murray, stepping through a door in one of the alcoves. The lieutenant was wearing a pair of protective gauntlets and carrying a large hunk of meat on a metal hook.

Opening a hatch in the side of the cage he threw the carcass inside and watched as the dragon devoured it with one bite.

'But you can't keep her locked up like this!'

Murray laughed, closing the hatch. 'It's too dangerous to release. His Majesty has asked the Royal Society for a suitable plan. Until then, she will be confined and studied.'

Looking around at the other empty cages, Lyra shivered. 'Is that what you do with all your captives? What is this place?'

'A holding facility for some of the more unusual and dangerous specimens that our department has encountered.'

'They're not specimens!' Lyra protested. 'They're sentient beings.'

Murray rolled his eyes. 'Ah, you're one of those,' he added in a patronising tone.

She crossed her arms. 'One of those?'

'A suffragette, one of those liberals that thinks everyone should have equal rights including beasts like this — until one tries to rip out your throat. We're the ones that have to protect people like you from the monsters.'

Sometimes Lyra forgot how deeply annoying travelling into certain periods could be. The past was not a place for free-thinking, intelligent women. She knew better than to rise to his taunt, although it was a little ironic that he was calling other creatures monsters, after what she witnessed the previous evening.

'So what are you going to do with her?'

He shrugged. 'Most don't survive in captivity. Those that do are eventually relocated to a distant corner of the Empire, as far from human civilisation as possible.'

'I don't want to see her suffer,' she said, walking towards the cage.

'It doesn't belong out there. It's too dangerous.'

Lyra put her hand through the bars, wishing, hoping that somewhere inside Shenlong's troubled psyche, the creature could hear her. 'It's not her, it's Crowley. He's driving her insane!'

The beast seemed to calm, settling at the front of the cage, resting its head so that it could keep one golden eye on its captors.

'Which reminds me,' said Murray, taking off his gloves and hanging them beside the hook. 'How exactly did Crowley's consciousness become trapped inside her?'

Lyra withdrew her hand. This was a question she would have to answer without giving away the existence of the Order. 'It's an ancient ritual,' she began, finding that the lie came easily, 'one that he discovered in a sacred text in Tibet. It's a form of astral projection.'

'And a mythical dragon?'

Shenlong rubbed her head along the bars, her horned ridges creating a sound like a stick along railings.

'He wanted immortality,' she said with a sigh. 'The blood of the spirit dragon was believed to have the power of eternal life.'

Murray scoffed. 'It's not all it's cracked up to be.'

'Who are you anyway?' she said, pointing at Davey. 'I saw you change.' Then turning back to Murray. 'and you turned to smoke.'

'We're different,' Murray snapped, walking away. 'It's classified.'

'I'm pretty sure he's a werewolf,' she nodded at Davey. 'I thought you were supposed to be the ones who hunted them down.'

'Poacher turned Gamekeeper,' said the King, coming out of the shadows. 'My brave lads have suffered much in the line of duty. We owe them a great debt.'

'You owe me nothing, Sire,' Murray said, bowing.

The King patted the lieutenant on the shoulder and smiled. 'George III may have been quite mad, but he was the first to realise that defending our realm against the supernatural would require a team of extraordinary gentlemen.'

'Vampires and werewolves?' said Lyra, unable to hide the disbelief in her voice.

'We prefer the term lycanthropes,' the King corrected her, 'and they have served me well. Dealt with situations that would make any normal man turn and run.'

Lyra wondered how they would fare against the horrors of the Maelstrom.

'Although it does seem you have the stomach for it too,' continued the King, lighting a cigar.

Davey winked at her.

Murray scoffed. 'She's not one of us.'

The King tilted his head from side to side. 'She's proven herself to be useful, and she doesn't appear to be daunted by the paranormal. What more does it take to qualify for this department?'

'She'll slow us down,' protested Murray, his face paling as his irises darkened.

The King ignored him. 'Well, it's been a while since we've had a psychic within our number, and we can hardly pack her off to the back of beyond. What say you Lyra? Do you care to join this department of the strange and unusual?'

Lyra watched the spirit dragon settle back into a coil in the middle of the cage. With her powers gone she was stuck in this time zone, their proposition sounded infinitely preferable to being their prisoner. Although, at some point they would probably realise she'd lost her powers, but until then she thought it wiser to play along, at least until Benoir came looking for her.

'What would I have to do?'

The King blew out a ring of smoke and smiled. 'Be ready to serve your country if and when the need arises, which tends to be quite regularly. But be warned this is not a job for the faint-hearted.'

She smiled. 'I've seen worse.'

Davey clapped his hands together, while Murray simply walked away.

The King shook her by the hand. 'Jolly good. There are a few formalities, traditions really, but I leave that to the Custodian, Davey here will take you to him.'

'May I have a moment with her?' she asked as the King turned to follow his lieutenant.

'By all means,' he said with a wave of his hand.

She put her hands on the bars once more and pressed her head against the cold steel.

'I will free you from the madman. I promise,' she whispered to the sleeping dragon.

58

VACCINE

Xenobiology Laboratory. Present Day.

Melanie sat back from the microscope and rubbed her tired eyes. She hadn't slept more than two hours in the last twenty-four and caffeine wasn't working quite as well as it should. Her body clock was completely out of whack; it was hard to measure time when you were in a permanent state of the now.

'Why don't you take a break?' Doctor Shika said, looking up from her laptop.

'I will,' she replied with a sigh, 'when I've finished checking over these latest results.'

Ignoring the dull ache behind her eyes, Melanie pressed them against the lenses once more. It was certainly an unusual experience to watch the molecular structure of the vaccine transform every time she made an observation in her notebook.

Kaori had called it an 'almanac', and explained that it was quantum entangled with a sympathetic twin twenty years in the past. So as Melanie wrote her notes into the book, they would appear on the pages of its duplicate and actions would be taken based on her findings, making the results instantaneous.

Doctor Shika smiled. 'It's addictive isn't it? This rapid development approach.'

Melanie nodded, scribbling down another note. 'We've made more progress in a day than most would in a lifetime.'

'It's a shame they haven't got access to quantum computers, it would be even faster.'

'Why don't they?'

Kaori shrugged. 'The basic laws of time. You can't use something that hasn't been invented yet.'

A few days earlier, Sim had returned from the Cretaceous with a sample of a similar creature's DNA and some fragments of a crystalline shell, which Kaori ran through a genetic sequencer. The results were showing a match with the toxins in Fred's system and was the first glimmer of a breakthrough.

The main challenge Melanie was facing was the unusual effect the virus had on the ageing of a cell, drastically accelerating its metabolic rate until it died. To make matters worse, the virus envelope went through a series of chimeric shifts, making it hard to establish a receptor profile.

But Melanie was close to establishing a pattern. She sketched out a new structure in her book, carefully labelling the base pairs and closed it.

'I think you're right. I'm hungry. Where do you go for some decent food around here?'

Doctor Shika smiled. 'Not just a case of where, but when.'

They took the elevator up to the canteen. Melanie didn't notice time shifting, but when she stepped out of the doors, she felt the warmth of the sun on her face and smelled the citrus of the orange trees that surrounded the quiet Mediterranean courtyard below them.

'Andalusia,' said Kaori, 'catering change the location every week.'

The view out over the glittering sea was breathtaking. Melanie could see the sails of three-masted trading ships leaving the port.

'How?' was all Melanie could manage to say.

'Temporal engineering. We can attach any point in time to our own. Most of the Guild houses keep at least ten centuries connected to their headquarters. It's a smart way for them to increase capacity in a building without having to actually do any construction work.'

Tables with white linen cloths were positioned around the courtyard where other members of Doctor Shika's team were already tucking into bowls of gazpacho.

'Looks like we missed the starter,' Kaori added, walking down the steps.

'So why can't we just go back and save Fred?' asked Melanie, putting her fork down. 'The founder said it wasn't possible.'

Kaori nodded, handing her empty bowl to one of the waitresses. 'Our chronologies don't follow the usual rules. We're non-linear, we exist in the now, so the idea of going back to our past is a little trickier — we don't exactly have one.'

'But you still age?'

The doctor sighed. 'We do, albeit rather slowly. It's one of the perks of being a time traveller.'

Melanie smirked. 'I can think of a few more.'

'Yes, most linears do. I've read a few time travel books. They usually involve stopping Hitler from being born, trying to get rich or changing some mistake that happened back in their past.'

'Like having your doctoral thesis stolen by your mentor and then him winning the Lasker award for it?'

Kaori winced. 'Ouch, that's a pretty bad one.'

'Yeah,' Melanie agreed, taking a sip of wine. 'Now there's someone who needs to have his timeline tampered with.'

'Adjusted,' the doctor corrected her, holding up a finger. 'And only once all the possible consequences have been considered.'

'Whatever. It wouldn't take much, just a little accident somewhere in his father's past. One missed opportunity in the sack and no more devious plagiarist to steal my work.'

The doctor laughed. 'But then you would never have met Fred.'

'True,' Melanie admitted. 'But I would've won the Lasker prize, a PhD and a research grant.'

Kaori shrugged, putting on her jacket and taking out her notebook. 'Not going to keep you warm at night though, as my mother used to say.'

Melanie frowned, but inside she knew the doctor was right. There was something about the dopey redhead that she couldn't quite put her finger on, but whenever she thought about him and his quirky little grin, she couldn't help but smile.

'Guess we should get back to fixing him then,' she said, getting up from the table.

Kaori didn't reply, she was too busy studying something in her almanac.

'What is it?'

'The American President has just announced that they have a vaccine.'

'What? That's impossible!'

The doctor turned the book towards Melanie, who just saw a page of fluctuating symbols and branching lines.

'I can't read your temporal code.'

'Ah, yes, sorry. It's basically a newsfeed I set up for anything related to the virus. It's literally just happened in the present.'

'Can you get hold of some?'

Kaori tilted her head, her eyes widening. 'Not without going through a lot of red tape, but I do know some Draconian brothers who might be able to help.'

59

KELLY

The study of the Grand Seer. Mortlake. 1585

E dward Kelly ran his long finger over the pages of Lyra's journal, following the lines of her paths across the paper. 'She was trying to map the unmappable,' he said, holding up the book. 'Like a hawk studying the world through the eye of a sparrow.'

'Enough of your riddles, man!' snapped Rufius. 'Give us a straight answer.'

'I know Lyra had a vision,' Benoir said. 'A bad one. And she came to you — that was the last time any of us saw her.'

The Grand Seer sighed. 'I warned her not to pursue this.'

'She's gone back into the shadow realm hasn't she?' Benoir continued, walking towards the long mirror at the other end of Kelly's study.

Pulling off the black cloth that was draped over it, he tapped on the glass. 'Is she trapped in there?'

Kelly stroked his beard into a point. 'She ventured into a stranger's dream. A madman by all accounts, one who wished to bring about Armageddon. City streets filled with the dead, not a living soul remaining, a global plague. When she described the man who had shown her this, I was struck by the resemblance to someone you might remember, Rufius — Aleister Crowley.'

Rufius huffed. 'The Exile?'

'Indeed. Lyra saw a man carrying the mark of the silver star, and I told her of the Argenteum Astrum.'

Josh looked confused. 'Who is the Exile?'

'Someone who I should have put out of his misery a long time ago,' growled Rufius. 'A seer who lost his powers dabbling in things he shouldn't have.'

Kelly went to a shelf and took down a book, the cover was black with a silver circle and a five-pointed star in its centre.

'He claimed to have spoken with an elder god: Aiwass.'

Opening the book, he read aloud.

'*Into my loneliness comes—*
The sound of a flute in dim groves that haunt the uttermost hills.
Even from the brave river they reach to the edge of the wilderness.
And I behold Pan.'

'He was nothing but a fraud and a charlatan,' added Rufius. 'A disgrace to the Order.'

'Where did he go?' asked Josh. 'After he was exiled?'

'Turned up in Egypt 1904, claiming to be a prince and started communing with spirits and writing that damned book.'

'*Liber AL vel Legis* — the Book of Law,' Kelly said, closing the book and placing it back on the shelf. 'He assumed the role of prophet, but his philosophy was not one that many aspired to.'

'So Lyra went to see him?'

'I fear she has. Alas, there's no way to trace her when she travels along the forgotten paths.'

'She can't stop him single-handedly,' said Benoir.

Kelly sighed, walking over to him. 'That is not why she went. She seeks knowledge, she wants to learn how Crowley lost his abilities.'

Benoir's eyes widened. 'Why?'

'She wants to be free of the burden of sight. To rid herself of this curse of knowing too much. Lyra wants to spend the rest of her life in blissful ignorance.'

The Frenchman seemed to inwardly crumple, his lip trembled and tears welled in her eyes. 'I thought she didn't want me.'

Kelly put his hand on the man's shoulder. 'She's prepared to give up everything to be with you.'

Rufius coughed, taking out a handkerchief and wiping his eyes. 'Well, we'd better be getting on with finding her then.'

60

BOSTON

Fort Detrick, Maryland. Present Day.

Wiping his mouth, Cooper looked down at the blood in the sink.

His time was running out and nothing had changed.

He'd been monitoring the daily reports from the CDC and still there was no mention of any serious outbreaks in West Virginia, Texas or Massachusetts. Miller assured him that the Project Contagion had been executed exactly as planned. Three of the infected crew from the Hercules had been sent out into the wild.

Were the models wrong? He wondered, *Or maybe the virus had mutated into something benign.*

Another bout of coughing put him on his knees. The doctor had warned him that the cancer would spread, that his lungs would be the most likely site for secondaries.

His body was waging a war with itself, one that it couldn't win. He tried to visualise the cancer like some kind of invading army, Soviet T-54 tanks rolling down through his spine, making forward operations in his liver and lungs.

'Get off your knees soldier,' he whispered to himself, pushing up off the porcelain.

Going back to his desk, the Colonel picked up the photograph of the skull. It was an elegant creature, a dragon straight out of mythology.

He'd spent over a year looking for the Emperor's fabled cure, only to find it too late.

The quest held a similar fate for him as it had for the First Emperor; having scoured the known world for a cure for death, only to find there was no way to unlock its secrets of immortality in time to save him.

Song Wuji said there would be a price to pay, that the gift would be protected by a curse. Little did Cooper know it was the most deadly virus known to man.

After his diagnosis, when Western medicine had no answers, Cooper had taken a prolonged leave of absence and headed for Asia.

He'd first heard of Wuji in Vietnam. The locals called him 'pháp sư' which roughly translated as "wizard". Rumour was he'd once been a physician to the Emperor of China, a claim made by most of the witch doctors that were selling herbal remedies and acupuncture from shacks in the Old Quarter of Hanoi.

Back then, Cooper had been given eighteen months to live, and the wizard told him he could live forever and there was something about the man's dark eyes that made him believe it.

'You must find the egg of a Yaoguai,' he told him in broken English. 'Shenlong, the spirit dragon.'

In his small wooden hut decorated with ancient texts, the old man told him the story of Emperor Qin's obsession with becoming immortal. How he'd sent his agents to every corner of the world in search of an elixir. That he himself had witnessed the terrible punishments that were meted out when they returned empty-handed.

All except one.

A weary fisherman was brought to court one stormy night, saying that he had travelled from Penglai which sat on the shores of the Bohai Sea.

He claimed that his great-grandfather caught a beautiful egg in his nets many years ago, that it took pride of place in the ancestral shrine for many years, until the night of the comet, when it began to glow with an unnatural light.

The Emperor was ecstatic, for the Bohai Sea was thought to be the home of the Island of Immortals, where, his alchemists told him, could be found the secret to eternal life.

The fisherman put down his straw basket and produced the egg. Kneeling before his master, he held it out as a gift. It was a large, crystalline object, bigger than a man's head. Its shell seemed to reflect every colour in the room.

But the Emperor was a wise man, he had been duped many times by the promise of magical gifts and refused to touch it. Instead, he commanded his most trusted advisor, Song Wuji, to collect the egg from the peasant.

When Wuji touched the shell, he told Cooper he could feel the creature's heart beating through the iridescent surface. A bond grew instantly between them, the energy from the creature warming the old man's hands until his arthritic joints were no longer sore, nor swollen.

Content that the egg was not dangerous, the avaricious Emperor leapt from his throne and snatched the prize from Wuji. Dismissing his courtiers, he took it into his royal chambers and was not seen again for several days.

When he reappeared, he looked drained. The dark shadows beneath his eyes told Wuji the man was gravely ill.

But the Emperor refused to believe his alchemists, saying that he felt rejuvenated, that the egg carried Shenlong, the spirit dragon, and that soon it would emerge and bless him with eternal life.

The man died two weeks later and as requested on his death bed, the egg was buried alongside him in the great mausoleum of a tomb he had built in Xi'an. Along with his court. No one who came into contact with the egg survived.

Except for Song Wuji.

'There it remained for two thousand years. As have I. Waiting for the rebirth of the dragon.'

The curse was obviously the virus, assumed Cooper. Somehow the old man had survived it and it had given him eternal life.

The sound of his sat phone broke his reverie.

It was Lieutenant Miller. 'Colonel. Switch on CNN.'

Cooper sighed, putting down the photograph. 'I'm a little busy right now Lieutenant.'

'Sir, you're going to want to see this.'

The colonel picked up the remote and switched on the TV. Helicopter footage of bodies on the streets of Boston flickered onto the screen with headlines like 'Zombie outbreak?' scrolling across the bottom of the picture.

'It was too fast for the CDC,' continued Miller, 'they missed it.'

'How many?' asked Cooper, getting up from his desk.

'The news is saying it's taken the entire city. That's seven hundred thousand people.'

In less than three days, thought the Colonel, flicking through the other news channels. They were all showing the same report.

'How's the vaccine coming along?'

There was a slight hesitation before Miller answered. 'We've hit a small problem.'

'What?'

'The medics are saying the virus is mutating too fast, they can't get a fix on the protein envelope.'

His desk phone began to flash, the number on the display was the private line for the Oval Office.

'Let's go with whatever they've got.'

61

THE WAR ROOM

Tower of London, London. 1914.

L yra followed Davey in a daze, still trying to make sense of this strange new world. He escorted her to the elevator and they descended into the cavernous depths. She was amazed to find that there were more than a hundred levels below the Tower.

'Where are you taking me?' she asked steadying herself against the wall. The loss of her abilities was disorientating. Without her temporal-enhanced vision, everything around her seemed dull and flat.

The big man smiled. 'To the Custodian,' he said, as if that were explanation enough.

The floors slipped past quickly, giving her brief glimpses of storage vaults piled high with wooden crates and barrels, workshops filled with strange mechanical machines and what looked like a Victorian theatre complete with velvet seats.

It reminded her of the storehouses of the Antiquarians, who had centuries of artefacts piled up in dusty corners waiting for the day when a traveller might need to visit a particular point in time. She considered asking Davey who built it, but something stopped her.

Too many questions would look suspicious and she had an inkling that the big man probably wouldn't know.

'Edward Grey,' the gentleman said, limply holding out a gloved hand. 'You may call me the Custodian.'

He was a tall man, with a thin face and sharp, haunted eyes. In his mid-sixties, his hair was silver, swept back and tied with a purple bow. Grey was dressed in a black morning coat and pinstripe trousers as if he'd just stepped out of the House of Commons.

'Lyra Cousineau,' Lyra replied taking his hand, trying to ignore the lack of timeline that should have unravelled from his touch. 'Aren't you the Foreign Secretary?'

The man sneered. 'And you are French?'

'By marriage,' she replied with a sudden pang of longing.

They were standing in what could only be described as a war room. Each of the walls were adorned with charts of the world and steps led down to a long table with a map of Great Britain etched into it.

Stern-looking assistants were busy taking messages from pneumatic tubes and handing them to orderlies who were moving military symbols across Europe.

1914, the beginning of the First World War. Lyra reminded herself. *Archduke Franz Ferdinand was assassinated in June, war broke out a month later.*

'His Majesty has instructed me that you wish to join our ranks,' Grey continued, raising one eyebrow slightly. 'I have to say that I find that a trifle rash, but then he is known to have a penchant for young mystics.'

Lyra let go of his hand, ignoring the innuendo. 'I'm considering his proposition,' she replied.

Grey's eyes narrowed. Without her sight, Lyra was finding it difficult to read him. His body language was guarded, if not bordering on rude.

'Well, perhaps I can assist you in your decision,' he muttered in a sarcastic tone. Turning back to the table, he picked up one of the pieces. 'Our department has listening posts stationed in every corner of the British Empire. Intelligence reports are sent directly to us via a secret telegraph network so we are able to make timely decisions and appropriate actions.'

'You're spies?' she asked.

Grey grimaced and puffed out his chest. 'No! We're defenders of the realm!'

'From the Nazis?'

He look at her quizzically. 'You mean the Hun?'

Of course, she chided herself, *this was the Great War.*

'No.' He held up the piece. It was a demon, carved from black ivory. 'Ours is a greater battle. We fight the denizens of Hell.'

Lyra looked at the table, there were pieces spread across the country, like a giant game of Risk.

'Demons,' she repeated to herself, imagining he meant the Nazgûl of the Shadow Realm or the nightmarish spawn of the Maelstrom. *Could they be dealing with a breach? Why weren't the Dreadnoughts dealing with it?*

He sighed. 'It is a never-ending struggle.'

'How many are you?'

The Foreign Secretary put the piece back on the table. 'Sadly, not enough. At last count: two hundred and twenty all told, but our losses are numerous.'

He turned his attention to the maps on the walls, where more symbols were being moved by the assistants using long poles.

'The battle is being fought on many fronts,' he added.

A bell sounded above the map of the Far East and Grey climbed the steps towards it.

Lyra followed him, watching the frenetic activity as various magnetic glyphs were pushed across the chart towards the northern part of China.

Recognising the symbol from Crowley's scrolls she asked: 'Is that a Yaoguai? '

The Foreign Secretary looked impressed. 'Indeed, apparently there's been a rather nasty outbreak in the Shaanxi province.'

She tried to contain her excitement. Shaanxi province was close to where Crowley said he met Song Wuji, in Peking.

'I've had some experience with Yokai, a similar form of spirit.'

Grey's eyes widened slightly and his expression softened. 'The King informed me you're something of a clairvoyant.' He folded his arms over his frock coat. 'We have need of such skills since Madame Georgiana passed on.'

'Passed on?'

'It was a terrible loss,' said Grey, lowering his head. 'Murray has never quite forgiven himself.'

Suddenly the lieutenant's animosity made sense, this was more than just the death of a colleague, Murray was grieving his lover.

'How did she die?' Lyra asked.

'That is not for me to say,' said Grey, turning away, distracted by another flurry of activity. He walked over to speak to one of his assistants who was busy checking a series of reports.

When he came back, he looked concerned. 'Returning to the subject of the Yaoguai, how do you feel about air travel?'

Lyra tried to recall what kind of air travel he could possibly be referring to. She knew it was too early for commercial airline flights, so the only other option would be an airship.

'I've never had the pleasure,' she said, which was not too far from the truth. As a member of the Order she could be anywhere in the world with a touch of the relevant object.

'And you never will,' said Murray, suddenly appearing behind them. 'Not on my watch.'

Grey's face hardened at the sound of his voice. Lyra wondered if he'd overheard their conversation.

'Lieutenant, that is your decision of course,' he said, handing Murray a slip of paper with the coordinates. 'The airship is being readied. A team will be waiting for you on the roof.'

The lieutenant nodded and went to leave.

'Wait! I can help,' she called out to him. 'Yaoguai aren't spirits of the dead, they're immortals from Diyu, the Chinese equivalent of Hell. The only way to exorcise them is to learn their true name. Crowley has a scroll in his study.'

Murray stopped and turned back to her, his eyes dark like coals.

'I've been fighting demons since before your grandmother was born. I don't need a lesson in how to deal with them from you.'

And with that he left.

62

SHADOW REALM

Shadow Realm.

The Shadow Realm was a desolate, broken land of forgotten things that smelled of dust and mildew, like an old abandoned house. It reminded Josh of the Maelstrom, except it was more stable and there was no sign of any Djinn.

'How the devil did she find this place?' asked Rufius, turning Lyra's journal upside down to look at the map from a different angle.

'She's been coming here for years,' replied Benoir, pulling the threads of another cobweb out of his hair. 'Apparently it's the only place she can get any peace.'

Josh took the journal from Rufius. 'Why are all the names taken from Tolkien?'

Benoir shrugged. 'She said it reminded her of Mordor.'

Rufius scratched his beard and walked over to a signpost. 'She's not far wrong.'

The wooden post was rotting and riddled with wormholes. There were various marks scratched down its length. Whatever lettering had once been etched into its boards was long gone, erased by rough weather and endless neglect. He ran his hand over the more recent marks like a blind man reading braille.

'It wasn't her,' he murmured, looking down paths that stretched out into the distance.

'How are we supposed to know where she went?' asked Josh, turning towards the Grand Seer.

With his usual theatrical flourish, Kelly produced a scrying ball from his cloak and held it out in front of him. Gradually, the glass sphere began to glow with an internal swirling mist in which forms began to take shape.

'She passed this way,' he said, teasing tendrils of smoke from the glass and weaving them into the ghostly shape of Lyra.

'What is this? Dark magic?' Benoir asked, watching it float off towards the east.

'An echo,' replied the Grand Seer, looking furtively around him. 'We should make haste — the Nazgûl are close.' Holding the sphere aloft like a torch, he followed after the ethereal image of Lyra.

Josh turned back towards Benoir. 'Nazgûl?'

'Wraiths,' said the Frenchman, taking the journal from Josh and putting it in his jacket pocket. 'Lyra called them that because they prey on the lost.'

Rufius snorted. 'Great,' he said, marching off after the Grand Seer.

The road to the east was littered with tiny skeletons of what Josh assumed were birds. He heard the chattering of teeth and claws in the broken walls of the tumbled-down buildings, but never saw a living creature.

'What is this place ?' Josh asked Kelly, who was trudging beside him furtively looking behind every few minutes and mumbling incantations under his breath.

'Old paths, built between times,' whispered Kelly.

'By who?'

The Grand Seer stopped and raised one long bony finger, drawing a glyph in the air. 'He has many names. The Old King, Lord of Shadows, The Wanderer, Abandon, to name but a few. I have never made his acquaintance, but Lyra tells me she has and it changed her — he gave her a gift that enhanced her abilities.'

The symbol hung in the air between them as if carved from fire. There was something vaguely familiar about it, a circle with a rune of five intersecting lines like a crude compass.

'And she's been searching for him ever since,' added Benoir.

Walking back to join them, Rufius had a stern look in his eye. 'This isn't the time to be standing around chatting like old women,' he growled, pointing back down the road they had just travelled. 'In case you'd forgotten, there's something following us and it's getting bolder with every step we take.'

Dark shapes shifted behind the shattered trunks of an old forest to their left. Josh hadn't noticed them until the old watchman pointed them out. The forms of shadow-like creatures solidified as they crept amongst the trees.

Kelly dismissed the rune with a wave of his hand and took out the scrying globe once more.

Whispering into it in a language that Josh had never heard, it began to glow brightly. Holding it aloft like a torch, the light expanded until it enveloped them all.

The darkness shrank back like a scolded child.

'Quickly,' ordered Kelly. 'I cannot hold this for long.'

In the distance the ghostly figure of Lyra paused at a crossroads formed by two bridges.

'To the bridge,' said Rufius.

They ran together, no one looking backwards, staying within the penumbra of Kelly's light until they reached the cobbles of the stone bridges.

Lyra floated in the air above them, looked down into the chasm and disappeared.

'Where did she go?' asked Josh.

Kelly shrugged, putting down the sphere and taking out a stick of chalk. 'I think we have more important things to worry about right now.'

63

PRESS CONFERENCE

Fort Detrick. Present Day.

Colonel Cooper sat in front of the world's media, their cameras trained on him like a firing squad.

The President had given him everything he asked for and more. The vaccine programme was now in full production and the first batches were being rolled out to the National Guard and healthcare workers.

Boston had been hit the worst, followed by Philadelphia and Washington. All of them were in quarantine now, but there were reports coming in of cases in every major city across the US.

'Colonel Cooper.' A reporter from CNN broke the silence. 'Can you give us an update on the current death toll and the projected numbers?'

He cleared his throat and leaned slightly into the bank of microphones. 'So far we have three hundred and twenty-thousand confirmed fatalities. We believe that it will reach five-hundred thousand by the weekend.' He kept his tone neutral, no hint of emotion.

'Do you believe we can produce enough vaccine?' asked the

woman from Fox News. 'We're hearing there maybe issues with production.'

There were more than just issues, Cooper thought, thanks to the President's trade stalemate with China, they were having massive supply chain problems.

He twisted his mouth into a reassuring smile. 'I'd like to take this opportunity to set the record straight on that rumour. We've been planning for this kind of event for years, stockpiling the raw materials necessary to scale up production for just this kind of emergency. There will be enough for every single US citizen.'

'And what about the rest of the world?' asked the man from the BBC. 'Will you be sharing the formula with your overseas allies?'

For a price, Cooper wanted to say, but bit his tongue. 'Our government is working with the global scientific community to ensure that every country will have access to the relevant data.'

'Do you have any idea where it came from?' asked a reporter from The Washington Post.

'We believe it originated in Russia,' he replied with a cool surety. *Nothing like a bit of commie bashing to get the media hyped up.* 'There are unconfirmed reports of a massive outbreak near the town of Belogorsk.'

'The military facility?' continued the reporter, hastily making notes.

'The bioweapons facility,' added another.

Suddenly everyone was asking questions at the same time.

Cooper stood up. 'Thank you, that will be all for today.'

Standing at the back of the room, William Ross watched the Colonel leave. His brother, Henry, was standing to his left behind a camera, pretending to film the announcement, but was instead using a Draconian longscope to scan Cooper's security pass and pull the necessary biometric codes from its NFC chip — as well as recording his voice.

Edward, who was three floors down dressed in a sergeant's uniform, was waiting for the data.

Electronics was not something most members of the Order were keen to embrace, but as members of the Draconian's most advanced unit, they were very familiar with such covert ops.

'You have clearance,' Henry said into his headset.

'Confirm,' came Edward's response. 'I'm in.'

Edward moved quickly towards the storage facility. He'd memorised the layout of the expansive sub-levels of Fort Detrick, most of which were built to withstand a direct nuclear strike. They kept every deadly disease known to man in the lower levels, cryogenically frozen to prevent any chance of infection.

This was also where they kept the antidotes and the vaccine samples.

He swiped the cloned pass in the security lock and the heavy safety door slid open.

'What am I looking for?' Edward asked, walking along the endless rows of glass fridges filled with small vials of colourless liquid.

'VBX-109-A,' whispered William into his ear. 'It should be in the section marked "I wish I'd listened more carefully at the briefing".'

Edward ignored the jibe, and walked slowly, reading off the labels as he went. He wasn't as clever as his older brother, but had a knack for getting in and out of places without being noticed. William would joke that it was because of his unremarkable face, but they both knew it was more than that. Edward could control his temporal movements to the microsecond.

'Got it,' he said, opening one of the doors and pulling out a tray and removing one vial. 'Can we go now? I'm freezing my balls off in here.'

'Just make sure you erase the video footage on the way out,' his elder brother reminded him.

64

DIRIGIBLES

Greenwich, London. 1914

The airships floated lazily in the late afternoon sun, like whales basking in the Sargasso Sea.

Lyra counted over thirty Zeppelins, each carrying the insignia of the Royal Navy. They were magnificent craft, much larger than she had expected. The silver cigar-shaped ships were over six hundred feet long and bristling with guns.

Refusing to be put off by Murray, she'd stowed away on one of their supply wagons and followed them to the Greenwich mooring mast.

An eight-sided steel structure rising over two hundred feet into the sky above Greenwich Royal Park and the Observatory, the mast dominated the landscape, as did the airship attached to it.

While the wagon came to a stop at the gates to the freight yard, Lyra managed to lever off one of the lids of a packing case and climb inside. Finding herself amongst a straw-filled box of assorted uniforms, she made herself as comfortable as she could and waited.

To her relief, the crates were unloaded carefully and winched up into the cargo bay of the ship. Watching the ground through a small knot-hole in the side of the case, Lyra began to wish she still had some of her talents — there were definite advantages in transportation for starters.

It was dark in the hold.

The crew had taken hours to finalise the loading. By the time Lyra thought it was safe to extricate herself from the crate, her joints were stiff and she need to go to the toilet badly.

She felt her way along the canvas sacking, barrels and wooden cases, until she managed to find the gantry that led up to the crew quarters.

Peering through a porthole in the hatch, she could see men in dark grey uniforms going through the final preparations for take off. It wasn't going to be easy to step out into the passageway without being noticed, and without her enhanced senses she had no way of knowing how to avoid them.

How do linears bear to live like this? she wondered, finding a fire bucket and squatting down on it. *It's like walking around with one eye closed.*

Her stomach growled, reminding Lyra that she hadn't eaten since breakfast. She had no idea how long it would take to get to China, but once they were in they air, she hoped she would be able to find a better place to hide, preferably near the galley.

The hunger pangs disappeared at the sound of heavy footsteps echoing down the passageway. Shrinking back into the shadows she watched as a detachment of guards passed by the hatch.

One of them paused by the door, his shadow blocking out the light. Lyra held her breath as the wheel on the door rotated and a familiar head poked through the gap.

'Hello there,' said Davey. 'Thought it was you.'

'How did you know I was here?' she asked as he slipped through the door and closed it.

He nodded towards the fire bucket. 'I have a very good sense of smell.'

Of course you do.

Davey looked confused. 'How did you get on board? The lieutenant said that you weren't coming.'

'I hid in a crate,' she said, pulling straw out of her hair. 'Are you going to tell him?'

The big man shrugged. 'Not unless you want me to.'

She shook her head. 'I'd rather you didn't.'

He smiled. 'It's okay, he tends to stay in his cabin during daylight hours. You'll be needing this,' he said, pulling a paper bag from his pocket.

She opened the bag to find it was empty. 'What's this for?'

'Just in case.'

Lyra followed Davey to the bridge where the Captain, dressed in a blue serge uniform, was issuing orders to the engine room through a brass tube. Three men sat at a mahogany control desk filled with brass dials and levers, while the helmsman stood at a large wheel like something from a sailing ship.

'Cast off and engage rotors,' the Captain instructed his crew. 'Full steam ahead.'

The drone of the engines changed pitch and the Zeppelin lifted away from the tower with incredible speed. As the ground disappeared beneath her, Lyra felt her stomach lurch, and realised exactly what the paper bag was for.

Flying was a very unusual sensation. Lyra had done it many times outside of her body, but astral projection didn't suffer from the physical effects of gravity or vertigo. Davey took her down to a large leather couch in the observation deck below the bridge and made her put her head between her knees while he went to find some brandy.

'We will encounter some turbulence as we ascend. Crew to remain at their stations,' came the voice of the Captain through a tinny brass speaker at one end of the room.

'Great,' muttered Lyra, raising her head as Davey came back with a glass of cognac and a plate of shortbread biscuits.

He smiled and looked towards the large window at the other end of the room. 'It'll be better when we get above the clouds.'

Managing a weak smile, she took the drink and sipped at it until the warm sensation calmed the fluttering in her stomach. Then devoured the biscuits.

Recovering from the sense of vertigo, Lyra got to her feet and went over to the window. The view was quite impressive; London was nothing more than a rapidly shrinking black smudge in the middle of a green map of England.

Suddenly the whole ship began to shake, and the country was lost behind a white veil of swirling cloud.

Davey grasped an iron strut of the bulkhead with one hand and held out the other to Lyra.

She took it, hers was like a child's inside his.

'Turbulence,' he said, speaking more to himself. 'Just rough air.'

They burst through the cloud and into a clear blue sky and the shaking subsided. Lyra realised she'd been holding her breath.

Davey's eyes widened in awe at the landscape of sculpted white towers around them.

'Like another world,' he whispered. 'Just for the birds.'

He let go of her hand.

'How long have you been a lycanthrope?' she asked, remembering to use the correct term.

The big man shrugged. 'A hundred years, maybe more.'

She went to sit back on the leather couch. 'Did it hurt?'

He shook his head. 'Can't remember. We were in the woods, looking for mushrooms. My sister always knew where the big ones were. It was late, the moon was full, which is the best time to harvest the silver caps, so Maggie used to say.' He took a deep breath and she saw his lip quiver a little.

'At first I thought it was a boar. I was big, even then. I found a stick and told Maggie to climb a tree, but she just laughed at me and walked off. I never saw her again.'

There were tears in his eyes.

'The wolf came out of the thicket all teeth and red eyes. I had never seen something so big. Bigger than me, even now. He took me by the throat and dragged me into the bushes.'

Davey pulled down his shirt collar to show her the white scars on his neck.

'When I woke up I thought I was in heaven, but then I heard my heart beating and the blood was everywhere. The wolf was dead beside me and a man was standing over it with a big gun.'

'A man?'

He nodded. 'A hunter. I think he thought I was dead too, but I was strong and he took me back to his lodge. Looked after me until I was better.'

'What about your family?'

'Sister was all I had,' he replied, wiping his cheek with the sleeve of his jacket.

'And the wolf infected you?'

He nodded. 'I didn't know until I came of age. Then it was too late. I would just wake up in different places, with no clothes.' The colour rose in his cheeks. 'Then Murray found me.'

'Was he a vampire then?'

Davey nodded. 'He taught me how to control the wolf inside me. He's one of the first.'

'First?'

'Murray is old. He was one of the first to be recruited by King George, but he'll outlive all of us.'

Lyra assumed they were all immortals, but that obviously wasn't the case.

'He doesn't like me very much.'

'He doesn't like anyone very much,' the big man said with a sigh, 'not since Madame Georgiana died.'

'How did she die?'

Davey narrowed his eyes and let out a low growl. 'She was the best of us, she didn't deserve that.'

Lyra could tell he was finding it difficult to control his emotions. *Have to tread carefully,* she thought. 'How did it happen?'

The ship lurched once more and Davey took a seat behind her.

'Well, we don't like to talk about it really. Especially not in front of Lieutenant Murray.' He took a deep breath. 'Madame Georgiana was a very beautiful, kind lady, and he loved her very much.'

There was a high-pitched whistle from the brass speaker.

'Engineering engage thrust turbines and commence deployment of the afterburners. Passengers to take to the acceleration couches,' said the Captain.

Instantly, metal shutters slid down over the windows and the furniture rearranged itself around them. Tables and chairs folded away and back into wooden cabinets and the leather couches lined up in rows.

Davey looked nervously towards the bridge. 'I'll tell you later,' he said, helping Lyra to strap herself in. 'Best if you stay quiet for now.'

Other members of the crew, including Murray and Cobham, came down the spiral staircase and took to their seats. Lyra shrank down in her chair, hiding behind Davey's bulk.

'What's happening?' she whispered.

'The best bit,' he replied with a wink. 'We're going to go very fast.'

The Captain began to count down from five and when he reached zero, Lyra felt her body being pressed into the cushioning as the ship accelerated.

65

PANDEMIC

Chapter House, London. 1982.

There were more patients arriving every hour.

The first ten floors of the Chapter House were now connected to hospital wards from the Crimea, each of their beds were occupied.

'We're going to need more,' Alixia demanded of her husband who was carrying a stack of bed pans up the grand staircase.

'I've instructed the Draconians to add the Royal from 1935. There was a new wing opening to combat the rise in tuberculosis. Should provide us with at least another hundred beds.'

Alixia frowned at him. 'Where's your mask?'

'In my pocket,' he said, putting down the metal pans and pulling a beak-like mask out from the inside of his long silk housecoat. 'It itches my beard and it makes me look like a plague-doctor.'

'Still better than catching the virus,' she reminded him.

The wards were full of guild members who'd been working in the present. Once it was clear how rapidly the virus was replicating, the founder initiated an emergency quarantine and ordered everyone back to the relative safety of the Chapter House circa 1982. Level seven protocols dictated that they would spend forty-eight hours in isolation before they could be allowed to leave.

Alixia had considered studying medicine when she was younger. There was a time, before she specialised in extinction curation, where she had toyed with the idea of becoming a doctor like her mother.

But temporal medicine involved more than just learning how to diagnose and treat; there was the paradox of losing patients to illnesses that would become curable within decades, and yet not be able to save them.

Something she found impossible to bear.

Caitlin walked out of one of the wards carrying a sealed bag of personal effects. She was dressed in the starched white and blue uniform of a nurse from the mid-nineteenth century.

'We've had another positive case,' she said solemnly, handing the bag to a passing orderly.

'Who?' asked Alixia.

Caitlin peeled off her paper mask. 'A Scriptorian, Rodrigo Alvira. He worked at the National Palace Library in Mafra. I've alerted Doctor Shika, they're taking him to stasis now.'

Alixia grimaced, Mafra was close to where she was born in Lisbon. 'How bad is it?'

Caitlin looked down at her notes. 'Cases in Portugal have risen thirty per cent in the last day, that's lower than the global average.'

'Not low enough,' replied Alixia through gritted teeth. 'We need to get this under control.'

'The US has relaxed the patent restrictions on the vaccine,' Caitlin added, trying to stay positive. 'The European pharma companies are already scaling up production.'

'It may be too late. Is there any sign that it's slowing down in America?'

'No, in fact they're showing the worst stats of all.'

Alixia scowled. 'I think you should take Zachary back to 1880, it's not safe for you to work here.'

Caitlin shook her head. 'You need all the help you can get.'

'Not if it puts you and your son in danger. Have you had any news from Josh?'

'Not a word — which is usually a good sign.'

Alixia sighed. 'Let's hope so, for all our sakes.'

66

NIGHTMARES

Shadow Realm.

The Grand Seer drew a circle in chalk around them and added warding glyphs at each of the main points of the compass.

'Does that actually work?' asked Rufius, staring down at the symbols.

'This isn't an entirely physical realm,' said Kelly getting back to his feet. 'The texts I have studied on the Old King say that he practised a deep, primordial magic when he created this world, something that I should be able to use in our defence. Not everything requires a physical force to be repelled.'

Josh stared at the approaching darkness. The inky fog folded in on itself as it rolled towards them over the broken landscape. Blinking to clear his vision, he tried to unsee the shapes of nightmarish creatures forming inside the cloud.

Benoir returned from the far side of the bridge, carrying a pair of boots.

'The bridge is broken, it leads nowhere, but I found these,' he said, holding them up. 'They're Lyra's.'

'We're running out of options,' said Rufius, turning to Kelly. 'Can you find her with those?' He pointed to her shoes.

'Faith, as you say, there's small choice in rotten apples,' quoted the Grand Seer studying the rapidly approaching storm.

Josh looked at Rufius who simply shrugged his shoulders as if to say *have you got any better ideas?*

He reached out with his mind, sensing the chaos approaching, searching for a coherent timeline, but there was nothing, just a haze of disconnected moments, echoes of past lives.

The world around them was built from redundant parts of time, a pastiche of the past, like random pages from an old scrapbook. Lacking the stability of the continuum, the discarded remnants had been stitched together with something intangible; as Kelly had said, a dark energy flowed under everything.

This was a world of ghosts.

Suddenly, an old man strode out from the boiling gloom surrounded by a flock of ravens. He leaned heavily on a tall staff while holding a lantern in his other hand. A cowl shrouded his head, keeping his face in shadow. Fiery red eyes burned from beneath it and Josh shivered at the intensity of their glare, this was the Lord of Shadows, that one that Kelly had spoken of, the creator of this world.

'Guys,' he said, unable to look away from the approaching figure, 'are you seeing this?' There was a small part of him that wondered if he was hallucinating.

'The Old King,' Kelly whispered reverentially. 'It seems we've attracted some rather unwanted attention — quickly, everyone inside the circle!'

'Can we leave now?' demanded Rufius, stepping quickly over the line of chalk. 'This place is beginning to get on my wick.'

With a flick of his staff, the Old King sent the ravens ahead of him.

The flock of birds wheeled around the perimeter of chalk like a black hurricane, their screeches drowning out any chance of speech.

Kelly pulled something from inside his feathered cloak and blew on it until it caught fire. The flames were an odd shade of purple tinged with blue. They curled around his fingers as he waved his hand in short arcs, making light trails in the air.

The black wings melted into a continuous wall of night, but Kelly continued to weave the ribbons of fire until Josh could see the shape it was taking. An arched doorway began to solidify between the lines of light.

The hand of the Old King broke through the wall, and holding the lantern out before him, he stepped out of the darkness and into their circle. His lamp burned with a similar hue to Kelly's hands. Dark tendrils that Josh had mistaken for a beard began to twist out towards them.

'Hell is empty and all the devils are here,' the Grand Seer murmured, making the final touches to the ethereal door.

'Gentlemen, I believe it is time to go,' he added, taking the boots from Benoir and throwing them through the doorway. 'Wherever young Lyra is now, we shall duly follow.'

With a bow to the Old King, he stepped lightly through the portal, followed quickly by the others.

67

GEORGIANA

HMS Intrepid, China. 1914

According to the Captain, the *Intrepid* was now travelling at over a hundred miles an hour, which he announced proudly as they reached 'cruising speed', forty-two thousand feet above sea level. After the initial acceleration, which Lyra found rather exhilarating, everyone unbuckled their harnesses and went about their business.

Davey waited for Cobham and Murray to leave before showing Lyra to his quarters.

It was a small luxurious cabin, with lacquered mahogany panels and velvet-covered chairs. The bed was turned down and a small leather valise sat on the dressing table. *An unusually delicate bag for such a big man*, Lyra noted as he closed the door behind them.

'You should be safe in here,' he said, taking off his jacket and hanging it on the only chair. 'I can bring you food later. The others will dine with the Captain, I'm never invited.'

She sat down on the bed and took off her boots. Blisters were forming on both heels and she cursed herself for leaving her own pair in the Shadow Realm.

'You were going to tell me about Madame Georgiana?' she said, tucking her legs under her skirt.

Davey turned up the gas lamps, seemingly ignoring her question. When they were all lit, he sat down in the chair and clasped his hands together in his lap.

'We were on a mission in Serbia,' he began, 'on the trail of a strzyga. Do you know what that is?'

Lyra knew very well what it was, but shook her head nonetheless.

He grimaced and took a deep breath before continuing. 'The peasants called them "Vampyr" because they have two sets of teeth, one hidden behind the other, but they're not, they're demons who've taken possession of the dead. We were sent to a village, Kisilova it was called. A man named Petar Blagojević had died, followed by nine others shortly after — each one drained of blood.'

And all of their memories to boot, thought Lyra. Strzyga fed off the lives of others, drinking the blood of their victims was one of the easiest ways to access their lifelines.

'The local priest had the body of Blagojević dug up, by the time we arrived he'd burned it and scattered the ashes into a nearby river.'

Lyra was confused. 'So you were too late?'

Davey shook his head, tears welling in his eyes. 'The killing continued, the lieutenant was convinced the demon had simply changed hosts. Georgiana volunteered to interview the villagers, convinced that she would be able to sense the strzyga and single it out.'

He took out a large handkerchief and wiped his face.

'On the third day, we were questioning a family of farmers who lived on the outskirts of town. They had lost their eldest son to the demon and were very afraid. In fact the whole town was hysterical, groups of men were patrolling the village at night with pitchforks and torches. If they had known who Murray really was, I think they would have put a stake through his heart without a second thought.'

'Does that actually work? I've always wondered.'

'No.'

'Sorry, carry on with the story,' Lyra said.

'The farmer was an old man with a young wife and three other children. We took them in one at a time to speak to the Madame in the vestry of their church. It was Murray's idea, thinking that it would immediately put the demon off guard. We assumed that it had moved into another adult, but we were wrong. Georgiana spoke to each in turn, alone, until it was the turn of their youngest daughter. She couldn't have been more than ten-years-old. When no one come out after twenty minutes we went in.'

Tears were now rolling down his cheeks.

'There was blood everywhere, and her body was ripped open, like a wolf had attacked her.'

'It was the girl?'

He nodded. 'Murray dispatched her on the spot. I've never seen him so angry. The demon bated him as he killed it. Used names for him that only Georgiana would know. It was like it had eaten her soul.'

Pretty close, thought Lyra.

68

GHAST

Xenobiology Laboratory. Present Day.

M elanie frowned at the screen, the three-dimensional model rotating on the display didn't make any sense. She paused the programme, reset the parameters and stepped slowly through the sequence again, watching as the virus attached itself to the host cell and the immune response that followed.

'Are you sure they stole the right one?' she asked, turning to Kaori, who was also studying the results.

Doctor Shika picked up the vial and studied the label. 'Yes, unless they mislabelled it in the lab.'

'Is it working in your model?'

Kaori shook her head. 'Nope.'

'So the Americans haven't cracked it,' Melanie muttered under her breath. She knew that she shouldn't feel relieved, that this was terrible news for all those that thought they were safely vaccinated.

'They've not solved the temporal instability,' Kaori observed. 'The mutation rate is too fast.'

'So how did Cooper get it past the FDA?'

The doctor shrugged and got up from her workstation. 'Presidential order. The military probably argued that there wasn't time to follow the usual clinical trials process. After Boston they could pretty much write their own cheques.'

'But it doesn't work.'

Kaori went to the coffee machine and returned with two dark espressos. 'But ours will, and the US have mobilised a massive pharmaceutical machine to produce the fake vaccine in abundance. All we need to do is find the answer and then give them the fix.'

Melanie sighed taking the cup. 'And let Cooper take all the credit.'

It was Kaori's turn to frown. 'Is that why you're doing this?'

'No,' Melanie snapped. 'Of course not, but I've been shafted before and it's not something I wanted to go through again.'

'You will know what you did,' Kaori reassured her. 'Fred will know too. What more do you need? History has a terrible memory. Unless you're a mass murderer or an Elizabethan playwright you've little chance of immortality.'

Melanie was growing to like the diminutive doctor. Her perspective was refreshingly quirky and her department was by far the most advanced lab she'd ever worked in.

'So, what's next?'

Kaori wound her long black hair into a bun and jammed a pen through it to secure it in place.

'I think you deserve a break. There's something I've been wanting to show you.'

Melanie glanced back to her screen. 'What about the vaccine?'

'Remember we are working in a null time field. No time has passed outside of it.'

'That's still a pretty hard concept to get my head around,' she said, getting up from her chair and grabbing her jacket. 'Feels like cheating.'

'You get used to it,' Kaori said with a smile.

The Hall of the Non-Corporeal was colder than Antarctica, but the thermal gear that Kaori insisted Melanie wear made it bearable.

Snowflakes fell from the distant ceiling, carpeting the floor with white.

'Gynaephora,' Kaori's voice explained through the speaker embedded in her hood. 'A distant relative of the arctic moth.'

Melanie scooped up a handful of ice in her glove and studied the crystals as they melted. Small wings dissolved in front of her eyes.

'Are they invisible?' she asked.

'To our visual frequencies, yes. We find that the cold slows them down, as with many of our non-corporeal specimens.'

The hall was a vast space with a high, vaulted ceiling. Around the walls stood large glass display cases filled with ice sculptures of monstrous creatures, like a frozen aquarium of nightmares.

Following Doctor Shika across the soft white floor, they approached one of the exhibits.

It was a shark-like creature, three times the size of anything the natural world could offer. The body was shaped from glass, allowing every internal structure to be studied.

'Is it alive?' asked Melanie, leaning towards it.

Kaori put a hand out to hold her back. 'Yes, but not in any sense that you would call life. This is a nethershark, one of the first specimens ever captured. Doctor Dangerfield nearly died bringing this one back.'

'Back from where?'

Kaori sighed, her breath turning to a white cloud as it left her mouth.

'There's a realm beyond the borders of the time continuum, we call it the Maelstrom. For many years we believed it was a chaotic space devoid of life, until the first attack.' Kaori lowered her eyes. 'A lot of Draconians have died protecting us from the monsters that have evolved in that realm.'

'Including Fred's father?'

The doctor nodded. 'The Draconians formed an elite guard specifically to combat breaches in the chronosphere. His father was a commander in the Dreadnoughts. There was an incident during the Second Punic War, a horde of monads broke through and attacked

Hannibal and his Carthaginian army at Saguntum. Wolfbeard died sealing the breach, but his sacrifice saved most of his squad in the process. His death was one of the reasons Doctor Dangerfield created the Xenobiology department, to study the monsters and learn their weaknesses.'

Melanie looked around the hall. 'How many species are there?'

Kaori sighed. 'There's no way to know. The Egyptians have a symbol for it, *Heh*, it just means "more than can be counted", another way of saying infinite.'

'And you've been into this Maelstrom?'

The doctor nodded. 'I have my very own memento,' she said, a white aura glowing around her. 'There was an accident, I was lucky to survive. Ophelia saved me.'

The shape coalesced into the ghostly form of a reptilian creature, horns and spikes studded its head and back.

'She's a form of ghast. The Japanese call them *Ikiryō*, a living spirit.'

Melanie took a step back, watching as the creature solidified around Kaori.

'Does it communicate with you?'

'It's more a sensation than actual thought. She feeds off my dreams at night, which can be a little disturbing, but you get used to it.'

The shape faded away like smoke, and Kaori's face beamed through the fur-lined hood. 'Would you like to see the rest of the freak show?'

Melanie was mulling something over and was only half-listening. 'Sorry, what did you say?'

'Do you want to see more of my fantastic beasts?'

Shaking her head, Melanie turned towards the exit. 'We need to find an intact egg.'

'An egg?' Kaori began to follow her. 'What for?'

'The amniotic fluid, I think it holds the key.'

69

DISCOVERY

HMS Intrepid, China. 1914

The next morning, Lyra woke to find Lieutenant Murray standing over her.

'Would you care to explain what you are doing on my ship?' he said through gritted teeth. His eyes hidden behind dark glasses.

'I told you I could help,' she replied, rising from the bed and feeling slightly under-dressed in one of Davey's shirts. 'But you wouldn't listen.'

'And I ordered you to stay behind!'

Lyra glared at him. 'I'm not one of your men. I can do as I please!'

He scoffed. 'This is not some pleasure cruise. I should have the Captain throw both of you off the ship.'

Davey was hovering by the door, his head hung low, staring at his shoes.

'It's not his fault,' she said, raising her voice. 'I'm the stowaway.'

Murray turned to the big man. 'You should have told me immediately. What on earth made you think this was a good idea?'

'She's clever b-boss,' Davey said with a slight stutter, something he never had while speaking to her. Murray obviously made the man nervous. 'And she did help us with the dragon, didn't she?'

'Shenlong,' Lyra reminded them. 'Which is the reason I'm here. I think there's someone in Peking who may be able to help her.'

Murray laughed, producing a telegram from his pocket. 'I think you'll find it's too late to help that creature. We've just received word. In the next few days it'll be on its way to the Antarctic.'

Sitting back down on the bed, Lyra read the note twice.

'Why?'

His eyes darkened, and his mouth twisted into a wicked smile. 'Because Shackleton's expedition needed the funds and Antarctica happens to be the perfect place to dump a psychotic three-tonne winged serpent. I'm sure it will be very happy there.'

Murray turned to leave. 'As soon as we dock, I'm putting you on the first train back home.'

She did her best not to cry. The sense of helplessness was overwhelming, never in her life had she ever felt so useless, so weak.

'Who was this man in Peking?' asked Davey, once Murray was gone.

'Someone Crowley told me about,' she said, between sobs. 'A wizard, his name was Song Wuji'

Davey sat down beside her. 'A wizard?'

Lyra nodded, now she said it out loud, it sounded ridiculous, but then again she was sitting next to a werewolf.

She sighed. 'He was my last hope.'

The telegram still in her hand, she read the words again.

++SERPENT BOUND FOR ANTARCTICA++ENDURANCE LEAVES AUG 1ST++STOP

++GOD SAVE THE KING++STOP

'Davey, if I gave you a message, do you think you could get it sent on the telegraph?'

The big man scratched his chin. 'I'm not great at reading and writing.'

'No, I'll write it. You just need to get them to send it.'

He smiled. 'Who are you going to send it to?'

Lyra thought for a moment. She'd once overheard Sim talking about a Draconian telegraphic code, one that was monitored by the Copernican dispatchers — listening for a temporal SOS.

She turned over the telegram and wrote:

TO: WHITEHALL-451
    PEKING 1914-07-30.
    HIC SUNT DRACONES.
    LYRA.

The *Intrepid* made good time to the borders of China. In just over three days the ship covered over eight thousand miles, eventually passing through the snow capped mountains of the Himalayas and over the steppes of Mongolia.

Lyra spent much of the time on the observation deck reading books that Davey 'borrowed' from Murray's personal collection. The lieutenant was absent for most of the day, only reappearing in the evenings to dine with the Captain and discuss tactics with Cobham.

There was little she could do but wait and hope that Benoir would find her soon.

70

PLAGUE

Fort Detrick. Present Day.

The estimated death toll had risen to just over four million.

Cooper insisted that the count be displayed in the command centre as a stark reminder to everyone on his team that this was an existential threat.

The wall of screens displayed a world map with reported outbreaks marked by red dots on most of the continents. The USA was almost totally covered in a miasma of red spots. China and Russia weren't far behind.

No one wanted to admit that the vaccine was failing, but the rate of the spread clearly showed it wasn't effective.

There was mounting pressure for the President to step down.

Fifteen states had declared martial law. The borders were shut, international travel was banned and some governors were making noises about federal restrictions.

The entire country was going into lockdown.

Hospitals were predicting they would run out of beds in less than a week and the police were starting to report looting and civil disorder.

Society was unwinding, anyone with any sense was packing up an RV and heading for the hills.

And so far, the survival rate was zero.

Standing at the back of the command centre, Cooper felt the dull ache at the back of his head begin to throb. The drugs were becoming less effective every day. Even doubling the dose, which he'd been doing for the last few weeks, wasn't working any more.

Lieutenant Miller appeared at the door and saluted.

'What've you got for me?'

'You're going to be called before a grand jury.'

Cooper laughed. 'The country's going to shit and they want to take me to court?'

'Seems like the President is looking for a scapegoat.'

The Colonel rubbed the back of his neck, trying to alleviate the pain that was threatening to overwhelm him. 'There won't be a country to preside over if we don't get this under control.'

Miller looked like a man about to deliver a death sentence.

'And the joint chiefs want answers, they're waiting in the conference room.'

71

THE TRAIN

HMS Intrepid, China. 1914

A day later they were floating above the city of Peking, the crew making ready to dock with the ornate spire that rose out of the city like the Eiffel Tower.

Lyra was told to wait on the observation deck while the crew went about the business of securing the ship. She watched the small figures slipping gracefully down the bow lines towards the iron platform, like the indexers of the Great Library, seeming to have no fear of heights.

She could hear Murray talking to the Captain on the bridge. Lyra hadn't seen him since their last confrontation. They were discussing the protocols around disembarking. It seemed that Duan Qirui, the commander of the Beiyang Army, had ordered all military personnel to remain on the ship, insisting that his own men would escort the "honoured guests" to their destination.

From his tone, Lyra could tell that Murray was not best pleased.

'We don't need babysitters,' he said, cursing under his breath.

'The Republic are still our allies,' the captain reminded him.

'We've been instructed to patrol the eastern border, apparently the Hun are deploying a second front.'

Lyra couldn't hear the reply over the sound of the gantries being lowered into position.

Under the lieutenant's watchful eye, she joined Davey and Cobham as they walked off the ship. The weather took a turn for the worse. Having spent four days above the clouds in bright blue skies, the dark grey world beneath was something of a disappointment.

Representatives of the Chinese authorities were waiting at the end of the gangplank to greet them. Dressed in western clothes, they bowed to their visitors and explained in a polite but insistent way that they were free to roam the city under the watchful eye of a bodyguard.

'For your own protection,' muttered Murray on the way down in the elevator. 'Keeping tabs on us more like.'

When they reached the base of the mooring tower, they were greeted by a Chinese woman in a plain grey tunic. From the way she greeted Murray, Lyra assumed she was from their department.

'Lyra, this is Mai Li,' Davey said, as the woman bowed to her. 'She's one of us.'

Lyra returned the bow. 'Pleased to meet you,' she added in her best Mandarin.

The woman looked impressed. 'The honour is mine,' she replied in perfect English.

'Mai Li will accompany you to the station,' Murray said abruptly. 'She will escort you to Shanghai and see that you get on a steamer back to London.'

'The next ship leaves tomorrow,' added Mai Li taking her by the hand, 'we must hurry if we are to catch it.'

Lyra nodded, it would be easier to slip away once it was just the two of them.

Davey hugged her while the others made arrangements for their bags. 'Don't worry,' he whispered in her ear. 'I will enquire about Song Wuji.'

The bustling streets of Peking were filled with traders and customers bartering over food, silks and spices. It was a riot of colour, smell and sound, which after the relative solitude of the journey made Lyra's head spin.

Mai Li led her through the maze of narrow alleyways until they came to the gatehouse set into the city wall. On the other side of it was Peking Station.

The clock in the ticket hall was showing five minutes to twelve as they joined the long queue.

'Shit,' she uttered under her breath. 'We're going to miss the twelve-twenty at this rate.'

Lyra was attracting a great deal of attention from the other passengers. She realised she was the only westerner in the station, and even the guards were beginning to notice her.

The line moved slowly forward, Mai Li becoming more agitated with every minute that passed.

An officer approached them, with two minions in tow.

'I think we should go,' whispered Lyra, through tight lips.

Mai Li turned towards the guards. 'It's okay, leave this with me.' She stepped out of the line and went over to speak to them.

Standing in the middle of a crowded hall, surrounded by total strangers was a new experience for Lyra. Their lives were closed to her. It was the most lonely feeling, hundreds of people staring at her, their eyes filled with questions about who she was and what she was doing here.

I should run. She thought, *they would never find me in this crowd. I would just disappear.*

Turning to look for a way out, she noticed the green uniforms of guards at every exit.

Mai Li was having a heated debate with the officer, waving various pieces of paper in his face.

Now, I should go now.

But something held her back.

She was too obvious, stood out too much, she wouldn't get more than thirty yards before they would be on to her.

Without thinking, she reached out to touch the satchel of the woman in front of her, hoping for the merest hint of a timeline, something she could use to move a few hours back but there was nothing.

'Stop that! Come with me,' ordered Mai Li, pulling her by the hand from the line. 'The sergeant is going to help you.' She glowered at the smug-looking officer. 'Even if it costs me a month's wages.'

Billowing clouds of grey steam poured from the locomotive as Mai Li and Lyra ran along the platform.

A shrill whistle sounded from the guard's van as they both leapt onto the steps of the first class carriage, only to find it filled with gap-toothed peasants and their animals.

'The glorious revolution,' Mai Li muttered under her breath as they forced their way through the compartment and into the next car.

The train jolted into motion as they took their seats. Lyra watched the station slide past the soot-stained window and wondered how long it would take to get to Shanghai.

Mai Li took off her jacket and folded it up into a makeshift pillow. 'Might as well get comfortable,' she said. 'It's going to be a long night.'

The rocking of the train lulled Lyra into a troubled sleep. Her dreams were filled with snatches of Crowley's memories — half-remembered moments of his travels through Asia, glimpses of ancient temples, abandoned palaces and dark-eyed shamans.

72

TOMBS

Mausoleum of the First Qin Emperor. 208BC

Rufius woke to find himself lying on cold stone, the screeching of ravens still ringing in his ears, and an unsavoury brackish taste in his mouth as if he'd eaten ashes.

'Kelly you damn fool,' he muttered, getting slowly to his feet.

It was dark and although the starless sky looked strange, he assumed it was night. Taking his tachyon from his waistcoat, Rufius switched on the torch and shone it into the darkness. The beam lit up columns and bronze statues on four sides of a square; he was standing in the courtyard of an ancient palace. The style reminded him of the Qin dynasty, carved dragons and phoenixes stared down at him from the pagoda roofs, their mouths holding seals of office.

There was no sign of the others.

He sniffed the air, it smelled old and stale like a tomb, and it was too quiet, no sound of birds or beasts to be heard.

Everything about this place felt wrong.

Cursing Kelly again for his ridiculous theatrics, Rufius made his way towards the nearest gate in one of the vast walls.

. . .

Josh felt as if something heavy was sitting on his chest. Rubbing his ribs, he sat up and winced at the pain. He'd cracked a rib before, climbing trees with Gossy when they were kids. His mother had been so angry, she hadn't let him out for a month. It was odd to think now he done it again, but this time from the tail of a dinosaur.

Gritting his teeth, Josh got slowly to his feet. Taking shallow breaths, he took out his tachyon and switched on the torch.

The corridor was full of stone statues.

Soldiers in full armour stared at him with blank eyes, their hands resting on the hilts of their swords. The statues were as tall as he was, with meticulously detailed armour. Their faces were so life-like it was as if they could have been real men inside the clay.

They look Chinese, he thought, touching one of them.

Its timeline confirmed it.

He saw the craftsmen's hands carving the rings of the mail, the small intricate details of the hilt of the sword. The overseer's cane stinging across the man's back when he made a mistake.

It was 208 BC, and this was the mausoleum of the First Emperor of China.

Josh was standing amongst an army of terracotta warriors.

'Hello?' he shouted into the darkness ahead. 'Rufius, Benoir?'

Benoir shook the dust out of his hair and rubbed his face.

It was pitch black and for a moment, he wondered if he'd gone blind.

His hands found the wall, and running his fingers along the coarse surface he teased out its chronology. The stone was old, more than three billion years. Its time-line spoke of metamorphosed island-arc igneous rock, which placed him somewhere in the tectonic region of Northern China .

There was a noise from somewhere ahead of him and he flattened himself against the stone.

A glow of light illuminated a door and Benoir relaxed as the unmistakable figure of Rufius came marching through it.

'Have you seen the others?'

Benoir shook his head.

'Do you know where we are?'

'China.'

Rufius scratched at his beard. 'Feels like a tomb. Only one thing I can think of that would be this size — the mausoleum of the First Emperor, Qin Shi Huang.'

'Why would Lyra come here?'

Rufius grunted. 'I'm not sure she has, that madman could have taken us anywhere.'

'She's here,' said Kelly, silently moving into the light.

Both Rufius and Benoir started at his sudden appearance. 'Where the hell have you been?' Rufius snapped. 'And what the devil are we doing here?'

The Grand Seer ignored his tone and whispered something as he drew a sign in the air between them.

Torches burst into flame around them, lighting up the entire complex.

They were standing in a courtyard. In the centre a shimmering silver lake reflected the glow of the torches on to a distant ceiling of glittering stars.

'Quicksilver,' said Kelly.

'Mercury?' asked Benoir, walking over to the edge. 'What is it doing here?'

'The alchemists of the first Emperor believed it had the power to extend life,' explained Kelly, coming over to join him. 'Although it most likely hastened his demise.'

Rufius huffed, picked up a rock and threw it into the silver pool. 'What has this got to do with Lyra?'

Kelly shrugged. 'I've no idea. I simply followed the path.'

'Where's Joshua?' asked Benoir.

73

SHANGHAI

Shanghai Station, China. 1914

When Lyra awoke, night had fallen and the world beyond the train was cloaked in darkness. It took her a moment to realise that they were stationary, and that Mai Li was gone.

In fact the entire carriage was empty.

She got to her feet and walked along the compartment to the exit.

Looking out of the window she could see the passengers lined up on the platform, soldiers with guns were searching their belongings. Blinking to clear her vision, she searched their faces looking for any sign of Mai Li, but she wasn't among them.

Suddenly a hand grasped her shoulder and dragged her back into the coach.

Before she could cry out, a hand clasped over her mouth.

'Be quiet or you'll get us both killed,' whispered Mai Li in her ear. 'They're looking for you.'

'Why?' Lyra mumbled from behind Mai Li's hand.

'I don't know.' She took her hand away. 'Maybe the officer I bribed grew a conscience, or got a better offer. You're worth quite a lot to certain interested parties.'

Raised voices were followed by a single pistol shot, stopping their conversation abruptly.

'Shit!' Mai Li cursed as the sounds of boots came towards them. 'One of the passengers must have told them.'

She pulled Lyra down the carriage and into one of the private compartments.

'We can't stay here, it's not safe.'

Lyra could feel her heart hammering in her chest, without her gifts she'd never felt so vulnerable in her life.

Mai Li sighed. 'I'm going to have to take you back.'

'How?' Lyra asked, looking around for another way out.

The woman took something from around her neck and wrapped it around her hand. Lyra could make out a series of charms on a silver chain, but not what was inside Mai Li's fist.

'I have a talent,' she began, taking hold of Lyra's hand. 'I can move between places. I'm not supposed to use it unless it's an emergency, but I think this counts as one.'

With that she closed her eyes and the carriage disappeared.

Bell Tower, Peking. 1914

The next moment they were standing in a basement vault, surrounded by statues of fierce-looking Chinese lions.

Lyra stumbled and put her hand out to steady herself. Mai Li caught it before she touched one of the stone guardians.

'Shishi don't like to be touched,' she said in a whisper, as if they were listening.

'Where are we?' asked Lyra, regaining her balance.

'Headquarters,' Mai Li said, unravelling the necklace from her hand and hanging it around her neck. Lyra caught a quick glimpse of a silver talisman before it disappeared under the woman's tunic.

'We're back in Peking?'

Mai Li nodded and walked out through an arched doorway.

'Wait!' Lyra ran to catch her up. 'How did you do that?'

She had a good idea how, but thought that was probably the kind of question a linear would ask after being transported eight hundred miles in the blink of an eye.

Outside of the lion's den, a tunnel stretched away in two directions. The curving walls were built from intricate blocks of sandstone with ancient symbols carved into each of them.

'I told you, I can move,' snapped Mai Li, clearly unwilling to go into detail. She marched with her head down towards a doorway at the far end.

'But, how?' Lyra continued, playing the part of an awestruck idiot. 'I mean, that was amazing!'

Mai Li shrugged her shoulders. 'We're all special in our own way.'

Lyra wondered if she was a latent; someone with temporal abilities that the Order had overlooked. Perhaps with a limited range, one that was so slight as to have gone undetected. *She can move*, teleportation or telekinesis, whichever it was Lyra was very thankful for it.

Before she could ask another question the door ahead of them opened and Murray stepped through.

His eyes narrowed at the sight of the two of them walking towards him.

'They were looking for us,' Mai Li said in way of explanation. 'I had no choice.'

Lyra assumed that she was referring to the government, but there was something in her tone that spoke of something else.

'It's no matter,' Murray said, ushering them through the opening. 'In fact it may be rather fortuitous. There's been a complication with our mission. I need your assistance.'

It took a moment for Lyra to realise he was talking to her.

'Me?'

He nodded. 'The demon has asked for you personally. Lyra Cousineau. I assume that's your real name? Although it also referred to you as a "Daughter of Time". Which may mean something to you?'

Lyra's brow furrowed as she tried to think of any reason for a so-called demon to name her.

'What does it look like?'

Murray's expression hardened, pointing to an iron-bound door a few yards from where they stood. 'See for yourself. We've restrained it, the priest is on his way, but until then all ideas are welcome.'

Something had changed in his manner towards her, he seemed anxious as he opened the porthole in the cell door.

Cobham was strapped to a heavy chair bolted to the floor, his arms bound with manacles and a leather strap between his teeth.

He was raving like a madman.

'The demon left the host. Cobham was too slow to defend himself.'

They had removed his legs, a pair of powerful mechanical limbs were set to one side. *Well, that explains his ability to leap so high*, thought Lyra.

'Daughter of time!' Cobham screamed from behind the gag. Rocking back and forth in the chair.

A chill ran down Lyra's spine.

'Abandon,' she whispered.

'You know its name?' Murray said, unable to keep the excitement from his voice. 'Can you help him?'

Lyra nodded. 'Bring me a mirror, a long one and some charcoal. Oh, and a hammer.'

74

WERNER'S THEOREM

Copernicus Hall. 1580.

S im stood in the Map Room, watching the numbers on the brass tumblers spinning rapidly, counting the death toll in real time.

The total was edging ever closer towards a hundred million.

Although there was a quarantine zone around the Frontier, news was reaching them of the general decline in social order. Except in dictatorships such as China, most democratic societies were descending into chaos. A lack of food and clean water had led to riots and looting of the supermarkets, which without a global supply chain were unable to meet the demand.

The army were being deployed to protect government buildings and essential infrastructure. The city centres were deemed no-go areas after the breakdown of the healthcare system, and there were now bodies lying in the streets.

In under two weeks many countries had reverted back to a feudal system, with towns and villages barricading themselves from outsiders. Trying to fend for themselves, there were reports of bandit-like raids on supply trucks by desperate people armed with home-made weapons.

. . .

Professor Eddington stood beside Sim, his usual stoic expression replaced with one of real concern.

'Werner's theorem seems to have failed,' he muttered to himself, referring to one of the most respected members of their Guild.

Gustaf Werner's models predicted that the proliferation of the virus would slow once societies introduced lockdown procedures and ceased all international travel, but if anything, the spread was accelerating — especially in areas like the USA that were supposed to have initiated a vaccine programme.

'Are we going to reset the timeline?' Sim asked, knowing that this was the option of last resort in such situations. It was something that had never happened in his lifetime.

His mentor nodded. 'The High Council are debating that as we speak. I have proposed a number of temporal scenarios, the obvious adjustment would be to intervene at 1914. Ensure that the *Endurance* never made it to Antarctica.'

'Why not simply adjust Colonel Cooper's timeline? Leave the virus buried in the ice.'

Eddington grimaced as the counter broke through the hundred million. 'And leave it to be discovered in another hundred years? No, the most prudent thing to do is to intercept the *Endurance* en route. The xenobiologysts are already preparing a containment chamber for the host. The rest of the world will believe the ship sunk without trace, another failed mission, one of many.'

'And Shackleton and his men?'

'Better twenty souls are lost in a storm than a hundred million die of the plague,' the Professor said, turning away. 'We must prepare for the intervention. If you would be so kind as to bring me your notes on the voyage we can calculate the coordinates for the intercept.'

75

THE MIRROR

Bell Tower, Peking. 1914

L yra stood before the prisoner as Murray removed his gag.
Behind her was a tall mirror, covered in a black cloth as per her instructions.

Cobham's eyes were dark, and black bile stained his chin. His mouth opened, widening until it made a horrible cracking sound as the jaw distorted.

'DAUGHTER OF TIME,' came a sound like many voices speaking at once from somewhere inside the dark maw. 'I HAVE WONDERED HOW LONG IT WOULD BE UNTIL WE MET AGAIN.'

Lyra ignored him, waiting for the others to leave before turning to the mirror and pulling off the cover.

It took a while to remember the correct sequence of runes the Grand Seer had taught her. On the glass she'd drawn the magical symbols designed to break the boundaries between this world and the Shadow Realm. She made the final glyph with a blackened finger and they all began to vibrate making the surface shimmer.

The reflection revealed his true face. An old man with fiery red eyes, his long beard writhing with snake-like tentacles.

'Abandon,' she spoke his name calmly.

Cobham's body tensed, shaking and rocking the chair back and forward.

'YOU DARE TO CHALLENGE ME! I GAVE YOU SUCH A GIFT!'

'It was a curse!' Lyra replied, keeping her gaze on the mirror as the background darkened.

'THAT YOU HAVE LOST! MANY WOULD HAVE GIVEN THEIR IMMORTAL SOULS FOR SUCH POWER.'

Lyra thought about Crowley, driven mad by his desire for immortality. 'It would have destroyed me, such power is not meant for mortals.'

'HAH! YOU HAVE NO IDEA WHAT YOU ARE CAPABLE OF! TOO AFRAID TO LOOK BEYOND YOUR OWN DEMISE!'

He seemed to rise out of the chair.

'LET ME SHOW YOU.'

The temperature in the room dropped, her breath turning to ice on the surface of the glass. She felt his mind reaching out towards hers.

Lyra knew it would come, he wouldn't be able to resist possessing her.

As the image cleared in the mirror, she saw Cobham's body go limp, the demon lord walking towards her, his eyes on fire.

'No,' she said, calmly taking a hammer from her pocket. 'Let me show you!' With that she hit the mirror.

Abandon howled as the glass cracked, trapping him inside the fractured portal, Lyra struck it once again, smashing it until it was nothing but shards of glass scattered around her feet.

Murray and Davey rushed in at the sound of the commotion.

'Is he gone?', the Lieutenant asked, checking Cobham for a pulse.

Lyra nodded, handing Davey the hammer. 'He's back where he belongs.'

'How did you know what to do?' asked Davey looking at the broken mirror.

'It's a long story, but I think he's responsible for the demons you've been fighting. There is a world beyond this, filled with unspeakable things.'

Davey nodded. 'Hell.'

'Well, that's one name for it I suppose,' Lyra replied.

Night was falling and standing on the upper terrace of the Bell Tower. Lyra watched the lanterns flickering in the city streets below.

'We'll be leaving on the *Intrepid* tomorrow,' Murray said. 'If you would care to join us?'

Lyra shook her head. 'Thank you, but no. I'm looking for some-one. He was once the Emperor's alchemist. Song Wuji.'

The Lieutenant looked at her blankly, but Mai Li nodded. 'I know of him, or rather the legend.'

'Do you know where he is?'

'If the myth is to be believed he's imprisoned with the Emperor inside the Forbidden City, but it will be difficult to get in, the palace is surrounded by the Revolutionary Guard.'

'But you could move me there?'

Mai Li looked over towards the walls of the Grand Imperial Palace. 'I could, but it would be certain death for you. The Manchurian banner men still guard the Emperor, they will cut you down the moment you appear.'

Lyra paused for a moment, considering her options. 'I think I have an idea.'

76

SONG WUJI

Forbidden City, Peking, China. 1914

L yra controlled her breathing and kept her eyes tightly shut. Instinctively, she reached out with her mind, trying to sense the environment around her, but it was no use, there was nothing but the smell of sweat and steel. Even without her seer's abilities it was obvious there were soldiers surrounding her.

She was lying face down on a soft-pile rug, her hands and feet bound tightly with a cord behind her back.

There was a quiet hush about the room, as if everyone was holding their breath.

As they planned, Mai Li delivered her and disappeared without a word. A gift-wrapped prisoner was much less of a threat, especially a blond-haired western girl in a kimono. Nothing could be more harmless or unusual to the Imperial Guard.

Her gamble seemed to be paying off, no one had killed her so far.

Slowly, she opened one eye.

The guards stood around her like statues, their swords lowered towards her. Lyra tried not to focus on the unwavering points of steel held inches from her face and concentrate' on the small figure of a man that stood behind them.

'Where am I?' she asked in English, before repeating it in Mandarin. Lyra knew full well where she was, but it seemed the most logical question to ask.

'In the Palace of Eternal Longevity,' the small man replied. 'I am truly fascinated to learn how you came to be here?'

'Who are you?'

Placing his hands together the man stepped forward and bowed his head slightly. 'I am Master Wuji. Grand Sorcerer to the Lord of Ten Thousand Years.'

He was wearing the most beautiful embroidered uniform, adorned with golden dragons on a sea of blue and green flowers. The ceremonial rank badge of a high court official.

'Master Wuji!' Lyra exclaimed, trying to turn over and failing. 'I was sent by the spirit dragon, Shenlong.'

The steely eyes of the guards showed no sign of understanding. These were Manchurian banner men and Manchu was the official language of the court, not Mandarin.

The old man smiled and signalled to the guards to put away their weapons.

With one swift movement the men sheathed their swords and stepped back. Their captain took out a dagger and sliced through Lyra's bonds.

Master Wuji shuffled forward, his long silk robes hiding his feet so it appeared as if he were gliding across the lacquered floor.

The man's face was heavily lined, his skin like rice paper. The white hair of his beard was plaited into a long tail, with delicate threads of gold woven through it. His eyes were a deep brown, they were kind, knowing, eyes that seemed to be able to see into her soul.

'Mistress Lyra?' he said in English, with a small bow. 'A thousand apologies, please forgive my men.'

Rubbing the feeling back into her fingers, Lyra gasped when the man lowered his head, the star shaped tattoo clearly visible on his bald pate.

'It is you,' she said.

He straightened and touched his hands to his forehead. 'I have been waiting a long time to meet you. Come let us talk in more comfortable surroundings.'

She followed him out of the golden hall and into a labyrinth of small passages, each one decorated with intricate illustrations of mythological beasts.

'You must excuse my guards,' he said in perfect English. 'The world beyond the walls of the palace is not as it once was, the revolution has created fear and suspicion in those loyal to the Emperor.'

Lyra had learned a little of Chinese history on the flight. She knew that Emperor Aisin-Gioro Puyi was only six when he was forced to abdicate in 1912, bringing to an end two-thousand years of imperial rule.

Wuji paused in front of an ornately carved wooden door and took out a small golden key. 'This is my sanctuary,' he said, turning the key in a hidden lock.

Inside, was his own private museum, a cabinet of curiosities collected over hundreds, if not thousands, of years.

The objects were beautifully presented in velvet-lined cabinets, each displayed with a simple card with a single Chinese character drawn onto it.

He sat down beside a low table set out with a tea service.

She sat cross-legged on the opposite side from him as he began to whisk the teapot.

'You knew I was coming?'

'I saw you in a dream,' he said, pouring steaming water into the pot. 'The world was dying.'

'A pandemic,' she agreed. 'I saw it too.'

He sighed. 'Sadly, I have lived through more than one plague, although this may be worse than all that have come before.'

Lyra wished she could read his timeline, wondering what it would be like to have experienced the rise and fall of an empire.

'How old are you?' she asked.

Song Wuji's eyes glazed over for a moment. 'I was born in the year of the Metal Ox, in your terms 259 BC. The second son of a magistrate, I spent my youth as most men do in the pursuit of women and status. When I was old enough, I was sent to the Imperial Academy at Xianyang, where I studied under Master Xu Fu. My dream was to become an explorer and join the search for the elixir of immortality, but the First Emperor, Qin Shi Huang, had other plans.'

The old man poured the tea into two bone china cups and presented one to Lyra, which she took with a nod of gratitude.

'I spent the next twenty years in his court, apprenticed to his alchemists, while Xu Fu took others to search for Mount Penglai and its immortals. I rose to the rank of upper first within his court and enjoyed the eight privileges that came with it. I had quite resigned myself to spend my days in service to his majesty, until the day they brought me the egg.'

'Shenlong's egg,' noted Lyra, putting down her cup.

Song Wuji's eyes narrowed a little, his pupils darkening. 'The dragon has given you her name, that is a great honour.'

'She told me to find you. She needs your help.'

He bowed his head, showing the star to her once more. 'Now this is not the reason you came to me. Is it? You must forgive my directness, but I fear I have little time left.'

Lyra told him about Crowley and what happened at the loch. She avoided too much detail about the Order, focusing more on the events of the last few days. Wuji listened intently, his inscrutable expression revealing no sign of whether he believed her story.

'I remember this man, Crowley. His was a tortured soul.'

'He said that you took away his burden. He was a seer like me.'

Song Wuji tilted his head to one side and then the other. His eyes glazing over. 'It is true that surviving the dragon's curse does more than extend one's life.'

Lyra bit her lip and tried to hold back the tears, but they came all the same.

'You have lost your gift?' he added.

'I thought it was what I wanted,' she said, the tears flowing over her cheeks. 'To be normal. To not have the burden of seeing their fates, but it's like looking at the world through a window. I can't feel anything.' Lyra held out her hand, palm first. 'It's as though I'm behind an invisible wall.'

The old man nodded, rising up from the floor in one gracious movement. 'This is the sacrifice that one must make to be mortal, to live each day as if it were the last. I too have wished many times for such release, but we were chosen for a greater purpose.'

'Can you help me?'

He smiled. 'Not I, for I did not take it from you.'

'Shenlong?'

The old man nodded.

Lyra felt frustration and anger building inside her. 'How am I supposed to do that? They've locked her up in a cage and Lieutenant Murray told me they're shipping her off to the South Pole!'

Wuji sat absentmindedly stroking his long white beard with one hand.

'In the present, yes, but you have all of time at your command, do you not?'

Lyra shook her head. 'Not any more.'

'Have you tried?'

She nodded.

He rose and shuffled slowly over to an apothecary's cabinet made from hundreds of tiny drawers. After a few minutes of searching, he produced a piece of iridescent shell hung on a silver chain.

'When the Emperor was brought the egg, the alchemists spent many weeks trying to break into it. Their sharpest tools could not scratch it, not even diamond would leave a mark. Yet one day, while I was examining the surface, this piece fell into my hand, like a petal from a flower.'

He handed the small fragment to her and she immediately felt the lines of power weave around her fingers — it resonated with pure chaotic energy.

'You can feel its *Chi*, can't you? I have often wondered if that is what has protected me all of these years. I've worn it around my neck for most of my life, as a reminder of my salvation, a talisman against evil.'

It was as though she was a child once more, feeling the power of the continuum for the first time. The temporal resonances of the tiny flake of shell were like holding an Infinity Engine in the palm of her hand. Strands of light twisted around her fingers and up her forearm leaving fractal patterns on her skin. She felt something awaken within her and probed its timeline with her mind, tentatively unwinding its chronology.

'I can see the egg,' she whispered. 'It's in a tomb?'

'Yes,' Master Wuji said, clapping his hands with delight. 'Crowley took it from the Emperor's Tomb.'

Lyra closed her eyes and focused on the moment and the palace faded away.

77

DEATH

Fort Detrick. Present Day.

The President had been evacuated from the White House and was airborne on Air Force One en-route to the Raven Rock complex in Pennsylvania. It was effectively a city inside a hollowed out mountain built during the Cold War.

The Joint Chiefs had relieved Cooper of his command and replaced him with an emergency committee made up of so-called experts, including Professor Wilks from the CDC.

The vaccine was a total failure, made worse by those who were treated believing they were now immune and breaking the lockdown rules regarding socialising and travel.

The latest estimates gave them less than a week before the majority of the population of the US would be wiped out. It was being called an "extinction level" event.

Cooper sat down at his desk and poured himself a large whisky.

'Now I am become Death,' he whispered, taking out his old Beretta M9 from the drawer and laying it on the desk. It was something that Oppenheimer had quoted after witnessing the first detonation of his atomic bomb.

The Colonel raised his glass to the skull of the dragon, now mounted on a plaque on the opposite wall. It leered at him through hollow eyes.

Throwing back the drink, he poured another.

Opening a metal container he took out the sample of the virus and a syringe, placing it next to his gun. His life had come down to one of two options: a bullet or a lethal virus.

In hindsight, the idea of tracking down the remains of a mystical creature seemed ridiculous, but it was better than nothing, if Wuji had survived, he could too.

When they told him about the cancer, he promised himself he wouldn't end up as a dribbling wreck, *better to go down fighting*, he thought, picking up the syringe.

He'd wanted immortality, and in a weird kind of way he was going to get it, *just not quite what I had in mind.*

78

MAUSOLEUM

Mausoleum of the First Qin Emperor. 208BC

Josh found Lyra sitting on top of a golden sarcophagus, cradling a large egg in her lap while she sang to it.

'You okay?' he asked, climbing the steps that led up to the Emperor's gilded coffin.

'Hi Josh,' she said in a wistful voice, giving him a quirky smile. 'Are the others here?'

Josh frowned. 'Don't you know?'

She shrugged and stroked the egg shell. 'It's complicated. I seemed to have lost my sight. I was hoping it might be in here.'

He was confused, but tried not to show it. The egg looked very similar to the one Josh and Caitlin had found in the Cretaceous.

'Where did you get that?'

'Here,' Lyra said, tapping on a cupola built into the coffin lid. 'From the Emperor's private collection.'

'He collects them?' he asked, looking around the chamber for others.

Placing the egg carefully back inside its holder, she climbed down.

'No, she's the last of her kind. Her name is Shenlong. The Chinese alchemists believed it to be a spirit dragon: "Master of Storms and Bringer of Rain". The Emperor thought it held the secret to eternal life. Which it did, if you were lucky enough to survive the curse it carried.'

'It's a dragon?'

Lyra laughed and gave Josh a hug. 'No silly, it's a dinosaur, dragons don't actually exist, not in this realm at least.'

'And you think it's cursed?'

She nodded. 'I met an old man. Song Wuji, who told me how it nearly killed him, but somehow he survived. He's at least two thousand years old.'

Josh looked around for the others, but they were nowhere to be seen. 'Did he say what kind of curse?'

Lyra shook her head. 'Just that it killed the Emperor, and most of his inner court. They're all sealed up in here.' She looked around the tomb and shivered, suddenly glad she couldn't see their ghosts.

'We need to get out of here,' Josh said, taking her by the arm. 'We've been looking for you. Benoir says that you had a vision about a plague. The Copernicans think it's coming true.'

She shook her head, pointing at the egg. 'I need to free Shenlong. Wuji says that she is the only one that can help me regain my sight.'

Josh touched the egg, his fingers feeling the timelines sliding beneath the outer shell. It was millions of years old and yet still fertile, a dormant life sleeping soundly within. Concentrating harder he felt the subtle signature of some kind of field enveloping it, similar to a stasis loop, holding the fragile embryo in a singular moment.

'I think we should get this back to Doctor Shika,' he said, picking it up. 'She will know what to do with it.'

'No!' Lyra exclaimed, grabbing it from him. 'I need it!'

At that moment, Rufius and Kelly strolled into the tomb.

'Ah there you are,' Rufius's voice boomed across the chamber.

Benoir appeared from behind him and ran towards her, stopping short when he saw the expression on her face and the egg in her arms.

'Are you okay?' he asked, the smile fading from his lips.

'My love,' Lyra replied with large, tear-filled eyes. 'I'm sorry.'

'Sorry? For what.'

She gave the egg back to Josh and went to him, letting Benoir gather her up in his arms and kissing him deeply. It was such a different sensation, to feel his lips on hers without the temptation to read his timeline.

'Where have you been?' he said, whispering in her ear.

Lyra smiled. 'It's a long story. I knew you'd find me eventually. Did Rufius get my telegram?'

He shrugged. 'No, ma cherie. I'm sorry it's taken so long.'

While the others went to inspect the egg, Lyra took Benoir to one side of the dais and explained how Abandon's gift had changed her, how she couldn't bear to be near him for fear of reading his fate and how she lost her sight when they captured the spirit dragon.

He sat on the steps and listened quietly.

'You wanted to lose your gift?' Benoir asked, unable to hide his disbelief.

'I wanted to make you happy.'

'I thought you didn't love me anymore,' he said, his hand brushing against her cheek to wipe away the tears.

'I was scared of what I was becoming,' she said, taking his hand in hers. 'But when I lost my sight — I realised it wasn't the problem. Linears live such limited lives.' She ran her fingers over his palm. 'They're trapped in a world of fleeting moments and physical sensations.' Her eyes lit up, running her other hand through his hair. 'Which has its benefits, but it's like living half a life.'

'And how are you going to get your sight back?'

She looked over to the egg. 'Master Wuji says Shenlong has the power to restore me.'

'We need to get you back home,' he said sternly, standing up. 'There's a plague, just like you saw in your vision.'

She nodded and got to her feet. 'You're going to have to carry me.'

Then turning to the Grand Seer. 'I see you have been travelling the old paths master.'

Kelly nodded. 'Indeed we have.'

Rufius shivered. 'Not something I care to repeat in a hurry.'

She laughed, holding onto Benoir's jacket and taking out his tachyon. 'So we'll take the more traditional route.'

79

EGG

Xenobiology Department. Present Day.

The interior structure of the egg floated above the laboratory table, rotating in a three dimensional holographic model.

Everyone watched the intricate simulation as Doctor Shika manipulated the image to get a better view of the foetus inside.

Melanie was fascinated by the egg itself, which sat on the table surrounded by scanning equipment. The patterning on the outer surface was fractal, similar to the rash patterns on the infected. Its colouring seem to change in the light, like fish scales, reflecting iridescent hues across its surface as her eyes tried to capture it. A star-shaped mark covered the apex of the shell, which glowed repetitively as if linked to the heartbeat of the creature within.

'There's some kind of temporal shielding,' observed Kaori, adjusting the field of view.

Lyra gazed wide-eyed at the creature, it was a perfect miniature of Shenlong, sleeping peacefully inside its time capsule.

'Where did you get this from?' asked Melanie, looking up to the hologram of the interior.

'The tomb of the First Emperor of China,' answered Josh.

'It has all of the same physical characteristics as the creature that attacked Fred in Antarctica.'

'And the one we encountered in the Cretaceous,' added Rufius.

Doctor Shika scratched her head. 'I need to run some more tests.'

'We need to take a sample of the amniotic fluid,' Melanie continued. 'There may be traces of the mother's immunity that we can use.'

'Can you penetrate the shell without disturbing the embryo?' asked Rufius, who Melanie thought looked like a cross between a pirate and a homeless person.

Doctor Shika tilted her head. 'If we disrupt the shield we risk releasing it from stasis, but there may be a way.'

She tapped a sequence of keys on her tablet and a thin laser-like beam struck the shell, scattering light in all directions. Everyone ducked.

'Okay, maybe not like that,' she said, adjusting the angle until the refraction stopped.

They watched the beam intensify, making the smallest hole through the glassy surface. The scanner showing the progress of the micro bore as it reached the inner surface.

Shika switched off the laser and attached a fine needle-like probe to a robotic arm.

With pinpoint precision the probe was inserted into the egg, and a yellow fluid ran down the transparent tube into a small silver box.

'The mitochondrial DNA matches the sample that Sim brought to us,' Kaori said a few minutes later, pulling up the profiles on a large screen behind her. 'Genetic markers are identical.'

'It's definitely from the same maternal line,' Melanie agreed.

Rufius scratched his beard. 'So it's sixty-six million years old?'

Kaori nodded. 'Although inside the stasis field, less than a day has passed.'

'Can you use it to find a cure?' asked Lyra.

Kaori studied the DNA sequence closely. 'The creature was obviously immune. If we can isolate the relevant antibodies we should be able to synthesise it.'

'Better still if we had a human survivor,' Melanie interrupted, 'someone with antibodies.'

'Except it's got a hundred percent fatality rate,' added Kaori. 'The current death toll stands at over a hundred million and it's still climbing.'

Lyra gasped and held up her hand like an excited school girl. 'I know someone!'

Everyone stared at her, but she ignored them and carried on. 'His name is Song Wuji. He was an alchemist to the First Emperor of China.'

'And exactly how did he survive?'

Lyra shrugged. 'I've no idea, but he says he's been alive ever since. I met him in the Forbidden City in 1914, which meant he was at least two thousand years old.'

Melanie scoffed. 'That's imposs—'

Doctor Shika held up a hand to stop her. 'You're still thinking like a linear. Rufius can you go back and collect a sample of the alchemist's blood?'

The big man nodded and took out his almanac. 'Of course.'

'As for you, young lady,' Kaori continued, turning to Lyra. 'I think we need to reacquaint you with your abilities.'

Lyra nodded to the egg. 'Shenlong?'

'My team are preparing for the extraction. I suggest you join them.'

80

BLOOD OF ALCHEMIST

Forbidden City, China. Present Day.

There were few men that Rufius would class as truly ancient. The founder was one, and there were a number of venerable Scriptorians who were rumoured to be over a thousand years old. Travelling through time extended your lifespan considerably, but it was still finite; there was no such thing as immortality.

Or so he thought.

Song Wuji sat in his small flat in the Fengsheng residential district . His apartment was on the twenty-third floor, giving him a bird's-eye view over the golden roofs of the Forbidden City and the Grand Imperial Palace.

When Rufius appeared the old man simply smiled.

'I wondered when you would come,' he said with a knowing smile, rolling up one sleeve of his silk tunic.

His arm was thin and withered and it took Rufius a couple of minutes to find a vein.

'You've been waiting here since 1914?'

Wuji nodded, turning his head away as blood filled the small test tube. 'Since Lyra left to find the egg. Tell me, has she found it?'

'She has, although I'm not sure what good it will do her.'

'She will know what to do,' the old man said with a smile. 'I have seen it.'

'You've seen quite a lot by all accounts,' Rufius said, exchanging the first test tube for a second.

The old man sighed, looking out of the window towards the walls of the Imperial Palace. 'Longer than I would have liked. I've witnessed the rise and fall of an empire, and now perhaps the end of the world.'

Sirens echoed across the street as a fleet of military vehicles sped past the building.

'They say Beijing has fallen.'

Rufius nodded. 'And many more besides.'

'The curse of the spirit dragon.'

'You survived,' Rufius reassured him, withdrawing the needle from his arm.

Wuji rolled down his sleeve and bowed his head to Rufius.

'What will you do with my blood?'

Rufius packed the test tubes carefully into the case that Doctor Shika had given him. 'Learn how to stop the plague. You might just have saved the world.'

This seemed to please Song Wuji. 'And Shenlong? The spirit dragon?'

'Lyra has a plan.'

The old man sighed and closed his eyes. 'Then my work here is done.'

Rufius went over and placed his fingers against the side of Wuji's neck. There was a faint pulse but it weakened with every beat.

He sat down beside the old man and waited, listening to the gentle wheeze of his last breaths.

81

CURE

Xenobiology Department. Present Day.

F red woke slowly, his eyes blinking at the bright lights.
'Hey,' Melanie whispered, stroking the hair across his forehead. There were streaks of white running through it now; a common side effect of stasis, Doctor Shika explained when she brought him out of the chamber.

'Hello,' he replied nervously, as if to a stranger. His eyes were full of questions, his voice dry and hoarse. 'Where am I?'

'You're safe,' she said, trying not to cry. 'We fixed you.'

He seemed confused, which Kaori had warned her about too.

'Thank you. I'm very grateful, but who are you?'

It was a form of temporary amnesia, his memories were out of sync, but it would pass.

'It's me, Melanie. You rescued me in Antarctica, don't you remember?'

Staring at her blankly, he shrugged. 'I honestly don't have a clue. Could I have something to drink? I'm a trifle parched.'

Doctor Shika walked into the room with a glass of water and a small cup of dark liquid.

'Hello sleeping beauty,' she said with a smile. 'Nice to see you back with us.'

She gave him the water and he took a long drink.

'Not too much,' Kaori warned, taking it and handing him the small cup.

He sniffed at the medicine and grimaced. 'What on earth is this?'

'A Doctor Crooke special, it'll help with your memory.'

'Smells like shit.'

Kaori scowled, placing her hands on her hips. 'It does, but it's the best tonic for your stasis fatigue. Unless of course you don't want your memories back?'

He drank it down in one go and nearly retched.

'Hell's teeth! It tastes worse than it smells!'

Refilling the water glass, Kaori handed it back to Fred. 'Drink a little more and then get some rest.'

He did as he was told and they left him to sleep.

'Are you sure he'll make a full recovery?' Melanie asked, looking at him through the window as he rearranged his pillows and snuggled down.

Kaori patted her on the shoulder. 'We tested your antiviral in over a hundred thousand simulations. It works, you need to believe in yourself! It was amazing work!'

Melanie turned away from the window. 'I know I should. I'm just not used to having a fully tested solution five minutes after I've designed it.'

The doctor laughed. 'He'll be fine. We've more important things to focus on now. My team's preparing the first batches of vaccines. The Dreadnoughts will be inoculated first, before they transport the rest into the quarantine zone. I take it you're going to want to come along?'

'Why can't we just keep the egg here? Surely if it's never discovered the virus won't get out into the general population.'

Kaori nodded, pulling up a series of intricate branching diagrams on her tablet. 'The Copernican's considered that option, but since we've no idea how many eggs might be out there, we think it's wiser to go back and deploy the vaccine in a suitable point to reduce the deaths to a minimum.'

Melanie studied the charts. 'You're still going to let people die?' she said, tapping on the estimated death toll.

'Professor Eddington's looked at every eventuality and calculated the lowest risk scenario. Even with the intervention of the *Endurance*, there's evidence to suggest there could be an outbreak in the near future. So we'll replace Shenlong with the infected carcass of the mother that Alixia brought back from the Cretaceous. It will be enough for Colonel Cooper to take back home.'

'And let him infect half of the USA?'

'No, but, it needs to become a wide enough threat for him to take us seriously when we arrive with the vaccine. We can't appear to have foreknowledge of what was about to occur. That's the curse of a time traveller, to know what is to come and not take action to avoid it.'

'I don't understand how you live with that.'

Kaori shrugged and put down the tablet. 'You tell yourself it's for the greater good. If we saved everybody we'd have a very different problem to deal with.'

'Overpopulation?'

Kaori folded her arms and sighed. 'We live on a planet of finite resources. Unchecked population growth is by far the greatest threat that humanity faces. Disease, war and famine are the best limiters of expansion. Our job is to ensure that there is a balance, and that they don't blow each other to kingdom come.'

Melanie looked surprised. 'Have you had to stop a nuclear war?'

'More than once. Ask Rufius, it's one of his favourite stories.'

They walked out of the ward and onto the main floor of the laboratory. Men and women in hazmat suits were carefully loading metal canisters onto a circular platform.

'We've created enough to treat a hundred thousand. Assuming that Cooper acts quickly, it should give them enough time to scale up the production.'

The cylinders were branded with a series of codes and a symbol of a silver star.

'What's with the logo?'

'It's a biotech company, Argenteum Astrum. Lyra came up with the name. We've based it in 2018 to make it look legitimate, they've been researching prehistoric pathogens as part of an antibiotic research programme. You're its medical director by the way.'

'Am I? Since when?'

Kaori patted her on the shoulder. 'Since yesterday. You've got twenty-five patents to your name already. You're actually a really wealthy woman.'

'Since yesterday?'

'You really don't get this time travel thing do you?'

Melanie shook her head. 'No, I don't.'

'Okay let's get cracking,' Kaori said, clapping her hands. 'Bailey, do we have a chaperone for Doctor Braithwaite?'

One of the hazmat suits turned towards them and nodded.

82

SHENLONG

Southern Ocean. December 1914

The seas were wild and rough.

Lyra held onto Benoir as the *Nautilus II* bucked and dipped between the dark, towering waves.

'What's it like?' he asked, as spray crashed around the conning tower of the ship. 'Not knowing?'

Lyra wiped the water from her face and smiled. 'Exhilarating and scary. I've no idea what's going to happen next! I don't know how you can stand it.'

Benoir kissed her. 'You get used to it.'

She laughed and kissed him back, her hands lingering on the sides of his face, fingers entwined in his beard.

'Are you sure you want to do this?' he shouted over the howling gale.

'Yes!' she whispered into his ear. 'It's my destiny.'

The silhouette of the *Endurance* rose on the horizon, the sails of its three masts billowing in the stormy winds.

Professor Eddington and his Copernicans determined that the fifth day after the expedition departed from South Georgia was the optimal time to intervene. The *Nautilus II* was finally declared fit for duty and Caitlin's parents were only too keen to help with the mission.

A special containment chamber was installed in the forward cargo bay, which Doctor Shika reassured Lyra was a temporary measure, until they were able to get the creature back to the lab.

The rotting carcass of Shenlong's mother was stored in a crate built to the same specifications as the one Fred and Melanie had seen.

A klaxon sounded, signalling that the *Nautilus II* was about to submerge and Lyra and Benoir moved quickly to the hatch and below decks.

Rufius, Doctor Shika and a team of Dreadnoughts were waiting for them on the observation deck, dressed in wetsuits.

'It's going to be dark and rough when we disembark,' Rufius began, 'but the storm will cover our approach, and ensure that most of the crew are below deck. The Dreadnoughts will go in first and secure the boat. The crew are to be incapacitated with as little fuss as possible. I wanted to use good old fashioned chloroform, but Doctor Shika assures me that her tranquilliser is more effective and has less side effects. Whatever happens do not enter the ship until we give you the all clear or you may end up missing out on all the fun.'

Doctor Shika took over.

'When the crew are neutralised we need to bring the *Nautilus* alongside so that the hoist can be used to transfer the creature and be replaced with the infected carcass. It's wise to remember that both are incredibly toxic at this point. The living specimen is also thought to be particularly unruly and may actually require sedation if Lyra cannot persuade it to comply.'

Lyra smiled weakly as all eyes turned on her.

'The most dangerous point of the mission will be when we lower the dragon into the containment cell. Two boats on a rough sea will be hard enough, but there will be storm force winds to boot,' added Rufius. 'Anyone falls into the swell, there's a very good chance we may never find you.'

'Definitely going to be you, Quirky,' Edward chided his younger brother, ruffling his red hair. Fred pushed his hand away and winked at Melanie.

'I'll bring her in as close as I can,' said Caitlin's mother. 'But it's going to be tricky.'

Fred watched his brothers climb the side of the heaving ship using grappling lines. *They make it look so easy*, he thought, taking the strain and launching himself from the conning tower.

The keel rushed towards him, covered in razor sharp barnacles. He planted both feet squarely on the hull as it dipped down into the swell, the gap narrowed between the two vessels, threatening to crush him, but he pulled himself up, hand over hand, gripping the knots in the sodden rope to stop himself from sliding back down.

Hands grabbed him roughly as he reached the gunwale. 'What took you so long,' whispered Henry.

Before Fred could answer, Rufius came up the rope behind him, his wild beard coated in ice and spray.

'Have you dealt with the watch?'

William nodded towards three bodies that were slumped against the mizzenmast.

'All accounted for. Eddy's on the helm. Just need to put the others to sleep.' He took out a canister and twisted the lid.

As the gas began to escape, William threw it into one of the hatches and took out another.

Rufius opened his tachyon and checked the time. 'Give it ten minutes to be sure. Let's get the winch rigged up in the meantime.'

· · ·

Lyra was strapped into a harness and winched aboard using a block and tackle attached to one of the lower spars.

It took nearly twenty minutes to haul her onboard, by which time she was soaked to the skin.

Rufius took her directly to the hold, where a large iron bound crate sat in six inches of water.

She could feel the cold draining the warmth from her legs as she waded towards it. The Dreadnoughts were busy attaching ropes to the top of the box, her job was to try and reason with the dragon within.

But she had another task to complete first.

Placing her hands between the rough planks of wood, she felt the touch of the tentacles on her fingers.

Hello child, Shenlong's voice echoed in her head. *Have you come to release me?*

It wasn't the spirit dragon, but Aleister Crowley.

Yes, Lyra responded, *I have come to set you free, but in return I need my sight.*

And you were so keen to be rid of it! He mocked her, *and yet now the little bird wants to fly once more.*

It is part of who I am. Who I'm meant to be.

Tentacles wove between the gaps in the crate, encircling her arms and drawing her closer. Two of the Dreadnoughts moved to intervene, but she shook her head.

We are all children of time. The gift you have received will become a burden.

This was the voice of Shenlong, somehow she'd managed to suppress Crowley.

I know, but I must learn to master it, she replied.

It will show you the deaths of everyone you love.

Lyra closed her eyes, she knew the price. *Death comes to us all. I must learn to accept what is to come.*

This is the fate of all Seers.

There was a sharp pain in her arm and one of the dragons tentacles buried itself under her skin.

Lyra felt her powers returning as the energy flowed through the wound. The dragon reignited a fire within her and she felt the substance of the ship fade away, her consciousness expanding beyond the boundaries of the physical world. Lines of light wove out of her and into everyone around her, their destinies weaving through space and time.

It was all there: the past, present and future mapped out in an intricate tapestry that glowed in beautiful iridescent colours.

Do you see?

She saw her life and her death, everything that she feared would come to pass. The pain and the sorrow, the love and the laughter. It was beautiful and terrible, but it was her life and now she knew what Abandon had meant when he said she must look beyond her demise.

Do you see? The dragon repeated.

Yes.

Feeling her abilities restored, she focused on the dragon's timeline. Lyra could see the twisted tendrils of Crowley's life wrapped around Shenlong's beautiful golden ribbon like a parasitic vine.

She plucked at it with her mind, teasing apart the dark strands that clung to it, separating the two. It took every ounce of power to force apart the bonds between them, until finally she heard him cry out as the last strand detached and his line disappeared.

When Lyra woke, she was back on the *Nautilus*.

Benoir was standing over her bed, a broad smile on his face.

'Hi,' he said, bending down to kiss her. 'How are you feeling?'

The lines of destiny wove around him, but she ignored them and pulled him closer. 'Like my old self.'

83

COOPER

Fort Detrick. Present day

Colonel Cooper sat at his desk, the throbbing pain in the back of his head was finally beginning to ease.

The telephone in his office rang. It was the Presidential line.

'I just wanted to congratulate you and your team Colonel,' the man's voice drawled. 'A fine piece of work, you've saved us from a terrible fate. I've recommended you for a Silver Star.'

The President continued, but it was just political hyperbole about funding and oversight committees. Cooper grunted in all of the right places, but he'd heard everything he needed to hear.

He was a hero, just like his grandfather.

Putting the phone on speaker, he poured himself a large whisky and put his feet up on the desk. The mission was a success, he'd found the cure, or rather he'd found the right people who could find the cure.

His team had discovered a small biotech company working on an antiviral which proved a hundred percent effective in blocking the receptors on the protein envelope. They found them quite by chance when they were running their initial research. It was a small team affiliated with Oxford University with a weird Latin name. They were working on a new antibody based on prehistoric material and had no idea what they'd actually found.

Cooper bought their patent for peanuts.

The vaccine his team produced was highly effective, stopping the spread in a matter of days, halting the initial outbreak in Boston. He got all of the funding he needed to scale up to a national programme.

The phone call ended and he knocked the whisky back, savouring the warmth as it ran down his throat.

Now if only he could find a cure for the cancer.

84

SHADOW REALMS

The Shadow Realm.

Lyra stroked the long neck of the dragon, feeling the warm scales beneath her fingers.

The Grand Seer was examining the mirror as Kaori's team finished their preparations. It was a large, twenty foot, silver circle, framed with glyphs that Kelly insisted were a requirement of the ritual, but everyone knew was simply another piece of theatre.

'What's it like in there?' asked Sim.

'Quiet,' Lyra replied.

'That's not the word I would use,' scoffed Rufius. 'Does it know what it's letting itself in for?'

'*She* does,' Lyra said, emphasising the word. 'There are paths that lead to beautiful places, like Rivendell. You just happened to find yourself in Mordor.'

'What about the egg?' asked Caitlin, trying to stop Zack from pulling Shenlong's tentacles.

'That stays with us,' Kaori replied. 'It's not every day you get to study a sixty-million year old foetus.'

The mirror surface shimmered as the field stabilised.

'Ready when you are,' said one of the technicians, handing Lyra back her journal. 'The coordinates have been set as you instructed.'

A view of green valleys covered in a thick forest replaced their reflection.

Shenlong turned her head, nuzzling into Lyra's chest.

Thank you, shining child of time. May the five blessings be upon you.

Lyra kissed her gently on the snout. *Thank you, spirit. I hope you find peace.*

Bowing her head, the dragon folded its wings and moved through the silver surface as if it were water.

85

FRED

Oxford. Present Day.

Melanie sat in her office, staring out over the spires of the city. The latest copy of New Scientist sat on her desk, with a picture of her holding the Nobel Prize for Medicine. She hated the photo, but the PR company said it would be good for the share price.

The patents that Doctor Shika set up in her name included the one that MacAllister had stolen from her. It was a hollow victory, as Kaori predicted, the fact that her name was attached to it made no difference to her, it didn't bring her any joy.

Not the kind that she experienced with Fred.

Even saving the planet from an extinction-level event paled into insignificance compared to the way he made her feel — unconsciously smiling every time she thought about him.

He was a Dreadnought now, spending days if not weeks exploring the deep past with his brothers. Either the virus, or the time spent in stasis, seemed to have reset his range. Whichever, it was the best present he could have asked for, she'd never seen him so happy.

The benefit of a time travelling husband was that he was always home for dinner, no matter how long the mission.

She was happy to stay where she was. The past was an interesting place to visit once in a while, but the paradoxes hurt her head.

Professor Eddington had offered to redact her, but she refused, it had been one hell of an adventure, which one day she hoped she would tell her grandchildren about.

And there were going to be more than a few of them, according to Lyra.

EPILOGUE

E dward Kelly sat at his desk, reading from a large grimoire. Lyra stepped lightly from the mirror, hardly making a sound as she approached the Grand Seer.

'I am not so deaf that I couldn't hear the tread of my little bird,' he said, without looking up from his book.

'I wondered if you were sleeping,' she replied.

'Indeed. What brings you to my study at such an hour?'

She handed him a notebook, one of her shadow journals.

'I couldn't sleep.'

Closing the grimoire, he took the book and held it up to a candle. An engraving of an old man was carved into the cover.

'You have found him? The Old King?'

Lyra shook her head. 'No, he found me. But that is not why I came. There is something very strange I wish to discuss with you.'

'Here be demons?' Kelly translated from the frontispiece of her journal.

She nodded. 'The group that rescued me from the loch have been fighting them for some time. At first, I thought they were creatures of the Maelstrom, but now I believe they may be Abandon's spawn. Somehow he is entering the continuum without causing a breach.'

Kelly stroked his beard and considered the idea.

'Curious. I have to admit he's grown more powerful than I imagined. It took all of my strength to escape him.'

'What should we do?'

The Grand Seer rose to his feet. 'To begin with. The Shadow Realm is out of bounds. No more galavanting through the mirror. I will speak to the founder about this in the morning.'

Other books in the Infinity Engines universe.

The Infinity Engines

1. Anachronist

2. Maelstrom

3. Eschaton

4. Aeons

5. Tesseract

6. Contagion

Infinity Engines Origins

Chimæra

Changeling

Infinity Engines Missions

1776

1888

You can download 1776 for FREE plus get updates and news by subscribing to my mailing list (simply scan the QR code below).

ACKNOWLEDGEMENTS

This was an interesting book to write, inspired in some ways by the effects of covid and how easily a simple virus can affect the planet. It feels as if we all experienced our own moment of history over the last couple of years and I think we've all been changed by it.

I hope you enjoyed the book, please feel free to join my community and let me know what you thought. And on that note, if you would be so kind as to leave a review on Amazon that would be most appreciated.

Cheers,
Andy x

ABOUT THE AUTHOR

For more information about The Infinity Engines series and other Here Be Dragons books please visit: www.infinityengines.com